CROSSROADS

CROSSROADS

STEPHEN L. BRYANT

[signature]

TATE PUBLISHING *& Enterprises*

Crossroads
Copyright © 2009 by Stephen L. Bryant. All rights reserved.

No part of this publication may be reproduced, stored in a retrieval system or transmitted in any way by any means, electronic, mechanical, photocopy, recording or otherwise without the prior permission of the author except as provided by USA copyright law.

This novel is a work of fiction. Names, descriptions, entities, and incidents included in the story are products of the author's imagination. Any resemblance to actual persons, events, and entities is entirely coincidental.

The opinions expressed by the author are not necessarily those of Tate Publishing, LLC.

Published by Tate Publishing & Enterprises, LLC
127 E. Trade Center Terrace | Mustang, Oklahoma 73064 USA
1.888.361.9473 | www.tatepublishing.com

Tate Publishing is committed to excellence in the publishing industry. The company reflects the philosophy established by the founders, based on Psalm 68:11,
"The Lord gave the word and great was the company of those who published it."

Book design copyright © 2009 by Tate Publishing, LLC. All rights reserved.
Cover design by Amber Gulilat
Interior design by Stephanie Woloszyn

Published in the United States of America

ISBN: 978-1-61566-545-7
1. Fiction / Mystery & Detective / General   2. Fiction / Christian / Suspense
09.11.11

DEDICATION

Any talent and inspiration I put forth is totally a gift from God. Without the Lord's mercy, grace, and forgiveness, I would have never survived. My life and my work belong to God, hallowed be his name.

I must also recognize my wife, Pam. I simply write stuff. She, however, types, edits, deals with agents and publishers, and handles all the other tedious requirements necessary to go to print. She is my love, my life, and my eternal partner.

And lastly, I dedicate this book to Brent Wildman, my friend and partner. It was with Brent that I found my own crossroad.

THE O'DOULS

A glistening snowflake the size of a nickel gently touched the slightly turned up nose of Annie O'Doul. She was a pretty girl in an unusual way, some might say. Auburn hair with thick, unruly curls surrounding high cheekbones and sea-green eyes with naturally red lips made dark by the bitter cold this Christmas Eve morning.

She stood quietly before the wooden foldout chair, unable to produce another tear. Annie O'Doul was all cried out.

Why? The question seemed to be the only thought her brilliant mind could contemplate. *Why?*

Annie O'Doul had been the apple of her daddy's eye. Oddly beautiful, number one in her class throughout high school at Sacred Heart Academy, and one semester short of graduating from the University of Louisville Law School.

Now the twenty-four-year-old honor student stood weightless before the ornate mahogany casket, unable to say goodbye to her adoring father. Why? Her mind begged for an answer. Why did such a gentle, caring man with a generous heart lay silently engulfed in creamy satin and polished wood this snowy Christmas Eve?

Why did a stranger, for no obvious reason, walk into the Hikes Point Lounge and place a .44 Magnum pistol to her father's head and blow his brains out across the antique stained-glass mirror? *Why?* she silently whispered deep inside. There was no answer to this haunting question.

Three long days ago, the police had surmised that Patrick O'Doul, lovingly known as Paddy, announced "last call" at precisely 1:45 a.m. Paddy O'Doul, as his closest friends called him, pronounced last call for the ten thousandth time. No one could have imagined it would also be his final call.

Police detective Donald Wilhelm, a veteran of twenty-two years as a Louisville cop, provided little in his investigation. His brief initial report read:

> *At approximately 1:59 a.m. Tuesday morning, December 21, Patrick O'Doul was shot at point-blank range with a high-caliber pistol, most likely a .44 Magnum, police department forensics determined. At last call, there remained three customers in the bar. Charles Yeager, a close friend and retired investment banker, Manny*

Matthews, an ex-convict whom Paddy had helped after his release from Bunker Hill Prison, and Skip Brown, an elderly black man and life-long alcoholic.

At 1:55 a.m. Tuesday morning, December 21, both Mr. Yeager and Mr. Matthews left the bar together. Mr. Brown locked the heavy glass front door covered with iron security bars. Mr. Brown stated that the bar area was empty with the exception of himself and Mr. O'Doul. Mr. Brown further stated that the boss sat on the corner stool.

Mr. Brown claims that he proceeded as he always did each night to the mop closet to fetch a broom to begin his nightly clean-up duties.

Mr. Brown further stated that as he stepped from the mop closet, he saw a young, white male, nearly six feet tall, maybe one hundred and sixty pounds and dressed nicely, walk from the bathroom, move quietly behind Mr. O'Doul, pull a big gun from his waistband, and shoot Mr. O'Doul in the back of the head.

Mr. Brown then stated that the young man with short, blond hair looked him dead in the eyes, smiled, turned, and disappeared into the darkness to the back of the bar toward the restrooms.

In the next several days, Detective Wilhelm and the forensic team from the Louisville Police Department went through the Hikes Point Lounge looking for any clues into the murder of Mr. Paddy O'Doul.

Detective Wilhelm carefully reviewed his handwritten notes, neatly printed in the small spiral notebook he always carried:

O'Doul shot at 1:59 a.m. O'Doul and Brown, the only two persons in the bar area prior to the shooting. Brown claims to have seen a young white male, nicely dressed, shoot O'Doul. Yeager and Matthews did not see said suspect at any time during the four hours they were at the bar. Major problem. Two doors to the HPL—both locked. Front entrance dead bolted, back door padlocked on the inside. Found $256 in paper bag under mattress of Brown in the basement of HPL where he lives. Brown did not call 911 until fifteen minutes after O'Doul was shot. No evidence of any young white male in the bar that evening. Brown is a drunk! He seems a little crazy! Fifteen minutes—time enough to leave and hide gun! Where'd he get $256? Brown—guilty as hell!

Cleophus "Skip" Brown was two weeks short of his sixty-seventh birthday the night Paddy O'Doul was killed. Born into a family of eleven children, Cleophus Brown moved from Mobile, Alabama, at the age of six. His family traveled throughout the south, finding employment mostly as migrant workers. Cleophus would brag that the only thing he'd never picked was another man's nose.

He often recalled that somewhere south of Jonesboro, Arkansas, an old rag-ass mule kicked him just above his knees. "Probably broke somethin' important." He laughed telling the story. "Can't say fer sure what that danged old mule torn up, but it still hurts plenty, and I can tell ya twenty hours before it's gonna rain."

The story ended with the fact that Mr. Brown's left leg bent slightly inward below his knees and fell two inches shorter than the right leg. Because of this, the old black man seemed to hop when he walked, thus the nickname "Skip."

Annie O'Doul watched the tent fill with sadness and almost found a distant smile as hundreds of men and women surrounded the gravesite. Most she didn't know, but all knew the late Paddy O'Doul, owner of the Hikes Point Lounge, a friend to thousands in his seventy-two years of life.

Annie had decided yesterday that she would defend Skip Brown just as soon as she passed the bar exam. It was impossible that the old black man her father loved could have committed such a heinous act. He was innocent, and she would rescue him. Her father would want it that way.

Paddy O'Doul locked the front door of the Hikes Point Lounge at 2:05 a.m. on New Year's Day, January 1, 1977, thirty years before his untimely death. His business was growing, and the bar crowd was becoming a great group of friendly regulars. It truly was a wonderful neighborhood bar.

Paddy pulled up the end barstool, lit his favorite Punch cigar, and sipped at his fifteen-year-old scotch while he counted the day's take.

"$1,256! Not bad for an old Irishman who quit school in the tenth grade!" Paddy proudly exclaimed to the antique mirror behind the bar, which smiled back approvingly.

Minutes before, the bar had been so loud as happy patrons danced, kissed, and drank in the New Year. Now there was silence. No sound but the ice cubes on his fifteen-year-old Chevis as they melted and moved. And yes, the *drip, drip, drip* of the faucet behind the bar. He smiled at the silence, proud of his dream, the Hikes Point Lounge.

As Paddy poured another three fingers of scotch into the thick glass, he heard something else. *What is it? Where is it coming from?* There it was again. It sounded like a moan. No, more like a plea. "Help me, please, dear God, help me." Paddy arose from his chair, grabbed the thick wooden baseball bat from behind the bar (he did not own a gun), and walked toward the pleading sound of a suffering soul. *Is someone hurt and still inside?* he wondered. "Who is it? Where are you?" His baritone voice was thick with concern but not fear.

"Help me, please, God, help me!" The sadness in the feeble cry brought urgency to Paddy's search.

"Where are you? Who are you? Are you hurt?"

"Help me; please help me."

Paddy realized that the hurting voice seemed to be coming from behind the locked steel door to the alleyway. He cautiously unlocked the heavy padlock, raised the bat high into the air, and pulled the big door inward.

A tall, thin black man covered in snow, nearly frozen, fell into Paddy O'Doul's big muscular arms. "Thanks be to Jesus," the graying, snow-covered black man whispered.

Paddy lifted the bone-thin man in his arms, kicking the back door closed, and placed him in one of the red fake leather booths that lined the enormous back room where the stage and dance floor were filled nightly. Now, no one was dancing; just an old half-frozen black man nearly unconscious occupied the dance floor.

Paddy ran to the basement, where a small area had been cleared for what he called overnighters.

Right after Paddy purchased the bar from his uncle, he fixed up a corner of the basement for friends who on occasion over indulged. There was a sink, a single bed, an old dresser short the bottom drawer, and a footlocker from his days in the army. Not much, but a good place for a friendly drunk to sleep it off. Paddy pulled the army blanket from the bed and rushed back up the narrow stairs.

The now damp black man lay curled up in a ball, shaking uncontrollably, teeth chattering as though they might break into a thousand bits of stained enamel. Paddy wrapped and tucked the army blanket around the thin body of Cleophus Brown.

After several minutes the man stopped his violent shivering, with only the occasional bone cold shudder.

"What's your name?" Paddy asked with genuine caring in his voice.

"They call me Skip, sir." His eyes fluttered several times. "Thank you, Jesus, thank you, Jesus," Cleophus Brown whispered. A minute passed in silence before the black man murmured, "Whiskey, sir, please, a drink of whiskey."

Paddy quickly raced to the bar, grabbing a bottle of Early Times Bourbon and a whiskey glass. "Here ya go, partner. Here ya go; have a shot of this."

The black man pushed the whiskey glass away and took a hard pull from the bottle of Early Times. He wiped his scar-covered right hand across his mouth and looked Paddy directly in the eyes. "Thank ya, sir; God bless ya, sir." Paddy had never seen such pain in a man's eyes before.

"Let me get you something to eat, my friend." Paddy started for the kitchen, stepped, and turned. "What's your last name, Skip?"

"Brown, sir." He took another big swallow of the bourbon. "And what do folks call you, sir?"

"All my friends call me Paddy. Call me Paddy, Skip."

A single tear slowly rolled down the black man's cheek. "Thank you, Mr. Paddy. Thanks for saving my life."

After three bowls of vegetable soup, the Hikes Point Lounge's lunchtime specialty, life seemed to return to Cleophus Brown.

During the next four hours, Cleophus told Paddy of his life. It would be the saddest story Patrick O'Doul would ever hear. Now homeless and a hopeless alcoholic, Skip Brown had laid down to die in the alley behind the Hikes Point Lounge. The man would believe until his dying day that Paddy O'Doul was an angel sent by God.

At six o'clock that morning, Paddy asked Skip Brown, "Mr. Brown, can I trust you?"

Cleophus, eyes clear and bright, looked into Paddy's soul. "With my life, sir." Paddy knew in that instant he could.

"Okay, Skip, here's the deal." Paddy's voice was firm but held a special quality of caring. "I've been needing someone to clean the place when I close each night. I can't pay you much, but I've got a place you can stay in the basement, you can eat lunch and supper from our kitchen, and I'll give you a pint of whiskey every night when we close. If you ever steal from me, you're done."

Several tears now streamed down the black man's hollow cheeks.

Paddy got up and went to the bar, opening the Citizen's Fidelity bank bag holding the cash from the previous day. He counted out $256 and slid the money across the table to his new clean-up man. Why $256 dollars? Paddy couldn't say, except maybe it was all the tens, fives, and ones.

"Tomorrow we'll go out and buy you some nice warm

clothes. Anytime you wish to leave or you lie to me, the clothes and money are yours to keep. Deal, Mr. Brown?"

"It's a deal, Mr. Paddy!" Cleophus "Skip" Brown smiled for the first time in many years.

Paddy showed Mr. Brown to his new living quarters, watched as Skip immediately went to sleep, and left for 6:30 Mass.

Two hours later Skip suddenly awoke. He was afraid and thought for a moment he might be dead. But then he realized he was warm and safe. Someone gave a damn.

The single light bulb overhead gave a comforting sense of security. Cleophus looked about his home, realizing the large basement was filled with assorted supplies. He arose and surveyed the room and its contents. In the corner was a large stack of paper bags utilized for carryout fish sandwiches, another famous Hikes Point Lounge specialty. He took a single bag and stuffed the $256 Mr. Paddy had given him that morning in it. He placed the bag of money underneath his mattress and the metal bed springs.

Mr. Brown smiled. "Someday I'm gonna buy something nice for my friend, Mr. Paddy."

Unfortunately, there were only two men who knew about the money. One was now dead, and the other awaited trial for murder and robbing the owner of the Hikes Point Lounge of $256.

Annie O'Doul sat beside her mother, Margaret, holding her small, gloved hand. Father McCall went on about all of her father's generous deeds. Nothing was registering, however, in Annie's mind. Nothing but freeing Mr. Brown, her father's long-time friend, from jail and the injustice waiting to be delivered.

Annie O'Doul knew it was impossible for Mr. Brown to have murdered her father, simply impossible.

Unfortunately, because of a well-known member of the community, loved by all, generous member of the Catholic Church and a contributor to the district judge's recent campaign, this outrageous murder must be solved.

After all, an aggressive police detective, Catholic prosecutor, and appreciative judge, must find justice and find it now!

In solitary confinement sat Cleophus Skip Brown, a poor black man without any property and no relatives. He was black, homeless, and a drunk. And no one was going to believe he'd kept $256 in a brown paper bag for thirty years.

Ms. Annie O'Doul could not know the morning of her beloved father's funeral that Cleophus Brown would go to trial and be convicted of murder before she even took the bar exam.

Three months later Mr. Cleophus "Skip" Brown entered cell block C on death row.

Finally, Father McCall completed his much-too-lengthy eulogy, and Annie held tightly to her mother as they left the burial tent.

And then, out of the corner of her eye, Annie saw a tiny flash of red. She focused. The snow now falling in great white blankets blurred the distance. But there, far off, standing just behind a large gray tombstone stood a tall young man. She could see that he was handsome between the falling snowflakes. His hair was short and light blond. And the red flash—there it was. The man had attended the funeral, wearing a red bowtie! *Strange,* Annie thought.

She turned her attention to her mother as Margaret slid

into the limousine. Annie turned back over her shoulder to see the tall young man with the red tie standing closer. He was smiling, and Annie O'Doul felt evil like never before.

LAST WILL & TESTAMENT

Three months and twenty-seven days had passed since Paddy O'Doul was laid to rest.

His only child and adoring daughter, Annie O'Doul, graduated one semester early from the University of Louisville Law School. She had done so with honors.

Annie sipped a steaming cup of ginseng tea as she sat at the window table of the Mandarin Tea Cottage, looking out onto Bardstown Road and the yuppie area now dominated by new lawyers, young doctors, and dial-me-up stockbrokers.

The nickname Cool Breeze Town, originated by nobody really knew whom, seemed to fit, the young woman mused. The Tea Shop sat next to and was surrounded by over fifty bistros and ethnic restaurants representing the United Nations of food fare.

Vintage BMWs, Audis, and assorted Volkswagen models lined the narrow streets for several square miles. Outside the Mandarin Tea Cottage, Annie could see the back wheel of her old Schwinn bicycle resting cozily against the brick exterior. It seemed to fit the scenic picture that could have been painted by a new-generation Norman Rockwell.

The young woman lived four blocks south of the bustling center street, where all cool people met and planned the salvation of the world, or at least their own yet-to-be-developed planet.

Annie O'Doul shared the bottom floor of a huge and grand old home, which must have been a great place to play hide-and-seek for the children who had occupied the house many years ago. She shared the ornate bottom floor with three other young women, all of whom where currently pursuing degrees at U of L.

Annie just yesterday had informed her roommates and the landlord of her departure in the next ninety days. She'd decided to move back in with her mother to assist in the planning of her very special wedding in late September.

Annie first met Joshua Franklin Berg two summers ago when she'd interned at the semi-famous law firm of Henthorn, Haddad, and Wildman. Joshie, as she loved to call him (he hated it), had been with the firm two years when they literally ran into each other coming out of the firm's law library. Joshua Berg nearly knocked the tall redhead flat that first encounter. However, when Annie O'Doul's green eyes locked onto Joshie's gold-rimmed spectacles, he almost fell over. Love at first sight? A match made in heaven? Probably a little of both. In the next few brief moments, Joshua Franklin Berg knew he would marry this oddly beautiful girl or die trying.

Annie smiled, recalling their first bumping-into-each-other moment, and realized how much life could change in mere seconds.

She was deeply in love with Joshie, who would soon be her husband. "Chance," she whispered. "A moment of luck, maybe," she considered attentively.

"Luck," she loudly stated unconsciously then blushed as the table to the right stopped talking, staring at her sudden outburst. Annie buried her face in the Appellate Law Journal she had been studying.

"Luck," she said, this time softly and in the safety of the law journal pages. Good luck and bad luck were real experiences she knew all too well.

Was it not good luck to have been raised by Paddy and Margaret O'Doul? Good luck to be born smart and beautiful, great luck to have found the love of her life. Yes, she knew that good luck surrounded her time on earth to date.

But there was the other side of the good luck mountain, the side where the sun never shined. No rainbows, no bluebirds singing, no love, no hope—only darkness and sorrow. That side where her father was shot dead for absolutely no reason! That black valley. Yes, Annie O'Doul knew both.

Annie asked the perky little Oriental waitress for a fresh cup of green tea. The waitress bowed in some Chinese ceremonious fashion and muttered something that might have been of Eastern dialect, although Annie seriously doubted so. The waitress, very young and pretty, had recently destroyed her long and beautiful hair with a new hip-hop, short, spiked, and tipped-in-purple do. Annie surmised that the young Oriental girl most likely lived in Shepardsville and the only real knowledge she carried of China was spelled with four letters and preceded by the word *minute*.

Annie looked at her gold Rolex, a gift from her dad when she graduated from high school. Josh was now twenty minutes late for their lunch meeting, very unlike Mr. Perfect. "Fifteen minutes more, Mr. Berg, and I'm calling you." She smiled, loving the fact that even Joshie could not always be that perfect.

The young woman sipped the fresh hot tea, returning to the task laid before her on the round table covered by crisp linen. She'd need more than luck to pass the upcoming bar exam.

Later today she and Josh would meet, along with Annie's mother, Margaret, at her father's lawyers' office to finalize Paddy's last will and testament. Danny O'Hara had served her father and family for nearly fifty years. He was their accountant, attorney, advisor, and friend.

Danny operated a small accounting and law office with his sister, Lizzy. Elizabeth O'Hara was a teetotaler, hating the evils of alcohol even among her sacred priest. Danny, on the other hand, could be seen daily at precisely 6:30 a.m. when the Hikes Point Lounge opened its doors for the twenty plus old codgers, all retired and all living within the neighborhood.

They called themselves the J.R. Breakfast Club, and like the postman—rain, snow, or shine—the boys were faithful to their task, which mostly consisted of heated daily bumper pool games and falling down drunk by 11:00 a.m.

No one knew for sure what the J.R. really stood for, but most believed it represented "just retired," even though the club's youngest member was seventy-one years old. As for breakfast? Well, you might see a half-dozen pickled eggs consumed on any given day.

All the members of the J.R. Breakfast Club loved the red-faced Irishman Danny O'Hara, and most were long-term clients. Danny had bailed them all out of jail at one time or another. "If you're going to get drunk and thrown in the happy tank, do it while the sun is shining," Danny O'Hara said on numerous occasions.

So every morning, except Sunday, because Paddy O'Doul did not dare open his tavern on the Lord's Day, Paddy's young nephew Dugan opened the bar to an enthusiastic group of elderly blue-collar retirees and one tiny, happy Irishman.

"Ah, nothing like a shot of good Irish whiskey to start your brain firing on all six cylinders!" Danny loudly proclaimed, and the twenty members would always propose the same toast. "Here's to Irish whiskey, redheaded women, and Paddy O'Doul! Hurrah, hurrah!"

Danny would stay for two more shots, one game of bumper pool, and twenty hearty pats on the back before opening the office of O'Hara and O'Hara.

Danny never really cared much about money, demonstrated by his long life of light workload. As a matter-of-fact, his largest client had always been the Hikes Point Lounge and other financial interests of his close friend, Patrick O'Doul.

Esquire O'Hara, attorney at law, would leave his office at precisely 11:30 a.m. each day and drive the four blocks to the tavern, as he liked to call it. Danny liked to beat the lunch crowd, which was substantial between noon and 1:45 p.m. It was the same fare every day: a large bowl of vegetable soup and three mugs of Irish draft. Danny seemed to be the only patron who enjoyed the Irish beer, although occasionally, both Paddy and Mr. Brown would indulge.

Danny closed the door to his overcrowded closet to his office each day at 4:00 p.m., wished his very large, unmarried sister "top of the evening," and returned to his safe haven, the Hikes Point Lounge. In the next three hours, Danny would have his dinner of grilled cheese, potato soup, five Irish drafts, and three shots of twelve-year-old scotch. Paddy always poured his friend doubles.

Danny would finish his last shot at precisely 7:00 p.m., rise from the corner barstool, and proclaim with a heavy Irish brogue, "Early to bed, early to rise makes a man a farmer! Good night to all. It's been one hell of a day!"

Danny would creep home in his fifteen-year-old rust wagon and quickly go to sleep. Danny O'Hara never dreamt about anything.

When he arose without the assistance of an alarm clock at 5:30 a.m., he knew today would be important. He dressed in the best of his three suits, placed a clean white hanky in the breast pocket, and went to the kitchen for his morning Irish whiskey kick-start.

Danny poured a double shot of single malt and looked deep into the golden calm that brought him love and understanding, not caring if his life meant nothing. And today he needed his whiskey more than ever. Yes, today Danny

O'Hara would complete his duty to his closest friend, Paddy O'Doul. Today Danny would tell Paddy's wife and daughter they were millionaires.

It had taken nearly nine weeks to gather all the assets of the late Patrick O'Doul. Twenty rental houses all scattered around the tavern and stocks worth more than fifteen million dollars. It appeared that Paddy had purchased IBM stock before there were computers and General Electric when vacuum cleaners had wooden handles. And of course, there was Paddy's love and his life, the Hikes Point Lounge, where he'd been senselessly murdered by a young handsome stranger, as Mr. Brown to this day proclaimed to all the C block inmates on death row.

Danny touched the glass of golden relief to his lips and stopped. Not today, Danny boy, not today. "Paddy's girls need you to be sharp." He set the single malt on the kitchen counter and left for his office.

Annie's face glowed with an obvious flush upon her silky cheeks as she watched Joshie cross the street. She met him as he entered and kissed him firmly upon the lips, not caring what the cool breezes might see or think. "I love you, Joshie boy. I truly do love you."

"One hot tea and a coffee, black," Josh ordered from the purple-haired hip-hop Chinese waitress.

"We've got a big day ahead, Shaggy." Josh ran his hand over and through his fiancée's very curly hair.

"Really?" she asked. "All I know about is Dad's will this afternoon at Mr. O'Hara's office."

"True indeed, my Irish angel, but after that we have to go back to my law office for a long night's work."

"Huh? For what?"

"You see, my precious, the partners of my most prestigious law firm have agreed to take on the appeal for one Mr. Cleophus Brown. And yours truly will be the lead attorney in this important death row case. Care to assist your future husband in saving your father's friend?"

She couldn't open her mouth for fear of losing all control of the overwhelming emotions building to overflow.

"I love you, Josh." Annie dabbed at the tears with her cotton napkin.

"Whaddya say, Annie? Let's get our pal Skip off death row."

"I'm there my sweetheart. I am there!"

Margaret O'Doul could not bear to leave her home after Paddy's death. She went to Sunday morning Mass and early morning trips to Kroger's for food. Beyond that she stayed inside the house, surrounded by the memories of her adoring, faithful husband.

Mrs. O'Doul arranged that day for Danny, Annie, and Josh to meet at 100 Maple Drive, where she believed Paddy's spirit might be watching.

"Can I get you a scotch or something?" Josh inquired to Danny O'Hara.

"No, thank you, sonny. I'll have what Maggie's having, if you please."

Danny took a long pull of iced Lipton. "Ah." He smacked his lips as if he really enjoyed this non-alcoholic beverage. "Tasty, yes indeed, refreshing! Got a nice color too!" he quipped, comparing the goldenness to that of twelve-year-old single malt.

"Please, everyone be seated. This won't take long." Danny opened a tattered portfolio and pulled a three-page document from it.

"Now, Maggie, you know dear Paddy was a man of few words. He said what he meant and meant what he said."

Margaret O'Doul nodded and smiled sadly.

Danny continued. "Six months ago, Annie, your father came by my office, which was a rare thing. He told me he was concerned."

"About what, Danny?" Josh interjected.

"Well, sonny, he couldn't really put his finger on it, but I could tell he was worried, and Paddy O'Doul was not a man to be about worrying!"

"Did he tell you, Mr. O'Hara, what had him concerned?" Annie felt she really didn't want the answer.

"Well, not really, in so many words. You see, for a while Paddy felt as if something might happen to the tavern."

"Tavern?" Josh quizzed.

"Sorry, sonny, the Hikes Point Lounge. Anyhow, Paddy sensed darkness outside the bar. Inside was a different story. That's where his friends and real purpose were each day. But outside? Hell, he even once said it was like something evil waited just outside the door."

"Evil?" Annie questioned.

"Yes, darling, and then there was the young lad whom Paddy kept seeing from a distance, always smiling at your father."

"A young man? Always smiling?" Annie's voice filled with anguish. "What did he look like?"

"Can't say, dear. Your father never mentioned it again; just seemed in a big hurry to redo his will."

Annie wrote down on the legal pad before her, *Young man. Mr. Brown saw him kill Dad, young man, Dad's funeral, smiling, afraid, evil, smiling.*

She pushed the pad in front of Josh.

"So about six months ago, Paddy and I drew up his last will and testament; he wanted it in two parts, one typed, and one he wrote and sealed in my presence, of which I can't speak of its contents. I've prepared a summary of his gifting to forego all the legal mumbo jumbo. So here are your father's final wishes."

"The house on 100 Maple Drive and thirteen million dollars go to my precious wife, Margaret Constance O'Doul."

Everyone gasped all at once.

"Excuse me?" Margaret whispered.

"Maggie, your husband was a very wealthy man, and no one knew it, including me." Danny handed her his white handkerchief. "Shall I continue?"

"Yes, please," Annie answered.

"Your father, Annie, also owned twenty houses scattered around the neighborhood in Hikes Point. All were lived in by the members of J.R.'s Breakfast Club. They'd lived there rent-free for years. I am to provide those men with clear and free titles to the properties."

"Wow," was all Josh could think to say.

"As to you, Annie, your father bequeathed two million dollars—one million at graduation from law school, and one million on the day of your wedding."

Annie O'Doul ran from the room in tears.

After several long minutes, Josh brought his fiancée

back into the living room. Annie sat next to her mother as they tightly held each other.

"Now," Danny went on to the sealed envelope. He read its contents.

"I, Patrick O'Doul, being of sound mind and judgment, do bequeath at the time of my death, the property, all contents, and the trade name of the Hikes Point Lounge to my dear friends, Daniel O'Hara and Cleophus Brown.

"They both must continue its operation. If they choose not to continue, or at their death, the business is to be donated to the Hikes Point Catholic parish. At that time, there is a separate trust at Citizen's Bank, controlled by Phil MacIntyre. The trust consists of one million dollars. The trust with the parish's assistance is to close the Hikes Point Lounge and convert it to a homeless shelter and soup kitchen for the needy."

This document was handwritten and signed by Patrick "Paddy" O'Doul.

Later that evening, Annie and Josh drove by the Hikes Point Lounge. It had not reopened after Paddy's murder. Several windows were cracked or broken. Trash blew around the entrance and clung to the exterior bricks like a magnet.

"Look," Josh whispered, "next to the door."

Annie gasped as she saw a ragtag man covered in filth and old newspapers. He was either dead or passed out. They really could not tell until they saw the man reach out for a half bottle of Mad Dog 20/20. Annie cried softly.

Neither saw the young man emerge from around the corner of the bar, tall, handsome, and wrapped in a dark gray cashmere coat. He walked over to the drunk laying helplessly at the entrance door. With highly polished, expensive Italian boots, the young man kicked the wino in the face and murmured with great hatred, "Die, you piece of crap!"

The man walked to the end of the strip mall and behind the new Pussy Cat Club with the gigantic sign flashing, "Girls, Girls, Girls."

He slid behind the large steering wheel of his black 560 SEL Mercedes, looked into the rearview mirror, smiled, straightened his red silk bowtie, and drove away.

The next two weeks would certainly come to prove Annie O'Doul's theory concerning good and bad luck. Yesterday? Two million dollars. Good luck. Today? It was time for the other side of the mountain.

At 9:00 a.m. Annie O'Doul walked into the big office her future husband occupied. She instantly knew something was wrong, very wrong!

"Honey, what is it?" She raced across the office and grabbed his hand.

"Annie, oh dear God, honey, they found Mr. Brown dead in his cell this morning."

"That's impossible! That can't be! How...what...why?"

"They don't know for sure, sweetheart. I talked to the warden an hour ago. He believes Mr. Brown might have choked to death."

Danny O'Hara could not even think about reopening the Hikes Point Lounge without Skip Brown. He guessed he'd just give it over to the Catholic parish. Probably what Paddy would want anyway.

Danny had not gone back to the office for six weeks now. After Mr. Brown died, he just didn't care. His new regimen was to drink all night and sleep all day. He had no friends, his sister disowned him, and she quit the family business. The only place he could find love was at The Pussy Cat Club… Girls, Girls, Girls.

That Friday night at 1:35 a.m., Danny attempted slurred conversation with two older dancers. He could barely see his hand in front of his face and did not notice one of the girls as she poured a packet of white powder in his glass of cheap rye.

"Good night, Danny boy; sleep tight." The gravity-challenged dancers giggled and left Danny facedown on the last table in the back beside the alley door.

The next morning, Joshua Berg sipped his coffee while watching the local news on WHAS. He stood as he watched the wrecker pull an old battered Chevy from the Taylorville Lake boat ramp.

The car, it seemed, had been spotted just before daybreak by two early morning fishermen.

"Local attorney, Daniel O'Hara was found dead this morning in his car at Taylorville Lake. Police cannot yet exclude foul play but believe the attorney was drunk and either mistakenly drove off the ramp or committed suicide."

Two days later, the police reported that Daniel O'Hara's blood alcohol level was three times the legal limit.

Danny had informed Phil MacIntyre of Paddy's will and what should happen to the one million dollar trust if he and Mr. Brown passed away. He'd promised to deliver the last will document by week's end. However, after Cleophus mysteriously died in his cell on death row, Danny left the document in a pile on the spare chair in his office. He also failed to notify the Hikes Point Catholic parish.

Danny's sister eventually went back to work after his death. His office contents were burnt in the fire barrel behind their office.

Phil MacIntyre resigned his position at the bank one week after the news of Danny O'Hara's driving off into Taylorville Lake.

He paid cash for the bungalow and the twenty-eight-foot sailboat swinging gently in the breeze yards away from the thatched beach bar, where he sipped his sixth umbrella drink.

The Costa Rican native poured Phil a fresh pink glass full. The bartender looked over at the new fully loaded sailboat, reading the large letters across its stern. He inquired, "Say, mon, where the hell's Hikes Point, Kentucky?"

"Somewhere over the rainbow, my man. That's where it is."

UNDER NEW MANAGEMENT

Annie O'Doul sat nervously beside her future husband, Josh Berg, facing the fifty-foot glass wall overlooking downtown Louisville with a perfect view of the Ohio River.

Annie watched the barge traffic amble effortlessly both east and west, as if taking a journey to nowhere. Maybe she was doing the same this gray dismal morning.

"You okay, sweetheart?" Josh squeezed her long, manicured fingers.

"Huh?" Annie broke her river trance. "Oh, yes, baby, I'm fine."

Richard Haddad, senior partner at Henthorn, Haddad, and Wildman, entered the large exquisite conference room occupying nearly 30 percent of the twenty-seventh floor of the new Imperial Towers complex, the tallest building in seven states.

"Good morning, young lady." His smile was warm and sincere.

"Good morning, Mr. Haddad. Thanks for helping us."

"Nonsense, glad to be of service, dear. And what's this 'Mr. Haddad' greeting anyway?"

"Sorry, Rich."

Richard Haddad treated Joshua Berg like a son. He'd hired Josh right out of law school and personally pulled the young man under his wing.

Haddad did not have children of his own. The joke around the office beyond his hearing was that he'd professionally adopted the young Joshua Berg as his own child to mentor.

Josh knew he was on the fast track, and he owed Rich Haddad a great deal in his third year with the firm. Josh Berg was now head of the tax law operation.

Annie, as Rich Haddad addressed the young lady in a firm yet caring manner, would also be joining the group as a criminal lawyer. *One big happy family,* Richard Haddad thought. *A son and a daughter.*

Richard Haddad took his normal position at the head of the deeply polished mahogany table that could seat thirty people. If you found yourself opposite the senior partners, you almost needed a microphone to speak to the impeccably dressed, handsome multimillionaire.

"So then,"—Richard sipped his mug of freshly ground

Columbian coffee—"here's the facts of our research." He stood like always and began to pace, exactly two steps west, a precise right turn, and back two steps east. He could do this all day and often did. "Let's review the facts,"—stopping to face Josh and Annie at step seven west.

"Mrs. Margaret O'Doul, Ms. Annie O'Doul, and Mr. Joshua Berg all have signed affidavits stating they were present when Mr. Daniel O'Hara, attorney of record for the deceased Mr. Patrick O'Doul, executed the reading of his final will."

Haddad took three steps west, turned, five steps east, stopped, and continued his summation.

"Now then, said will was a separate handwritten document supposedly signed by your father, Annie, and read aloud to all present by attorney Daniel O'Hara." Three steps east and a quick tap on the green speaker phone button. "Deloris, two black coffees and a hot tea, ginseng. Thank you."

Thirty seconds later, Deloris Graybill entered the throne room with coffee, tea, and a tray of fresh pastries. "Anything else, sir?"

"No thanks; hold my calls, Deloris."

"Yes sir, Mr. Haddad."

Annie noticed she bowed her head slightly in the senior partner's direction. Not out of subordination, rather out of awe for the man she'd served as personal assistant for nineteen years.

Haddad waited until the heavy oak door clicked soundly shut and headed west again. "Unfortunately, Mrs. O'Doul, her daughter, and Mr. Berg all heard attorney O'Hara read the handwritten will, but all admit to not actually reading the document. Not good."

Haddad stopped, sipped his hot Columbian brew, and took four steps west.

"As well, it is my legal assumption that said handwritten will was neither witnessed, nor was it notarized. Strange, one might think, since the document was given to an attorney who also employed a CPA at his law office."

Walking east now. "Further, there is no record of a million dollar trust at Citizen's Bank, and the suspect trustee, Mr. Phil MacIntyre, has vanished from the known world."

Back to the west, head down, right hand slowly rubbing his chin. "And lastly, no one at the Hikes Point Catholic parish office has any knowledge of the late Patrick O'Doul's final wishes."

Contrary to normal Haddad movement, the senior partner returned to his high-back throne. "We are three lawyers. Can we believe for one second, based on the facts, that there is one chance in a million that any probate judge would waste a moment of court time hearing our argument of 'he said, we heard'? Hearsay? A million dollars vanished? A Catholic parish turning a beer joint into a homeless shelter?"

"It wasn't a beer joint," Annie said softly.

Haddad rose, walked to his left, and gently placed his hands on Annie's slender shoulder.

"Sorry, my dear, for being insensitive. However, a judge would think it so and quite honestly, look for a scam inside the smoke."

Haddad stood silent for a long moment, circled the throne chair, and headed west. Five steps, then stopped. "You know our investigator, Mr. Hyde, and you know he is very good."

"The best," Josh added.

"Yes, well, Mr. Hyde informed me yesterday that Danny O'Hara's sister cleaned her brother's office of every single piece of paper, burning same in a rusty barrel behind their office. Stupid, but nonetheless, your father's wish for the Hikes Point Lounge went up in smoke for naught."

Another click of the green button. "Deloris, order lunch, please, sushi."

Heading east two steps. "And lastly, Ms. Lizzy O'Hara informed Mr. Hyde that her brother, attorney for the late Patrick O'Doul, never mentioned such an idiotic proposal as to give a bar full of old drunks to the blessed church. She further added that her late brother was prone to invented clients and great legal challenges only he could accomplish."

Haddad turned with a sad look on his face. "Honestly, young people, do you really want this firm to present this in court? Can you just see the front page of *The Louisville Times?* 'Well-known law firm laughed out of court.' Do you really want that?"

"No," was all Annie could offer.

"Well, sir,"—Josh looked first to his bride-to-be and then back across the half mile to the other side of the table—"isn't there anything we can do?"

"Yes!" Haddad made a sudden and surprising move by turning a chair backward exactly in the middle of east and west, sitting down facing the young couple. "We can buy it ourselves!"

"Really?" Annie immediately perked up.

"How … I mean, well, how?" Josh chuckled, as he knew he just sounded like a first-semester law student.

"Easy." Haddad up again, heading east.

"Mr. Hyde has learned of the impending auction of the property for back taxes. The auction will be by sealed bid day after tomorrow at the Hikes Point Township's clerk's office."

"How much?" Josh asked with excitement in his voice.

"That's the good news." The senior partner went all the way to the end, west, all the way back east before stopping. "Taxes owed are $18,200.66!"

"Piece of cake!" Annie O'Doul exclaimed, jumping into the air with arms stretched high. "I'm a millionaire."

All laughed loudly. "Hold it there, kiddo." Haddad looked serious. "It is a sealed bid, and even though the neighborhood is now overrun with druggies and hoodlums, the bar is still worth something and probably more than the taxes owed."

"How much is it worth, do you think?" Concern returned to Annie's porcelain face.

"Well, any bidder can easily find out the tax amount; it's public record." Rich Haddad was deep in thought now. "But one could surmise that any potential bidder would probably go in a bit higher, say twenty grand, just to be on the safe side."

Annie jumped to her feet again. "Let's go fifty thousand!"

"Wow!" Josh raised his eyebrows. "That's a lot of money, Annie!"

"Not if you're a millionaire!"

"Let's have lunch and celebrate the new bar owner!" A rare exuberance from the senior partner.

Annie O'Doul gave Haddad a frown.

"Oh, excuse me, Annie; let us celebrate the new owner of the Hikes Point Lounge!"

Two days later, at precisely 9:00 a.m., Annie O'Doul and Joshua Berg entered the main branch of Citizen's Bank. Annie placed the certified check for fifty thousand dollars in a bank letter-sized envelope, sealed it, and gave it to Josh.

Their plan was for Josh to attend the auction, surprise all the other bidders that would be there to steal her father's business, and return for an early dinner and celebration.

Mr. Hyde, the law firm's investigator, provided a key to the Hikes Point Lounge. Josh, without telling Annie, decided to give the place his once-over before going to the Hikes Point town hall and securing the bid.

Their future plan was to open a homeless shelter, funding the startup by a one hundred thousand dollar donation from Annie O'Doul and a matching check from the account of Henthorn, Haddad, and Wildman. Mrs. Maggie O'Doul would provide eight hundred thousand dollars as well.

At noon that day, Josh pulled his 300 series BMW into the strip mall anchored by the Hikes Point Lounge.

When he'd left his downtown office, the sun was out and the day warm; the air crisp, and the deep feeling that all would be fine. No, not fine, it bordered on great!

Now, in the parking lot of the Hikes Point Lounge, the sun hidden by low dark clouds, a misty wetness in the air, the young man felt cold as he reached into the BMW for his Brooks Brother's raincoat.

Josh stood there for a moment, surveying the strip mall that at one time he thought was probably a cool little neighborhood center.

Next to Annie's dad's establishment was Mamma's

Diner. You could still see the red, white, and blue letters in the cracked glass: "Real Home Cooking." Beside Mamma's Diner sat Harvey's Hardware, followed by Big Al's Barbershop, Tina's Sewing Center, and a used bookstore. *A good place,* he thought, *for older, retired couples living in the nearby neighborhood; a good place for the old boys belonging to J.R.'s Breakfast Club. Get a haircut, a shine, pick up a Zane Gray cowboy novel, have a few beers with Paddy, Danny, and Mr. Brown. Not a bad way to live out the last few years,* he considered.

Now all the family-owned businesses were closed, broken and cracked windows at every storefront. Trash littered and hid in every doorway; broken bottles, beer cans and even human waste covered the parking area. Yet to his right, even in daylight, the gigantic neon sign flashed twenty-four-seven: *"The Pussy Cat Club... Girls, Girls, Girls."*

Josh pondered, *If ever a place needed a homeless shelter... better yet, one great big fire would be even better.*

The young man could not help the queasy feeling deep down in his gut as the yellow police tape flapped in the wind, still partially attached to the entrance of the Hikes Point Lounge.

Josh turned the brass key in the lock and pushed the heavy door open. The musty odor, mixed with the smell of stale beer and who knew what else, would gag a garbage man, he felt sure.

The place was dark. No, not dark, it was black, pitch black. He flicked on the flashlight wisely taken from the glove compartment. He moved slowly forward.

"Gee, this place is an icebox." Josh couldn't remember ever being this cold. It didn't make any sense. He shivered, stepping closer to the old hand-carved bar with the great brass railing, now greenish gray with mold. Then he turned the light to the antique mirror and froze in his steps. Red stains covered the left side. It looked like old dried blood, more black than red. At that moment, he also recognized something else on the mirror—parts of Annie's father's brain and scalp.

Josh dropped the light and vomited. He could not stop after emptying his entire stomach. He continued to dry heave, falling to the floor.

He ran, fell, stumbled, crawled, and pulled his way out, praying with every step. "Please, God, please get me out of here!"

His flashlight left behind, the only light in the darkness directed its beam on an old tan hat, brim turned up all around. It was the hat that Mr. Brown always wore Friday nights at the Hikes Point Lounge.

Josh closed the door and bent over at the waist, still gagging and gasping for air.

"Little boy got a tummy ache?" The harsh voice caused Josh to look up. "Would you like us to call your mommy?"

Joshua Berg raised his head to see six very large and sinister men before him.

"I'm okay," he said in a low voice. "I just—"

The man with a red tattoo of the devil on his ham-sized forearm hit Josh squarely in the face, breaking his jaw and knocking out four teeth with his powerful blow.

"Grab his wallet," one of the evil-looking thugs demanded, "and his car keys."

Another pulled his raincoat from his body as the toothless man howled like a demon from hell, pulling off Josh's shoes.

Joshua Berg faded into blackness after the last of many heavy booted kicks caught him squarely in the temple.

Borack Abbadon entered the Hikes Point Township's city hall at 1:58 p.m. He'd arrived by armored limo. On each side stood two Arab men dressed in heavy coats with bulges just below their armpits.

Borack Abbadon presented his card to the clerk. The card, slick black with gold embossed lettering, read, "Borack Abbadon, Purveyor." At the bottom were three addresses: New York, Paris, and Turkey.

"We are here, madam,"—his voice was strong and almost musical—"for the auction of one Hikes Point Lounge."

He smiled, and the young overweight clerk with short greasy dirty blond hair nearly fainted. "Can you direct us, dear, to the proper place?"

"Yeah!" she squealed, showing a mouth with too many teeth. "Right this way, uh, sir!"

Two doors down, Mr. Abbadon walked through the door marked Township Clerk.

Timmy Trout stood behind a cheap podium standing on a box to make his five-foot-two-inch frame larger. The little man, nearly bald, wearing a powder blue sweater vest and yellow bowtie, swallowed hard when Mr. Borack Abbadon walked in with the very tough-looking bodyguards.

"Can I help you gentlemen?" Timmy's voice squeaked. It reminded Abbadon of a mouse, and he momentarily thought of the great pleasure possible by stepping on the blue-vested rodent's tiny bald head.

"Yes sir, I certainly hope so." Timmy's fear subsided with the beauty of the handsome stranger's pronouncement. "We are here for the Hikes Point Lounge property auction, I believe."

"Well, of course you are!" Timmy giggled. "And my goodness, it's five past bidding time!"

Timmy touched his little thin fingers to his blushing cheek.

"Now, let's see." Timmy surveyed the empty room. "The bidding process for the Hikes Point Lounge has officially begun. All bidders, please bring your offers to the podium."

Borack smiled and considered killing the little rat somewhere down the road for the fun of it.

"Okay then." Timmy was on his tiptoes now. "I guess, Mr., uh, Abbadon, you have the single sealed bid. Should we open it?" Again, the mousy squeal.

"Mr. Abbadon's bid is … $18,200.66."

Timmy's voice squealed as he once again touched his fat little cheek. "Oh my goodness, that's exactly the amount owed in back taxes!"

"Excuse me, sir." Abbadon touched Timmy on the shoulder, and the clerk nearly fainted. "Do you believe in supernatural miracles?"

"Well, Mr. Abbadon, I've never really thought much about it."

"You should start, Timmy. You never know when something new and strange might happen!"

Abbadon pushed the armrest button, and the bulletproof glass dividing front and back slid open. Next to the limo driver sat a very beautiful woman.

The exquisite beauty turned silently toward Borack. "Here, Grey, take care of this." He handed the deed for the Hikes Point Lounge to his personal assistant.

"Anything else, sir?"

"Yes, Grey, call Polly and tell him to meet us in New York tomorrow."

"Done," she said.

The glass closed off the front. Abbadon closed his eyes and whispered something in a very strange language that neither bodyguard understood.

The morning newspaper and all three local television channels were filled with the news of yet another murder in the Hikes Point Township. The *Courier Journal* headline read: "Hikes Point Going to Hell!"

"The sanitation department discovered the body of Joshua Berg this morning in a dumpster behind the Pussy Cat Club. Mr. Berg was employed as a lawyer at the prestigious firm of Henthorn, Haddad, and Wildman. Preliminary police reports indicated that Mr. Berg had been bludgeoned to death."

Polly watched the report on the overhead television just beyond the Delta gate bound for New York from Louisville. He brushed his hand over his short blond hair, straightened his red bowtie, and smiled.

Two days later, the news would report the death of Timothy Trout, a clerk for the Hikes Point Township. Mr. Trout's body was recovered in a wooded section of forest south of Louisville. Police reported that his head was crushed. No suspects at this time.

Annie O'Doul did not cry at Josh's funeral, and not a tear at the burial either. She'd buried the pain so deep that it could never surface. Her innocence, love, hopes, and dreams left her as she dropped a handful of cold red dirt on top of Joshie's casket.

Annie refused the arm of Richard Haddad and remained at the gravesite long after the last mourner had gone. She waited. She watched. She looked in all directions for a tall young stranger with a red bowtie. He wasn't there.

Annie finally walked away from the end of her dreams, now six feet deep in a cold, dark hole. Head down and void of any lifelike feelings, she sensed someone. To her left and several hundred yards away, a woman stood upon a hill just next to a single old oak tree. It was dead. From that distance, Annie could see long, thick, white hair, yet the woman looked young. She also noticed the red scarf wrapped around the woman's neck. This woman looked lovingly at Annie, turned and walked out of sight.

THE MASTER'S WORK

Ms. Annie O'Doul returned to the offices of Henthorn, Haddad, and Wildman one day after the love of her life was laid to rest. She must work now. There was nothing left but to hide in the massive law offices.

Annie would give her all to become a criminal attorney dedicated to defending the scum of the earth. She needed murderers and rapists.

Annie would bring forth an awesome defense for every lowlife she represented, and she would secretly pass on to the police and prosecutor that one little bit of information that would determine the execution of the guilty without them ever seeing it coming.

New York, New York

The hefty bodyguard, born and trained in Iran, looked through the thick door's sight hole for several long moments.

"It's Polly, Father."

"Let him in, Turk! It's Polly's turn to have a real job."

Grey sat motionless next to her employer, lover, and master on the enormous hand-stitched couch made in China by real artists with needle and expensive threads of silver, gold, and pure silk. The embroidered furniture depicted the entire story of Lucifer's war fought with Michael the archangel. However, in this beautiful display of rare artistry, Lucifer decapitates Michael's head from his angelic body, standing above the heavenly host in heaven.

"Enter," the Iranian muscleman capable of killing you with a finger stated flatly.

"What's happening, Turk?" Polly enigmatically shot back with his usual gleaming smile. "Good to see you, old man."

Polly spoke with a perfect English accent only to annoy the Iranian maniac. Turk hated the Brits almost as much as Americans. Timmy Trout was the last US citizen to see that hatred as the heavy boot of the Muslim killer crushed his skull with one fatal stomp.

Polly proceeded into the living area of the palatial penthouse. "Good afternoon, Father." Polly's voice sounded humble and in awe of the man he both loved and feared.

Polly then tilted his head in reverence to the beautiful young woman with the thick waist-long white-streaked hair.

"Grey, my honor to see you again."

This time Polly spoke with a thick Russian accent, his native tongue. The young man could actually speak six different languages, with numerous dialects for each language.

Grey, likewise, spoke six languages, preferring Russian, as both she and Polly came from a prison orphanage in the former Soviet Union. She was the older and protective sister of Apolyon, or Polly, as his adoptive father, Borack Abbadon, had named him. His sister, however, didn't have a real name that anyone knew of. At the age of thirteen, after a Russian prison guard raped her, the young Soviet beauty with blond hair similar to a lion's mane returned to the freezing dungeon where she and her brother starved. Her golden hair turned white after being violently molested. That night the prison camp burned to the ground.

The next day, 256 burned bodies, consisting of men, women, and children, were unceremoniously bulldozed into a frozen pile of humanity in the black wilderness to be devoured by Russian wolves.

Two days later, the Soviet Union's Ministry of Prisons contacted the KGB. Sixty-six guards had also been found outside the barbed-wire enclosure in a stacked heap. All were executed by a single gunshot to the head. All but one, who had been decapitated. That guard was the man who earlier had raped the young girl now known as Grey. The KGB would find no clues as to who may have executed 6,600 Russian soldiers.

Polly could remember nothing of his childhood before the age of seven, the age when he and Grey were rescued from their frozen hell. Grey, however, remembered everything—the men running everywhere dressed in white long coats, the gleaming black pistols, and the man in the long fur coat, the man with the wide-blade sword that glistened in the full moon's light. Grey watched as her savior clearly separated head from body from the filthy, hairy man who not moments before took the only innocence that remained within her tiny soul.

Forty-eight hours later, Grey and Polly sat beside a great fireplace, safe and warm in the grand palace buried deep in the mountains of Pakistan.

Borack Abbadon was royalty of unknown origin, but nonetheless a man of great power, wealth, and evil.

Grey recalled his first words, "My children." His voice still left her speechless. "I have many homes around the world and many children just like you, little children forgotten and thrown into the trash pile of man. Hopeless babies that the God of weakness has discarded."

Borack circled the young girl and her brother, moving without sound. He stood behind Grey and stroked her beautiful blond-gray hair. "Ah yes, my dear ones, I will raise you to be strong and powerful. I will give you love, and you will worship me. Together, the world will become our kingdom."

Grey, remembering and attempting not to, could recall that moment as she turned her head up to see her savior's eyes roll back in his head. He swayed slowly as if in a trance and whispered a language only he knew, although he spoke many. She remembered being afraid, only for an instant.

And even today, on the rare occasion when her master and lover spoke the unknown words, Grey chilled.

"Sit, Polly; sit, my son!" Borack's voice was loving and welcoming. "Good work in Louisville. I'm very proud of you."

"I am here to serve you, sir." Polly's commitment and admiration were clear in the proclamation.

"Would you like to have a brandy with me and your sister?"

"No thank you, sir. I'm fine, sir. Nice place, Father." This was the first time Polly had been invited to one of Abbadon's personal residences, although Grey knew all thirty locations well.

"Thank you, son. We try to live above the crowd." Borack's laughter felt warm as Grey reached out and caressed his long, strong fingers. "Please forgive me for my negligence. A father wishes all his children to share in his ambiance!"

Grey knew better. She believed Borack laid claim to over a hundred *children* such as Polly and herself. But in twenty years of being Abbadon's constant companion, she'd seen maybe ten or twelve of her adoptive siblings actually be welcomed to Borack's private sanctuaries.

All were male, approximately Polly's size and age, and all with the trademark short, closely cropped blond hair. Each of the young men were articulate, well schooled, and impeccably attired. And each one looked at you with eyes as cold as the Soviet prison camp where her savior had pulled her from a living hell.

"I am honored, sir, for the pleasure of your presence, be it penthouse or, well, the Hikes Point Lounge."

Borack laughed warmly, stood, and pulled Polly into

a loving embrace. "You are indeed a good son. I have prepared you for the great moment yet to come for *The Beginning*." The words trailed off in a hiss.

Grey moved nervously as her master began to sway. "That moment when the God of nothingness will seek to add to his horde of worthless souls. Those slugs that serve no one but themselves. 'Save me, Lord, save me,' they'll cry out to a worthless God."

Borack spoke in the unknown language. Grey pulled her knees to her chest, pressing her forehead to herself in fear. On the other side of the table, Polly swayed in rhythm, eyes closed, listening to the musical tone of the unknown language. Polly whispered, "Ali, ali, ali luc, ali am ali luc, death for the master."

Several silent moments passed before Grey opened her eyes. Polly stood before the large glass windows overlooking the great city of New York. Borack stood beside the young man, arm across his shoulders.

"Look before you, my son. Millions of lost souls living in their self-made prison of lust, greed, pride, and deceit, lost, helpless, and empty. Void of purpose, my dear boy. Void of a true God to serve. It is our battleground, and it shall become our harvest."

Polly looked adoringly into his father's black scintillating eyes. "What must I do to serve you, my father?"

"Patience is a virtue, my son!" Borack laughed. "I believe I recall that quote. Let me think; yes, from the children's book called Proverbs. I believe a Jewish king of a weak people wrote that. Not much of a king, but I must admit I loved his lifestyle!"

Borack poured brandy into the sparkling crystal glasses

for himself and his adopted children. Polly couldn't refuse the offer this go around.

"Now, boy, listen carefully."

Polly moved to the very tip of his chair, which was also finely embroidered with the biblical scene of Job covered in sores and dirt.

"You must return to Louisville. We now own the entire property attached to the Hikes Point Lounge, the girly club, and twenty houses in the neighborhood providing homes for our unsuspecting senior trash."

"When should I return?" Polly was ready to get back in action.

"Today, my son." Borack smiled softly at Grey. "You are to return and give the entire strip center a makeover. First class all the way!"

"And the money for my work, sir?"

Borack laughed heartily. "There is an account with $750,000 in the business name of Hikes Point Party Center. It seems we received a wonderful donation from a weak soul residing in Costa Rica recently. Poor fellow, I heard a local native bartender slit his throat!"

"Awesome!" Polly rubbed his hands together.

"Anyway, my son, continue your work as assigned until further instructions. This is but a small piece in the beautiful puzzle that awaits the final calling."

Polly bowed to his master and father and promptly left the penthouse.

Borack gently held Grey's hand and pulled her from the couch. "Come, my darling. Your brother has made me weary, and I need your touch."

ANNIE O'DOUL

Time passed quickly for Annie O'Doul. Exactly 365 days since Joshua Berg's funeral. She could not, she would not, visit his grave, nor did she visit her father's.

Annie moved back in with her mother after Margaret O'Doul suffered her second light stroke. Two months later, Mrs. O'Doul was relegated speechless when the third massive stroke rendered her helpless.

Annie made the ten-mile trek to the Rest Haven nursing home almost daily. She believed her mother could hear but was not responsive to any other modes of communication.

After Maggie's first stroke, the thirteen million dollar inheritance from Margaret's dearly beloved husband transferred to Annie.

Annie O'Doul, now the youngest criminal lawyer at Henthorn, Haddad, and Wildman, was also a multimillionaire. Brilliant, beautiful, and very rich, Annie O'Doul however felt soulless and desperately alone.

The young woman now lived in the family home at 100 Maple Drive. The place still gave her a feeling of warmth and safety.

All the furnishings remained exactly as her mother left them. Annie pretended that Mom, as she remembered her, would return someday, yet in her heart she knew better.

She remained in the bedroom where her childhood and teen years were lived. It was a large room with an attached bath.

Late each evening the young woman attempted to find comfort in the pink lace window treatments, hand sewn by her precious mother. At last count the room contained eighty stuffed bunny rabbits, all given to her by her father over the course of eighteen years. Big fluffy rabbits, crystal rabbits, why, she actually had a black rabbit made of silky mink. It was that one, her favorite, that Annie O'Doul held to tightly each night, struggling to find sleep.

The right nightstand displayed a silver frame and a picture of Paddy and Maggie O'Doul. Her father was in a wide-lapelled gray suit and fat tie, his arm around her mother lovingly as they stood in front of the Hikes Point Lounge. It had been grand opening day. Beside the picture of her parents so young and full of hope stood the eight-by-ten picture of Josh in front of the county courthouse, new Hartman briefcase in hand and huge smile on his face. *So handsome,* she thought. *So brilliant, so perfect in every way.* A tear moved down her cheek as she whispered, "And so dead."

On the left nightstand sat the bunny lamp that also served as a rotating music box, little girl rabbits dressed in tiny pastel dresses moving up and down as the lamp turned round and round playing "Here comes Peter Cottontail, hopping down the bunny trail…"

In front of the lamp rested her white Bible, the one her mother purchased at her first Holy Communion, the Bible Annie read a verse from each night before she dreamed of pretty things to come. Annie O'Doul did not read the Bible anymore. She did not open its white leather cover because Annie knew there was no God.

Richard Haddad booked the entire restaurant atop the Galt House Hotel after Ms. Annie O'Doul passed the bar exam first try, and with the highest score of any attorney now employed at the firm of Henthorn, Haddad, and Wildman.

Mr. Haddad closed the firm for the first time in history to celebrate Annie's accomplishment and her acceptance to the firm as criminal attorney. Every single employee, 314 in total, was present and accounted for.

There was a twelve-piece orchestra, all members of the Louisville Symphony. The mayor was there, the chief of police, and the prosecuting attorney. The *Louisville Times* even ran a front-page story on the event. Unfortunately, they also retold the story of her father and Josh's murders.

There were speeches made, congratulations in abundance from people Annie didn't even know, and just before the filet mignon was served with very expensive wine, Richard Haddad stepped up to the microphone.

"Welcome, and thank you all for joining me in this grand celebration. We are honored to have you with us, Mr. Mayor," which was followed by much applause.

"As well, I thank you, Chief Maddox, and our own very talented prosecuting attorney, Forrester Bingham, for taking time to be with me on this important and personal occasion."

Haddad reached out his hand. "Annie, would you please join me on the stage?"

Annie hesitated then nervously moved up beside the man who was responsible for this lavish and unprecedented event.

"Now I know," Haddad began smoothly, "that there might be one or two of our talented and hardworking associates that question this event and its expense. You might even hear a whisper like, 'Who is this girl anyway? Big deal, she scored higher than most on the bar exam.' I can understand such thoughts, so allow me to clarify several key points."

Haddad moved closer to Annie, gently placing his arm around her waist. "For those who have yet to meet this beautiful and smart young woman, all know of the tragedies she has endured in the last few years. She has done so with dignity, grace, and perseverance, all qualities we hope to personally attain in our lives." The room was silent and attentive.

"Yet through it all, Annie O'Doul maintained a toughness I have yet to see even from the strongest men I've known. I respect that immensely, as we all should." The guests stood to their feet and applauded for several long minutes. Annie blushed and bowed her head.

Haddad raised his hand, and everyone quietly returned to his or her seat.

"Furthermore, Ms. Annie O'Doul will be representing this firm as a criminal defense attorney for the poor souls unable to afford proper legal counsel. She will do so pro bono, and this firm plans to support her efforts with our full array of resources. Sorry, Mr. Prosecuting Attorney!" Haddad smiled innocently.

"I salute you, Ms. O'Doul, and know I'll be facing a worthy adversary in the courtroom." The prosecutor bowed, and everyone laughed cheerfully.

"As well, Annie is financially secure and has requested her salary in total be directed to the West End Catholic homeless shelter!" The second standing ovation.

"Please, please," Haddad continued. "And there remains one final point. As all of you know, I have no children of my own. Since meeting the beloved Joshua Berg, his soul resting in heaven, and this wonderful young lady, I felt like a real father for the first time in my life. I am proud to take claim to my fatherhood with this wonderful girl. I am proud to call you my daughter!"

Annie threw her arms around him and whispered, "And I'll be proud to be your daughter."

Rich, looking over Annie's shoulder, nodded toward a young intern in the back. Then six interns rolled a massive array of burgundy-colored law books on large flat carts. "Turn around, Annie," Haddad spoke tenderly.

"The partners of Henthorn, Haddad, and Wildman are honored to present you, Ms. Annie O'Doul, with the newest, most up-to-date criminal justice law library in this city!"

"I can't believe you did this. Thank you, Rich, and thank you for making this day so wonderful."

Rich kissed her cheek. "And lastly, before we dig into

some great filet and very expensive wine, our accountants need to know that none of today's festivities were paid for from the coffers of our firm. This is my gift to my adopted daughter as her graduation present. Let the party begin!"

The next day, Ms. Annie O'Doul moved into the massive office of recently retired partner, Franklin Masterson, the office just across the hall from Rich Haddad.

One week later, around 9:00 a.m., Mr. Haddad knocked on Annie's open door. "Can I come in, Annie?"

"I don't believe you need to ask, sir."

Rich chuckled and pulled the black leather chair closer to Annie's enormous stainless steel and beveled glass desk. "Here you go, kiddo, your first case." He tossed a file across the polished glass surface. "Let me know if I can help!"

That was what she really needed, real action. For the first time in a long while she felt alive again. She opened the file. "Nick Yarborough, age thirty-three, black male, seventeen priors for possession, terroristic threatening, concealed weapon charge, attempted rape, breaking and entering, and now attempted murder.

"You're going down, scumbag," she whispered.

Annie O'Doul, attorney at law, sat across the gnarly and scratched wooden table inside room three at the county jail.

Across from her sat Nick Yarborough, hands cuffed in a blue jumpsuit with numbers stenciled front and back.

"So, Mr. Yarborough, let's hear your side of the story."

"Hey, what your name, man? Uh, sorry, I mean, what's I supposed to call you?"

"My name is Annie O'Doul. I am your court appointed attorney."

"That's cool, man. I mean, Annie, cool name, man. My momma used to be called Annie sometime. Call me Little P."

"I think I'll stick with Nick, if that's okay."

"Hey, baby, whatever floats your boat. Nick be cool!"

"So then, Nick, what really happened?"

"Man, I mean, Annie, the man set me up on this bogus charge, man. I mean look, like, I'm innocent! I'm bein' framed by that undercover redneck cop, Rusty somebody."

"How so, Nick?"

"Well, you see, I was over at my peep's house, Dante. Hanging out, you know what I mean? Watching the Pistons get their butts kicked and enjoying a few Colt 45s, and in come this fat sister. I don't know her from Santa Claus' old lady. And you know she starts bustin' my stuff, saying I owe some money for some weed or something. Man, I'm clean. I don't even do no drugs. So I tell the whore to get out of my face before I pop a cap in her Cadillac behind."

"You did have a gun, then?"

"Nah, Annie, that's just street talk! I just wanted all two hundred pounds of her fat self to chill and let me watch the game with my brother, Dante."

"No gun, then?"

"Nah, I already told you! It was that ignorant big momma's boyfriend did the shootin'!"

"Do you know him?"

"No way, man. Just some big black dude new to the hood from Detroit I heard. He came bustin' in Dante's place waving a .45 screaming, 'Give Yolanda the money, boy, or I'll kill you dead!' Man, the brother was for real, and I don't have no idea what he or his fat girlfriend are talking about!"

"So what happened, then?"

"Man, I was scared, you know, man waving a big .45 in my face like that. So I hit him with a quart of brew upside the head, and the fool started shooting up Dante's apartment. Crazy!"

"So the big black man shot Yolanda?"

"Yeah man! Shot her twice in her big butt. Hard to miss!" Nick laughed. "He booked, and big butt go running down the hallway, screamin,' 'He shot me! Little P done shot me!' Man, she's lying trying to protect her boyfriend. Just ask Dante; he saw the whole thing!"

"I understand the police are having a problem locating your friend Dante."

"Tell 'em to go look in Gary, Indiana. That's where he live sometime."

Detective Rusty Judd had been in the neighborhood at Thirty-Fifth and Lincoln, two blocks into the west-end projects. He was there undercover on a drug buy.

His report claimed that he heard four rounds fired on the second floor of building D-62 around ten thirty. Responding to the gunshots, he found Yolanda Brown screaming in the hallway, her backside covered in blood. The detective knew the wounded victim from previous drug arrests. She was one of his best informants in the rat nest, as he called this part of town.

Entering apartment twenty-one after a quick search, Detective Rusty Judd found said suspect, Nick Yarborough, hiding under the bed. He did not, however, locate a firearm.

She picked up the receiver after the first ring. "Annie O'Doul."

"Ms. O'Doul, Forrester Bingham, prosecuting attorney, good morning!"

"How can I help you today, Mr. Bingham?" Her voice was serious and businesslike.

"May I call you Annie?" His voice was sugary.

"Please do, Forrester."

"Well, Annie, I don't normally get involved with the usual mundane trash cases, but I thought since the case in question was one at your firm, and well, I'm personal friends with Rich Haddad, you deserved a heads-up."

"Please continue, Forrester."

"Well, it concerns your representation of one Nick Yarborough, a career criminal, as you know I'm sure, and a very bad cat."

"And?"

"Well, Annie, one of my associates will be prosecuting, and with the testimony of Yolanda Brown that Yarborough shot her, attempted murder, I thought I'd offer you a plea deal and move on to more important cases."

"How thoughtful, Forrester. However, my client is innocent. I believe what you have is a 'she said, he said' situation."

"You don't really believe that, do you, Annie?"

"Have you found the weapon? Has anyone talked to the eyewitness, Dante, yet?"

"Well no, but I don't believe—"

"See you in court, Counselor." Ms. O'Doul hung up the phone.

Forrester Bingham just stared blankly at the dead phone in his hand. "I don't believe what just happened. Of all the arrogance!"

The DA looked across the desk of one of his superstars. "Tom, I want you to bury Nick Yarborough! Charge attempted murder. Go for life!"

"Yes sir, good as done."

Bingham rose from his chair. "Okay, little girl, you want to learn about courtroom action the hard way? Lawyer up, honey!"

After a six-month search, Annie secured the services of a private investigator shortly after Josh was murdered. The firm's main office was downtown Atlanta, and her contact, Macklin, ex-FBI, worked only for her now. With fifteen million in stocks, cash, and bonds, she could afford him.

To date, Macklin, ex-FBI and CIA agent, worked on finding her father and Josh's killers. So far, nothing.

It took the investigator two days to locate Dante Stallings in Gary, Indiana, and thirty minutes to get the truth out of him.

Annie sat next to her handcuffed client, Nick Yarborough, dressed in a Walmart suit two sizes too big. She'd purchased the clothes and purposefully bought the garments large. She wanted this thug to feel small.

The young assistant DA called Detective Rusty Judd to the stand. Sandy hair to his shoulders, reddish full beard, and deep blue eyes, he looked anything but a cop.

Rusty, undercover cop extraordinaire, took the stand and locked eyes with Annie O'Doul. She froze. His look was sad yet strong. She could see pain and love inside this man. Annie forced herself to look away.

Then Exhibit A: one .45 caliber pistol was produced with Nick Yarborough's fingerprints all over it. The cop, Rusty Judd, testified that after going back a second time to search for the weapon that shot Yolanda Brown, the pistol had been located in the freezer, pushed inside a box of frozen White Castle hamburgers.

Undercover police officer Rusty Judd failed to share with the court that he knew where to look after finding a typed note on his desk telling him the location of the gun.

The judge pronounced Nick Yarborough guilty of attempted murder and sentenced the thirty-three-year-old man to life without parole.

Annie pulled the file from the fireproof combination locked file cabinet marked "scumbags." She dropped Mr. Yarborough's court sentencing documents inside.

"One down." She smiled.

MACKLIN

Six months passed quickly as Annie O'Doul prepared for the fourth scumbag representation in district court. Annie was zero and three.

No one seemed to notice that in each case there seemed to be that one surprising piece of evidence that convicted the accused at the last moment. Nor did anyone question that Rusty Judd, undercover cop, was the arresting officer in all three cases. Not that unusual since two of the three cases were drug related and the last an armed robbery of a west-end pharmacy. All three offenders were repeat criminals, and each received life without the possibility of parole. Attorney O'Doul's secret scumbag file was gaining girth.

Mr. Haddad, senior partner at Henthorn, Haddad, and Wildman, stood quietly, arms crossed, leaning against the door frame of Annie's colossal office. "Got a moment, Annie?"

"All the time you need, Rich. What's up?"

"Well, Annie, please don't take this the wrong way, but I've had several calls recently..." Rich hesitated.

"Please, Rich, what is it? I think you know I'm pretty thick-skinned. Fire away!"

"First, let me say that I'll support whatever you do, and I recognize that the lowlifes you've represented were all guilty and deserved what they got!"

"And, Rich?"

"Well, Annie, the *Louisville Times* editor called me—we're close friends, you know."

"Yes, sir. Mr. Tate is a fine newspaperman."

"Anyway, Bill told me that one of his best crime reporters is proposing a story on our firm!"

"And that's bad?"

"Yes, dear; it seems the story 'Rich Man, Poor Man' is how this firm always seems to win every case when the client has a lot of money. But when the poor down-on-their-luck criminals come our way, they have all received life terms!"

"As you said before, Rich, they deserved what they got."

"I know, I know, and they did, but, honey, guilty verdicts, no matter who goes to jail, could have a negative effect when a big client is considering who best to save his neck! And you know, Annie, we're not the only game in town!"

"I've done my best, sir." Annie hated lying to this man who truly cared for her.

"I know you have, dear. You're a darn good lawyer, all agree. The judges love you, the cops love you, even Forrester thinks you are terrific. But, Annie, they don't bring in the big-ticket clients. See my point? And now I hear the ACLU is looking at the case you're currently involved in! I just don't want to see you get hurt, Annie."

Annie knew that to be partially true, but she also knew that Richard Haddad loved his law firm more than his wife, Annie O'Doul, and probably God, if the truth be told. "I understand your dilemma, Rich; I honestly do. Can I have a day or two to think about a good solution?"

"Absolutely! Take your time, Annie. Actually, I'm looking for an assistant in large civil actions that I personally represent!"

"That's sweet, Richard. Give me twenty-four hours."

"We'll make it work, Annie; I know two great minds will find the right answer!"

"I'm sure we will." Annie smiled as Mr. Haddad walked away, wiping a tear from his eye.

The next day Richard Haddad stepped on the lavender envelope as he entered his office, no doubt slipped under his office door either very late or very early.

He quickly, still standing, opened the envelope. *A faint odor of flowers,* he thought and instantly recognized Annie's signature handwriting.

Dear Richard:

Thank you for being a man of love and great honor. I don't imagine I would have endured the past several years without your genuine kindness and undying support. I will be eternally grateful.

I have given considerable thought to our conversation of yesterday. You have every right to be concerned. Here I am, a young attorney with zero experience. No doubt the criminals will not improve, nor will my ability to represent them. To be truthful, I'm just not cut out for this.

I have given Tom Conway my files on the recent case you assigned me. It's in the early stages, and I've yet to even meet the client. This will be good for Tom, and I'm sure the ACLU will love his liberal bleeding heart!

Last night I cleaned my office of all personal stuff and thought a silent departure best.

I have a new direction, something I've thought about for a long time! Rich, it will be exciting, and it will be fulfilling. Can't ask for more than that!

Again, thanks for everything. I'll be in touch.

With respect and love,

Annie O'Doul Haddad
Adopted Daughter

Richard Haddad slumped in his desk chair, turned to look out across Louisville's skyline, and cried like a baby. He felt gutless and very lonely.

Macklin sipped his scotch on the rocks and listened carefully to Annie O'Doul. Annie, likewise, sipped a chilled glass of red wine as she leaned forward across the small table in the very back of Tratorrio Mateen's, an expensive restaurant in the Buckhead area of Atlanta.

Annie did not know if this man had any other name or if it was his first or last name. Maybe he only used one name because of his sensitive work, or maybe because of his past. She just didn't know.

His white business card with raised black letters simply read, "Macklin, Investigator."

Macklin was a very quiet man but carried an intensity you could actually feel. Short military haircut, salt and pepper colored, black eyes hard and sensitive, ever changing.

Dressed in faded blue jeans (not the store-bought stonewashed kind), black highly polished combat boots, a black mock turtleneck, and a waist-length brown leather flight jacket, very worn, he looked the part of an old 1940s movie private eye.

"Ms. O'Doul." His voice was deep and masculine.

"Annie, please. I'm not an old spinster, you know."

"That's a given." A slight smile exposed very white and straight teeth.

He continued. "I know you must be disappointed in my results, or should I say lack of, in finding those responsible for Mr. Berg and your father's deaths. All I can say is that the killer or killers are not your average thugs like those we've recently, shall we say, assisted in their demise."

"Not so, Macklin!" Annie interrupted. "I have great faith in your ability; that's why I wanted to meet you here tonight."

His black eyes sparkled, and his expression was quizzical.

"You see, Macklin, I quit the firm yesterday and have a new plan."

Macklin, folding his big hands, resting his strong chin on top, leaned forward. "New plans?"

"Yes, and I hope you'll help me see it through."

Macklin did not respond, but his facial expression said to continue.

"I want us to join forces. You know, an ex-FBI investigator and criminal-hating attorney. We'd make one heck of a team."

Macklin smiled like a father might smile at his young child who's screaming, *Daddy, please, why can't I ride the roller coaster? Please, Daddy, please!*

"Annie, let me share a little background that, with what few people I know, only a handful have heard."

The excitement brought chills to the young woman as she unconsciously put her hands under her arms.

"I began my life one of six children poor as dirt. We lived on an eighty-acre farm in south Arkansas. It was all we could do not to starve.

"I joined the Marine Corps the day I turned seventeen, with my father's blessing. Since the age of six, my daddy taught me to shoot a rifle. I could place a .22 bullet right dead in a running squirrel's eye from seventy feet. Dad said I was the best shot in four counties." Although Macklin felt badly about telling Annie this made-up story of his young years, he knew for sure she was not ready to hear about his true background. The truth of his youth made him shudder to himself and almost made him sick to his stomach.

He sat silent for a long moment. "The Marines learned real quick that I was a shooter. However, I did not know way back then that I could also be a killer."

The waitress interrupted. "Yes, please, J&B on the rocks, double." Annie ordered another glass of wine.

"So the Marines made you a killer?" Annie felt stupid before the words left her mouth.

"No, Annie, even the Marines can't do that kind of brain washing. I think you're born to it. Either you can or you can't, and in my case I could, and sadly enough, I liked it."

Macklin downed his double shot of scotch and waved his glass for another. "Four years of killing sprees across the globe. In that time I was promoted to staff sergeant, probably the youngest in the Corps."

"My God, Macklin, that had to be extremely dangerous." Again, an *I'm so stupid* moment.

The powerful man, once killing machine, laughed. "It had its moments, Annie! Let's see now, three Purple Hearts, two Silver Stars, and the Navy Cross. Why, the commandant called me a one-of-a-kind hero!" He laughed sarcastically.

"Then one day I quit killing. I guess you could say it wasn't fun anymore. As luck would have it, the CIA recruited me."

"The CIA?" Annie was incredulous.

"Surprised me too!" A genuine laugh.

"And what did you do for the CIA?" Annie was deep in the suspense of this man.

"Mostly low-level stuff. Got my college degree while I was there. That was a good thing."

"In what?"

"Psychology. Last four years I trained newbies, weapons, hand to hand, how to rip someone's lips off."

"Really?"

Macklin laughed again. "Just kidding about the lips thing. Then they asked me to do something I didn't want to do—leave it at that—and then I resigned."

"You are one amazing man." The awe was clear in her voice.

"Not really, Annie. From the FBI, where I worked undercover, mostly boring nights of nothing but surveillance, and then too much bureaucratic BS and I quit. Four years Marines, eight years CIA, two years FBI, and now I work for a girl."

"That really must suck!" Both laughed large.

"Annie, let's be real. I'm an old, burned-out gumshoe PI; not much talent, not real smart, and not real ambitious. I live alone, no family, no friends, and I hate golf. You're wasting your money, kiddo. So whatever your plan, I promise you can do much better than me."

"It's my money to waste, isn't it?" There was a bit of fire in her voice.

"This is true." Macklin's eyebrows raised.

"Actually, Macklin, I think you are 1,000 percent what I need. And, sir, I trust you!"

That statement touched the tiny little spot buried deep in his tarnished soul. "What's your plan?"

HIKES POINT PARTY MALL

Polly often wondered what he might have been if his father, Borack Abbadon, had seen the other side of his soul early on.

He was an artist! He loved classical music! Didn't Grey love the portrait he painted of her just last year, the portrait that his father destroyed? Now his great artistic talent and skill as a painter was relegated to exterior and interior buildings, soon to be appropriately named Hikes Point Party Mall.

"Oh well," he mused. "Killing people isn't bad if you have a choice in careers. Both require special talent."

And that's what he was. Trained, developed in mind, body, and soul, he and one hundred more just like him, killers, and the devoted sons of Borack Abbadon, scattered across the globe awaiting *The Beginning*.

Polly had once heard Raoul refer to the future moment as "the Revival." Raoul was one of the ten male children adopted by Abbadon whom he had actually met.

Polly, dressed like a French politician, stood in command as he supervised the crew of twenty-two illegal Mexicans, all pretty good painters, no doubt.

The two lead Mexicans were paid five bucks per hour. The rest of the tomato pickers received $3.50 per hour, cash.

Although Borack had more money than God, a statement proclaimed often from the master, he expected a wise accounting all the same. So why pay a bunch of union drunks when you could bus in some wetbacks, give them phony papers, and move them anywhere quickly. "Plus, I'm helping the poor," Polly shouted, and two Mexicans spit outside of the young artist's eyesight.

If not for the special assignments, Polly often wondered if he'd still be performing such menial acts of servitude for the master. However, the young man so loved destroying the lives of others, those smug, simple-minded people who believed in a God, or better yet, themselves. Greedy, self-important, "got the world on a string" types until out of nowhere up pops Polly, and their self-protected world comes to a shocking, brutal end. Simple as that.

This would be the thirteenth project entrusted to Polly. In every case, some innocent moron stepped in the path of progress, and when they did, Polly sent them straight to hell.

Borack frequently, and with the pride of a satisfied father, spoke of his many children around the world. Polly could not be exactly sure how many there were or if they were adopted like Grey and himself or natural offspring. He did, however, have a sense that all were brought into the fold just as he had been.

Children of a lesser God, so to speak. Hopeless, miserable, and deprived little creatures already down the road of mindless hate. Each would have longed for the same things Polly needed at the young age of six, when Abbadon saved him. Love, protection, a feeling of security, and mostly, a purpose to live.

Borack provided all of this and more.

Polly's first memories began in a great castle surrounded by enormous pine trees that stretched as far as he could see. And the snow, always snow. He thought back for a moment and went deep in his memory bank, trying to remember a day at the castle when he'd actually seen the sunshine or heard a bird sing. There was nothing.

After being saved, as Grey recalled the rescue, he awoke in a warm bed inside the castle. That's where all his memories began. He recalled being frightful and calling out to Grey in the darkness. Then a small boy about his age with sparkling blue eyes stood beside his bed, holding a very large candle. "Don't be afraid." The little boy's voice was soft and comforting.

"Who are you? What's your name?" he'd asked the new boy.

"My name is three," the boy stated, as if having a number for a name was perfectly reasonable. "You'll probably be called six."

"Six?"

"Yes, six, because you are the sixth boy in our class, and six completes our covey."

Later that morning Polly recalled the beginning of the lessons.

On one side of the castle, little boys were taught the lessons, and on the other side were the girls. Both were placed in coveys of six and taught separately.

Studies started at 6:00 a.m. in private classrooms, each holding an individual covey of six children. The class was conducted by old, old women dressed like nuns but all in red. The old women were addressed as Mother Ravens.

The boys wore black pants, shoes, and long coats buttoned from the very top to the very bottom. All bedecked their shaven heads with wide-brim black hats.

The lessons, beginning at 6:00 a.m., ran all day to precisely 9:00 p.m. and then off to bed. During the day, both midmorning and late afternoon, the coveys would engage in the arts, which consisted of very strenuous strength and agility exercises. As well, from the beginning, the boys were taught the ancient art of killing. Weapons, explosives, and the great art of fire did not begin until age twelve and were called the duty lessons.

All would graduate at the age of sixteen, except those not smart enough and the crybabies. They simply disappeared at night.

There were but a few simple rules. One: Do not talk to anyone at any time except Mother Raven or the deacons, the older men who taught the arts. Two: Trust no man but those with the mark. Three: Dedicate your life to the purpose given you. Four: Worship the master.

Polly had been an excellent student in both the lessons and the arts, especially the arts. He enjoyed hurting the other children.

Anytime one of the coveys broke a rule, which was almost always for talking, that infraction was punished by a covey member choosing to beat the offender with a long agile cane or by burning his hands and feet with the heavy punishment candle. Polly was almost always selected to carry out the chastisement, an assignment he enjoyed so much that at times he'd lie on a covey member just for the opportunity to castigate.

Polly finished the lessons one year early and was rewarded by a visit from his sister, and for the first time in nine years, he was free to talk. The boy had not seen Grey until that moment and quite honestly could find little feeling for his sibling.

Grey was not a covey member, nor did she study the arts as all the other girls did. She lived with and was taught by Borack Abbadon. Furthermore, in one year she would become a prophetess serving the master, and there could be only one at any given time.

Because of this great honor, her brother would also be considered a special child of the father. As well, the master told her that number six was an elite pupil and would be called Apolyon. Grey shortened it to Polly, and the master liked it.

Polly, now a grown man utilizing all he'd been taught, would see his sister from time to time, rarely in the New York penthouse, and occasionally on sites as he did the master's work.

When they met, Grey was always in Abbadon's presence and seemed distant, maybe even cold. Polly even thought she might be frightened, but that was ridiculous. How could anyone be afraid of their father?

Polly once asked her about *The Beginning* while briefly alone as Abbadon spoke by phone to someone in a language he did not know.

Nervously, he thought, Grey quickly told of 666 young men such as himself who had all been covey students and were scattered all across the world preparing for *The Beginning*. That was all she could and would say, and for Polly to never mention it again. The master knew the time, and Polly would know when the master told him.

Now Polly sensed this project might be his last before Abbadon proclaimed *The Beginning*. He certainly hoped so, as this type of work was nothing short of boring. He was even getting tired of killing the odd soul here and there.

He longed for something bigger. Polly ached for phenomenal, an unimaginable act. He prayed for *The Calling* or *The Beginning*, whichever it was really called.

The chill of Indian summer blew across the newly paved parking lot. The colossal neon sign placed where all could see from three different directions was in place.

Polly offered up a smile filled with pride. The Hikes Point Party Mall, a work of art by Polly Abbadon, artisan from an unknown world.

This would be Polly's thirteenth masterpiece. Although he felt it his best, he hated this ragtag town of hillbillies. The excitement of New Orleans, Vegas, Miami, why, even Jersey City, brought additional pleasures that Hikes Point clearly lacked.

Now, closing in on completion, although the town itself sucked, the work he'd done was indeed a sight to see.

Like every project in the previous twelve cities, all went through and by a corporation exclusive to the property, i.e. Hikes Point, Inc. "Borack must own a million such properties," he pondered.

This property venture included the Hikes Point Lounge, the final jewel in the crown, Biker Town next door, where only the hardcore would come to shop, Wolf's Tattoo and Piercing Parlor, Triple X Toys for Boys, Suzie's Massage Salon, and the magnificent Pussy Cat Club... Girls, Girls, Girls.

"I love it!" Polly proudly proclaimed.

And what a group of tenants! All handpicked by Polly himself. Biker Town would be managed by Mikey Klanski, a real biker's biker, former West Coast Hell's Angel with fifteen years of solid prison time. Plus, he really did like to hurt people. "My kind of guy," Polly exclaimed.

Wolf's Tattoo and Piercing would be well served by Homie McCall, a very astute businessman who knew how to make a buck by using the same needle as many times as possible.

Triple X Toys for Boys would be manned sufficiently with the perv Randle Pridenone, who not only read all the porno but could, if he wished, write some true stories.

Suzie's Massage was of course managed by Suzy, a forty-year-old hooker and heroin addict. For a hundred bucks you could get the primo massage and stood a fifty-fifty chance of walking out with HIV.

The Pussy Cat Club brought in a great man of experience all the way from New Jersey, or so he claimed, where he'd managed a club with fifty dancers, most of whom worked in his Newark Laundry in the daytime. Richie Prunnaire was one of a kind.

And last but not least, Polly requested and received approval from Abbadon to open the Hikes Point Lounge himself. Just a couple of months of sprucing up the interior and he'd be ready.

Later that day Polly would order the massive banner: *Grand Opening: Hikes Point Lounge. New Year's Eve—By Invitation Only. Let the Party Begin!*

MACKLIN & O'DOUL

Twenty years ago, the Hikes Point area looked much like any other across America: middle-class people doing middle-class things.

Hikes Lane crisscrossed Breckenridge Lane, providing easy access to a variety of businesses. Heading east on Hikes Lane and to the north sat the Hikes Point Lounge and the other local stores providing services to the neighborhood. Behind this center of basic commerce lived a neighborhood of older houses occupied with retired thirty-year employees of General Electric and Ford Motor companies. Sprinkled here and there you'd find younger white-collar families paying their first mortgage, all living in peace and harmony.

On the south side, the Kroger grocery store, Walgreens, and Pizza Hut dominated the strip center to the north anchored by the Hikes Point Lounge. Tucked into an alcove between Kroger's and Walgreens, the locals could find Doctor Welch and the second-generation dentist office of George Ransdell, who once killed a man pulling his tooth!

All in all, a quiet, peaceful community moving slowly into the hell that now was, without ever seeing it coming.

The Pizza Hut, now relegated to an all-you-can-eat Chinese restaurant, Kroger's, Dollar General, and Walgreens, now a giant wholesale auto supplier, Dr. Welch, long dead, housed a gun and pawnshop. Next to the pawn and gun, where laughing gas and pain killer shots were the norm, the new residents proudly surveyed the sign above the door, *"Macklin and O'Doul: Private Investigators."*

The new residents, former FBI, CIA, Marine sharpshooter, and previous public defender, smiled as they stood before their office ready for truth, justice, and the American way. But then they really had no clue of the evil awaiting them on the north side of Hikes Lane.

Annie O'Doul's father had been murdered, followed by the killing of her husband-to-be. No clues, no witnesses to speak of, no hopes in either case. Nothing to hang your hat on, as Macklin often said. Nothing but a glimpse of a young, tall stranger in a red bowtie, moving like a ghost just inside the Hikes Point Lounge.

Macklin found a reason to get up each morning in his new job. Working with Annie brought sunlight into his dark past. *Call it love,* he thought, *not like girlfriend-boyfriend stuff, but love all the same.* Thirty years her senior, Macklin wondered what kind of love he felt.

Is she like my daughter, he'd asked early in their relationship. *No that wasn't it.* She wasn't like a daughter or a potential lover. All he knew was that Annie O'Doul was special to him. She was tough yet vulnerable. He, on the other hand, needed a reason to live, and Annie O'Doul gave him that.

Their first day in business, the obvious odd couple sipped coffee in the small compact kitchen area and discussed the future of their joint endeavor. Money, generally being the first concern for any new small business, was not the case here. Annie, a multimillionaire and well-advised investor, thanks to Rich Haddad, would not have financial concerns for the rest of her life. Besides, she was not in this for the money. Annie O'Doul wanted desperately to find her father and Josh's killer. After that, who knew?

Annie, with Macklin's approval, selected this location to begin their new endeavor for three simple basic business reasons: location, location, location!

You could walk twenty feet from their front office door and see across the highway to the left the Hikes Point Lounge, where Paddy O'Doul was shot in cold blood. Look three hundred yards east, and the twenty-four-seven blinking neon of the Pussy Cat Club ... Girls, Girls, Girls, where Josh's battered body was found in the garbage dumpster.

Macklin told her after she'd leased the dentist office, "If you're looking for pigs, you gotta put your nose in the mud." And now they were about to get knee deep.

GOOD COP, BAD COP: RUSTY JUDD

Detective Rusty Judd, a fifteen-year veteran of the Louisville police department, was well respected by his peers. Smart, fearless, and always had your back.

In his tenure as a uniform cop for five years and undercover narc for the past ten, Detective Judd had been awarded numerous accommodations for bravery, shot three times, and heralded for the most arrests and convictions in the entire police department.

Some said he was lucky. Others spoke of his back-street methods. Prosecutors wondered just how deep his contacts in the dark world he roamed. And Rusty did not much care what anyone thought. He caught bad guys—dead or alive, didn't make a whole lot of difference to him.

He mostly worked alone, not totally due to his wishes, but after his third partner was shot and almost died, other cops began to believe the man bulletproof, but not necessarily so for his fellow officers alongside.

Rusty didn't much care for his nickname, Quick Draw, but he agreed it applicable. Seven shootings, seven Internal Affairs investigations, and seven dead criminals. If you pulled a pistol on Rusty Judd, you'd better be quick and you'd better be good. He was both.

The undercover cop was also a loner. Married at twenty, divorced two years later, no children, no brothers or sisters, and no friends to speak of.

Rusty was well respected; he just wasn't that sociable. His simple life revolved around being a cop. Nothing else really gave him a rush.

For the past eight years he'd resided at Third and Oak Streets above Turner's Tavern. The small, one-bedroom apartment was clean and sparsely furnished.

Rusty liked the area because of its proximity to his many snitches and informants. Although transient by nature and trade, the lowlifes seemed to trust and respect the narc. He was a cop willing to give you a break, talk to the prosecutor, get you a deal, even loan you a few bucks when you were down and out.

The quiet narc with superman vision often sat at the back table facing forward, always looking through the thick haze of smoke inside Turner's Tavern below his humble abode, looking only at things he could see. It was his office.

The locals, never changing, always had a smile, a gentle nod, or a "what's up, Rusty" whenever he walked in, which was often.

Rusty was like the godfather of the lowlife underworld, holding court at the small table with two chairs, his against the wall and facing forward with a full view of their home for the hopeless.

If nothing was cooking on any given night, which was when Rusty did his best work, you'd find him in his chair looking out across the dying, a sad expression upon his weary face.

The same group of old men and old women sat about the tavern drinking dollar drafts and buck fifty shots of Old Granddad, looking for nothing, hoping for nothing, content in their shared misery. All knew and liked the cop in the back.

Rusty too sipped dollar drafts and occasionally might even take a hit from a slender well-rolled joint, if he knew the roller well.

Then sometimes, each and every night, someone would walk in or his cell would vibrate—"so and so at such and such"—and he'd be off. Another drug dealer unaware that the longhaired, bearded man driving a 1977 rusted out Caddy was indeed Quick Draw Judd. Busted, locked up, a new thug captured. All in a day's work for a lonely cop with little but this to live for. It was starting to get old.

THE PARTNERSHIP

Annie spent the entire day at the courthouse looking through property ownership records for the newly acquired and soon-to-be opened establishments across the highway from her office. Each business had been purchased in the last year at auction by an LLC. As well, many of the old homes behind her father's business were also now owned and rented by the same group.

The Hikes Point property management company's true ownership was impossible to track and spider-webbed through many DBAs and other corporations, ending with an investment company in New York City.

"What a fruitless wasted day!" Annie snorted as she plopped down, exhausted, into the over-stuffed chair against the window in Macklin's office, where dentist Ransdell had once committed dental torture. "How was your day, Mack?"

"Bout the same."

"Worthless?" Annie stated flatly.

"Mostly, but I did find a couple of tidbits to work on."

"Give me hope, kind sir. Give me hope."

"Well, all the new businesses across the way have managers, not lessees. So whoever owns it is running it."

"Interesting." Annie sat up.

"I have some of the new managers' names, so I plan to run background checks tomorrow. I also asked about a tall young guy with short blond hair."

Annie leaned forward, giving Macklin her undivided attention. "And?"

"Well, the managers I could find and a few employees working on the big grand opening are either really stupid or paid to act really stupid."

"Lowlifes?"

"Uh, in-between. However, I did talk to this Spanish guy who seemed to be in charge of the painting crew inside your father's old place. He knew who I was talking about."

"Who, as in who?"

"The blond-headed dude, duh. Are you with me?"

"Go on, smarty-pants."

"So anyway, the painter tells me he thinks the big boss is this young kid with short blond hair, or at least that's the guy who has been paying them, in cash no less."

"Interesting." Annie mulled this over.

"Indeed, the Spanish man said he heard someone call him Polly."

"As in 'Polly wants a cracker?'" She smiled.

"That's weak," Macklin chastised. "No, as in the young blond dude is in charge of the Party Mall, and the painter said, 'Watch him, man. There's something evil surrounding that gringo!'"

Annie, for no apparent reason, felt the hair on her neck rise.

"So anyway, that might be a pig worth digging up a little mud to find." Macklin smiled.

Annie fired back. "Mack, did you ever in your life hurt any pigs?"

"My dear, young innocent, do you really want me to answer that question?"

"Guess not." They both laughed.

"Hey, another interesting unrelated thing I read about in today's paper. Some cop, undercover variety, busted a gang of bikers behind the Lounge. Half-million dollars of coke, street value. Sounds like seriously good undercover."

"Did they say who the undercover cop was?"

"Yes, but I don't remember; here it's right here in the paper. Rusty Judd. Isn't his first bust, or so it seems."

Annie was smiling ear to ear. "Rusty Judd, well how do you like that?"

"Annie,"—Macklin giving her his fatherly voice—"do you really think this is a good idea?"

"Well, of course I do, or else we wouldn't be doing it!"

"A woman's logic, geez-o-pete." Macklin surrendered and pulled Annie's Mercedes into a parking spot next to Spalding's Drycleaners, a half block from Turner's Tavern.

"Now let's review this one more time." Macklin sounded like an FBI agent. "You and this cop, Rusty whatever, framed a couple of bad guys when you were supposed to be their attorney, right?"

"Wrong, we did not frame anyone! I only helped; just a little bringing justice to her glory."

"You framed them, and you know it, which could have gotten you disbarred and the cop kicked off the force. Simple as that, little girl."

"Little girl?"

"Yes, little girl... and pretty clever too!"

"Thank you, my hero, for recognizing my contribution to the legal system."

"Whatever." Macklin looked her in the eyes. "Now remember, I do the talking, you do the listening. Got it?"

"Yes, sir, Mr. General!"

The narc saw them before they reached the door as the big man and beautiful young woman passed the window with faded green lettering, "Turner's Tavern: Ladies Invited."

The place was packed. Friday night neighborhood pool tournament. Both tables crowded and loud. Juke box blaring *"Walk the Line"* by Johnny Cash. Ten-dollar bills stacked neatly on the table next to the scoring pad of Willie Stone, ex-con, old man, and a friend to no one. Each Friday night he'd get a cut from the pool games.

The bar full with cheering fans guzzling draft beer, chain-smoking Camels, their big night out. *What a life*, Rusty thought.

He watched the big man stand silently just inside the door, shielding the young woman professionally with his right arm. Black leather jacket, dark mock turtleneck, blue jeans, laced-up military boots, highly polished. Rusty smiled as if secretly watching a comrade from a distant war returning home.

The woman wore black jeans and a denim jacket. Her hair was pulled tightly back, exposing a natural beauty never seen in this place.

Tonight the couple went unnoticed. Any other and the place would have come to a screeching halt. But not this night, no, not on Friday night, when your ten dollars begged for an eight ball bank shot, corner pocket.

Through the smoke, the smell of wasting life, the cheers, the groans, and the ever constant "'Nother draft over here," Macklin locked eyes with Rusty Judd. In a split second, truth was told, the depth of real men shared. No fear of either man, yet ample caution that comes from walking in danger, day in and day out.

Macklin put Annie in front of him and silently moved to the back table. The narc sat as usual, back to the wall with two empty chairs just waiting for this unusual couple to enter the wasteland.

It had taken several phone calls for Macklin to get Rusty's cell phone number. No conversation, just a short message: "We need to talk. I'll see you at the tavern."

Stranger things, the cop thought when retrieving the message, but now he must admit, this could get interesting.

Annie reached her chair facing Rusty and quietly sat down. Macklin moved his slightly to the left, where he could see both Rusty and the wasteland people.

"Nice to see you again, Ms. O'Doul." His smile felt warm yet sad.

"Thank you for meeting with us, detective." *His deep blue eyes are piercing,* she thought.

The narc turned to face Macklin. "Cop?" he asked.

"Not really." Macklin studied Rusty carefully.

"FBI and CIA," Annie stated with a note of pride in her voice. Macklin frowned.

Rusty looked at Macklin, not changing his expression, as if he'd not heard the woman at all.

The heavyset barmaid pushing fifty and looking every bit of sixty sat three frosted mugs and three shots of Early Times on their table. "On the house," she exclaimed from a red mouth with too few teeth. Rusty nodded. "Thank you, Ethel."

He turned to Annie. "So how's the legal business? We've missed you in court."

Annie blushed. "I'm not doing that kind of work anymore."

"So I've heard. Too bad."

A man of few words, Macklin thought. *I like that.*

Rusty turned to Macklin, and Annie O'Doul could not help but recognize how young and how old he looked at the same time. *Handsome,* she thought. *A raw ruggedness, like an old western hero.*

"My name is Macklin. Please call me Mack." A first, Annie noticed. "Yes, I am ex-FBI and CIA. You can throw a lot of other meaningless crap into the mix. Some good, some bad. I'm now a private investigator and partner with Ms. O'Doul. We look for bad guys."

Rusty's warm smile again. "And what do you do when you catch them? The bad guys?"

"Bad things of course." Mack couldn't hold in the smile, and Rusty chuckled and seemed to relax.

"Good job?"

"It has its moments." Annie could see the boy thing beginning to blossom.

"And this means what... to me?"

Macklin continued. "I know that you and Annie had a, let's say *common interest,* in the past."

"Common interest?" Rusty chewed on that a moment. "Fair enough."

"We read today about your drug bust in Hike's Point."

"Publicity, just what an undercover narc yearns for."

"Guess not," Macklin stated in agreement. "But we are after the murderer or murderers of Annie's dad and fiancé. Both were killed in or near the Hikes Point Lounge."

Rusty looked sadly at Annie for a long moment, not saying a word, and then returned his attention to Macklin.

"I, we, believe you may be able to assist us in our efforts." Macklin sat back and relaxed.

"I think I'd like that."

Annie broke into a wide grin, not noticed by the two men saying much with their own eyes.

Rusty's phone vibrated. "Yeah, okay, thirty minutes." He turned back to Macklin and Annie. "One of my candy bars."

"Candy bars?" Annie acted confused.

The narc laughed. "Yeah, candy bars! Snickers are snitches, informants Milky Ways and M&M's."

"What's an M&M?" Annie was again confused.

"Mostly Mickey Mouse." All three smiled at that one.

Rusty was the first to stand. "Give me a couple of days. I'll get back to you. Let's go out the back way."

"Uh, here, detective, is uh, my card. In case you need,

you know, my number, our number." *She sounds like a schoolgirl,* Macklin thought.

"No need." Rusty smiled and met her eyes once again. "I know how to reach you."

He turned before moving into the alley and smiled again at Annie. "Caller ID, kiddo. I'm a cop."

THE PLAN: UNIFIED EVIL

Grey knew with great certainty that no man, woman, or child knew the father, Borack Abbadon, better than she did.

So many others, as he called them, served him around the world. As they moved freely between continents, Grey had met kings, queens, royalty of all known varieties. And there were the leaders of nations in faraway places and political powerbrokers coming and going from the ends of the earth. All had wealth, and all had power. But for her, the most bewildering were the religious people who also seemed to glorify in the presence of Borack Abbadon—bishops, rabbis, Muslim leaders, and television evangelists. Why, she once even sat in the jungles of Africa with the grandest of witchdoctors, all eager to spend time with the great man she also served with every minute of her life.

Often she would sit quietly as Borack would meet with the high and mighty. Many languages she did not know or comprehend, and often, most often, just out of her hearing range.

His wealth was not measurable, if castles, villas, penthouses, jets, and yachts around the world were any indication.

In the past few weeks she had traveled to Paris, Madrid, Istanbul, and New York, always in the lap of luxury and always surrounded by the great and powerful. She'd lost track of all the palaces and great mansions. *It used to matter,* she thought, *but great wealth without great love leaves one empty.*

Grey knew with the accelerated travel and secret meetings across the world that something of great magnitude was about to spring forth. Of what nature, she had no clue.

"Sit here beside me, my purest angel." Abbadon's soft low voice was hypnotic to Grey's senses. "Let me share my soul."

He stroked her thick long gray hair with strength and gentleness. Borack permeated power beyond comprehension, at times so loving and gentle. But below the surface, an earthquake of unholy magnitude waited. *Waited for what?* Grey often wondered and feared.

Borack was ageless to Grey. He could be thirty or three hundred. Gentle and terrible. Close and distant. Good and oh so evil.

Abbadon served no natural man and feared nothing. He stood alone as a great mountain casting its shadow across the landscape of mankind. No human weakness, not a single flaw, except one. Earthly love was great sin to the master, a sin not allowed in unholy communion with the master's plan.

Abbadon was forbidden to feel the childish emotions that destroyed men so easily—love, hope, tenderness, or a belief in a worthless God. He served a greater purpose, a higher calling. He exalted to the highest forum. He was preparing *The Beginning*, and he would win the battle of souls with the true king.

Grey laid her head on his massive shoulder covered by his gold and pure-silk robe. A spoken word or a gentle stroke and the beautiful woman fell into his trance.

In a dreamlike state she could feel him. He whispered, "The final calling will begin. We are prepared."

In an instant, Abbadon stood thirty feet away, moving from side to side, speaking rapidly in the unknown language. She pulled her knees to her chest, burying her face in fear. In all their time and travels she had never felt such evil.

Minutes later, he was again at her side as a different being. "Why do you tremble, my angel?" Almost a hint of love in his voice.

"What is *The Beginning?*" she whispered.

"My child, do not fear so." He pulled her tight. "It is *The Beginning* of the end and the end of *The Beginning*."

"I don't understand."

"Not to worry, my precious little one. It is the first of the calling of souls. It is the start of a new heaven and a new earth, where you may rule as a goddess by my side."

Grey found no joy in his proclamation, only fear and confusion.

Borack Abbadon's plan was soon to begin after so many years in the making, a worldwide event of untold proportion. No one but he knew the details.

So unique was the plan, such simplicity. Six years of chaos. The calling of souls not noticed or cared for by their worthless God until it was too late, too great to hold back, building until all hell and all heaven would meet and the souls of the dead would fight their most unholy war.

The first year would start small, unnoticed. Lost souls abandoned by their God would seek refuge in filthy bars around the world. Lonely, lost, and hopeless, they would die and find new life serving the master, their souls captured by the love of money.

The second year, lust would take over. New diseases would spread like wildfire among those abandoned and looking for love in the arms of strangers. Sex would rule.

Then the political rulers would grab for power around the world, many in the name of religion. This would be followed by greed, which was controlled by oil. Deals to be made. Let's see who cares about the Jews when America is out of gasoline.

Year five would bring the holy war, the great battle between the sons of Abraham and the sons of the prince of the air.

And lastly, the final weapon, loss of hope and a reason to live.

In the end, the final calling would be complete. Millions upon millions of lost souls would turn to the master, mad as hell and ready to fight, both the living and the dead.

"All of this! This great chaos! This great calling of souls for the master!" Borack swayed in musical movement and whispered, "All of this to the end, beginning with ten, simple, godforsaken souls losing life but gaining eternity at the selected birthplace of the calling… at the Hikes Point Lounge."

"Luc a od, luc a od, luc a od…" His chant lasted until sunrise.

ALL GOOD PLANS...

Abbadon secluded himself in the study of the century-old New Orleans plantation mansion for two days. Grey read the writings of Nietzsche while listening to ancient Cajun recordings.

Turk, the Iranian bodyguard, stayed in the darkest spot he could find, as if dead, only to awake when the master called.

On the second ring of the only phone with a very private secure number, Turk picked up. "Yes," he said in a heavy voice.

"Turk?" the caller asked.

"Yes." The huge man spoke in a deep bass.

"Turk, this is Polly; we've got a problem."

"Hold." Turk moved as in great pain up the spiral staircase to the great room where his master worked. Two firm knocks upon the solid oak door. Borack knew the power of the knock and the man behind the fist.

"Enter."

Turk, a man of great power and no fear, slowly opened the door. Rarely did this Iranian allow trepidation to enter his mind. But today, this moment, panic and unholy terror rose slowly from his belly, squeezing breath from his lungs, leaving a metallic taste on his tongue. He carried bad news from one of Borack's many sons, a son he knew that Abbadon only tolerated, allowed to exist, because of his love for the bastard child's sister, Grey.

The room was enormous, the size of a small house, Turk thought. The east and west walls were floor-to-ceiling bookcases. There were thousands of ancient leather-bound writings in every known and unknown language. In the middle of the west wall, three shelves up and center, Turk recognized the Koran and the Bible side by side.

Abbadon remained with his back turned from the Iranian. He was bent forward, arms stretched out, as very large hands spread architectural drawings across a beautiful hand-carved cherry table, some twenty-five feet long and maybe ten feet across.

Turk's anxiety subsided as he studied the delicate carvings of the magnificent table where his master worked. Demons and devils danced. Little children with horns and tails rode animals with wings. *The artwork seems to be alive,* he thought.

The south wall, one hundred feet across, was solid glass. Glistening windows were beveled and sparkled like fire, and the drapes were thick, blood red, or possibly deep burgundy. Golden embroidery also depicted scenes from an unknown world, such as the table displayed.

This was but the third time that Turk had entered his master's sanctuary. Each time great fear had gripped his soul, and for this Iranian killing machine, fear never crossed his mind. Yet in this room, it became almost overwhelming.

Without turning from his concentric focus, Abbadon motioned with his left hand. "Come."

Turk moved forward as if his feet were now great stones. The massive fireplace roared as if stoked by the fires of hell. Logs eight feet long snapped and crackled as if singing for the hand-carved demon children. Yet the room felt icy cold. Turk could see his breath, and he forced back the memories of a Russian prison camp.

He now stood just several paces from Abbadon's left. Neither moved, which only increased the Iranian's consternation.

Sound began to move up into the room from what seemed a thousand miles away—crying, begging, and pleas of mercy, torturous supplication to no avail. The sound was so horrible even Turk put his hands to his ears, raised his head, and looked out the great windows. He realized this was the first time in Abbadon's domain when the massive drapes had been opened.

As far as his eyes could see, there were hundreds, no thousands, of black men, women, and children. Black men under the whip, dragged through cotton fields by powerful horses with white riders. Young boys hanging limp from massive oak trees swinging in unison with blood-drenched

Spanish moss. Women ran through the fields holding babies against their chests until they were run down, clothes ripped from their bodies.

Such undiscovered horror without comprehension, the Iranian wiped away a single tear from his tightly drawn face. And then the torturous screams went away.

Turk realized he had closed his eyes. It was too much even for him to witness. When he opened them, the drapes were tightly closed and Borack, dressed in fine linen, stood alongside the roaring fireplace, brandy in a crystal glass in his left hand and a hand-rolled Cuban cigar in his right.

"Turk, my loyal servant and companion, what is it you need?"

The scene had changed so suddenly that for a moment Turk wondered if he might be awakening from a dream, not the first time for such an experience in the strange world they traveled.

"Sir, your son Polly is on the phone. He has a problem."

For a split second, Abbadon's features turned hideous, grotesque. Turk blinked his eyes, and his master was again most beautiful.

"A problem? A problem you say?"

"Yes, sir, Polly has a problem."

"Well then, dear Turk, let us get about what we do best." Borack hesitated before adding, "Eliminating problems!"

Grey, in Turk's absence, positioned herself closer to the table where the gold and ivory phone rested.

"Polly, my son! Turk tells me you have a problem. Let us hope it will not delay our plans for the Hikes Point Lounge celebration!"

"No, Father, no. I have everything under control, really.

I can handle it; you can trust me!" Polly sweated like a Mexican cutting tobacco in the August heat.

"Under control, my son? But yet you call and take me from my most important work? You know *The Beginning* is near, don't you?"

"Yes, sir, yes, sir! But you have always taught me to be prepared for the smallest problem. Eliminate, never live with. Correct, sir?"

"You've learned well, Son. So share your concerns with me, your loving father."

"Well, sir, there's these people who've been snooping around, asking questions about me and who owns this place."

"Snoops? Oh my!" Borack chuckled. "And who might the snoopers be, my boy?"

"Well, one of them is the daughter of Paddy O'Doul, the same girl who was engaged to the guy we left in the dumpster."

"Go on." There was a calmness in Borack's voice that built false trust.

"And now there's this cop. I think he's a narc or something."

"I see. Such an unholy alliance, one might assume. And this girl and a silly cop concern you, boy?"

"Well, it's not really them I'm worried about, Father."

"Then who, my son?"

"It's the third guy, older guy. He's working for O'Doul's daughter, and you know she has lots of money now. You know she can hire the best!"

"Lots of money? Hire the best? All things are relative, my boy." Borack's voice was taking Polly deeper into his trust level, fear escaping with his smooth, calming word.

"Yes sir, I remember. But this guy, this guy is different. I think he's ex-FBI or CIA. Something bigger than a Louisville cop anyway."

"I see, and do you have a name?"

"Yes sir. I did some detective work of my own."

Borack rolled his eyes and placed his powerful hand over the telephone, whispering, "God save us" in mock sacrilege.

"His name, please."

"He goes by Macklin."

"Macklin!" Abbadon shouted and filled the mansion with his voice. "Macklin!" he screamed into the phone. "Are you sure, boy?"

"Absolutely!"

"Now listen to me, boy, and hear every word." Borack's intensity caused Polly to pee his tailored suit pants.

"Go to the safe house."

Polly interrupted, "But, Father, I want to be there at *The Beginning*. I really—"

Abbadon cut him off. "Do not say another word." He hissed the words, and Polly found more fuel in his bladder.

"The safe house immediately. I'm sending Sean and Turk today to clean up your mess."

The phone went dead, and Polly crumbled to his knees. He could do without a visit from Turk.

MACKLIN: THE CONNECTION

Grey stood behind the door inside the sunroom adjoining the downstairs study, where Abbadon finished his tense instructions to her brother before storming out of the room and back to his upstairs sanctuary.

When Abbadon first filled the mansion with his furious proclamation of Macklin, Grey fell to her knees. Gasping for breath and close to losing consciousness, she fought for composure.

"Macklin." Abbadon proclaimed the name again as if announcing the arrival of an archangel.

"Macklin," Grey whispered. "Could it be? Is it possible?"

Grey quietly exited the mansion from the sunroom and walked through the flower garden meticulously kept by the "darkies," as Borack called them.

She often wondered why in all her years never once had she met an adopted child of dark color. In Africa, New York, and especially here in New Orleans she'd seen and even spoken to many of the dark-skinned people. Always a sense of deep something, she thought. A gentleness, maybe even knowledge of something she could never possess. What was it she felt when close to the darkies? It certainly wasn't dark. No, it was light, it was warmth. She could feel their souls.

Abbadon sensed something outside his mansion's top sanctum. *It,* that *it* that stole his concentration, the thing that could bring unholy questions to his purpose, the *it* he hated and would destroy.

Peeking through the colossal draperies, he stared out and down to Grey sitting among the pale tiny tombstones a century old. A ray of sunshine broke through the branches of the great pecan tree as old as the graves the living wood protected. The beautiful Grey was holding a red rose to her chest.

Grey felt the sun upon her face, a rare event, as she never ventured outside. Why, she couldn't be sure; however, Grey sensed Borack wished it so.

The rays of this magnificent sun brought life into her being, the fragrance of the roses alerting long forgotten senses. And she felt love, love as if the souls of the darkies rose up from the graves and surrounded her as a mother would protect her children. "Love," she whispered. *Love,* she thought of Macklin.

Borack could watch no longer, nor would he show his soul to Grey in fear of losing her. He moved back from the heavy drapes and began to sway. "Luc a od, luc a od, luc a od…"

The sun withdrew behind black and somber clouds. The wind began to blow the ageless dry dirt once mother to a million fields of white cotton. She felt the darkies retreat to the safety of their graves as the red petals of the roses flew away into dark obscurity.

Grey returned through the front door of the mansion, feeling as cold as the day Borack had pulled the prison guard from her body in the Russian snow. She felt dead all over.

"Macklin." She moaned his name.

MACKLIN: THE EARLY YEARS

His father was a light-skinned freedom fighter living in the hills of Lebanon. His mother was a well-educated RN working for the United Nations, attempting to save lives in the war that never ceased and never would.

The child, just three months old, lay quietly in a tiny handmade cradle as his mother and father shared a bowl of very old rice.

The soundless and poorly aimed mortar shell hit their tattered tent embossed with the cross of noncombatants. Eighteen wounded warriors, nurses, and refugees were killed in the senseless attack in a senseless war by senseless people. The child would be the only survivor.

Borack found the boy in one of the many refugee camps scattered across the bloodletting region.

The child of eight belonged to no one, yet he seemed to thrive in a hostile environment.

Borack remained in the camp for several days, observing the human refuge. But everywhere he went, the boy would be moving about. Stealing, lying in three different languages, and fighting children twice his size, usually winning.

After two days, Borack offered the boy a candy bar. The child looked into the man. He was wise beyond his years. Careful, trusting no one, the boy watched Abbadon for a long while before responding, "No, but I'll take a cigarette," spoken in very good English. He gave the child a British cigarette, igniting it with a solid gold lighter.

"Not bad," the boy replied in Hebrew and walked away.

Several hours later, Borack reached for his lighter as he spoke to a man who appeared to control the camp. It was gone. After a lengthy search, he found the boy sitting among a group of older men, dealing like a camel trader with Borack's gold lighter. It was at that moment that Abbadon knew the child was special.

After paying the camp leader one hundred US dollars, Abbadon returned to the castle, boy in tow, where his finest and brightest children were taught the master's lessons.

Early on in his training, Borack pulled the boy from his covey, deciding he should join those very special children and be taught by Abbadon personally. He gave the boy his first real name, Ishmael Abbadon.

Ishmael excelled in all the learning. As well, in his physical disciplines, no boy could beat him. He was very special.

Borack had no natural children and felt no love for the adopted. They were there to learn, to develop, to prepare for *The Beginning*.

But even Abbadon the man, if man he be, held some emotions, albeit dark and wicked. Therefore he was hopeful when he watched Ishmael grow in knowledge and skill. Ishmael gained the master's love, and only one other child would do so.

Abbadon took to traveling with his two children, the ones he loved, Ishmael and Grey. Around the world together, always together, and always learning the lessons of the master.

Grey was adoring and Ishmael obstinate, even to the point of showing disrespect, which no child of the master could be allowed to do. No child, that is, except Ishmael.

Grey was five years younger than Ishmael but in many ways much more mature. Brother and sister, Borack called them. The perfect family—loving father, brother and sister inseparable.

Just after turning nineteen, Ishmael and Grey walked hand in hand through the gardens located outside the sunroom of the New Orleans plantation mansion while their father traveled to Asia.

Borack returned two days early that spring afternoon, going directly to the sanctum. As he worked and planned, that rare sick, unholy feeling began to engulf his spirit. His sixth sense took him to the wall of windows.

There below in the garden were his children, brother and sister, walking hand in hand.

Ishmael stopped as they strolled among the graves. A brilliant warm sun illuminated their presence. He turned to face the young girl and pulled a tiny gold ring from his pocket.

"Where did you get that?" Grey's excitement was building.

"Right here, Grey! Right here next to this grave."

She took a white handkerchief covered with lace from her dress pocket and wiped the dirt from the stone's inscription. She read, "Sarah Jones 1901–1921. I wonder if the ring belonged to her."

"Can't say for sure, but it belongs to you now!"

Ishmael slipped the ring upon her slender finger.

"Grey, I love you," he whispered softly. "I have always loved you, and I will until I die."

Tears like tiny pearl drops rolled down Grey's ivory cheeks as she too whispered, "I will always love you too. I will love you until I die."

They kissed so tender, so innocent, the kiss of children moving forward into adulthood, the kiss of lovers lost in each other's embrace, the kiss of lifetime love.

Borack exploded with a rage not seen by mortal man. He felt betrayed.

In an instant he stood in their presence, red with anger, lost in his own tortured soul.

"You unholy creature! You motherless bastard! Is this how you repay me? Is this a son's love?"

He hit Ishmael hard in the face and with great strength pulled the tombstone of Sarah Jones from the ground and over his head, his intent to crush the life from the boy he'd let get too close.

"No, Father, no!" Grey's voice was calm but strong. "If you destroy him, you must also destroy me."

Borack looked first to Grey. He could not fight her love, a sin of major proportion in his world. He then gazed down at his betraying son with hatred mixed with love. Ishmael looked back with steady defiance.

"Kill me, then! Kill me!" The boy spit the words.

Borack tossed the tombstone like any other man might throw a brick.

Abbadon spoke in measured words. "You will leave today, and you will do so as I found you, penniless and owning nothing but the clothes on your back. If I ever see you again, I will kill you. This day your sister saved your life. Now go!"

Ishmael rose slowly, showing no fear, which was remarkable. The boy stood nose to nose with his father. "I hope you burn in hell!"

Abbadon smiled. "Be careful what you wish for."

Ishmael turned back to Grey. "Remember my promise" was all he said and walked away.

Twenty feet away, as if realizing something distant, he turned, reached into his pocket, and threw a gold lighter that landed at Abbadon's feet.

Borack, for the first time in ages past, held back his tears.

For the next six months, the nineteen-year-old stole, robbed, and mugged to survive. No family, no friends, nobody who cared. He had come full circle.

Early one morning, the boy sipped his coffee at the counter of a Texaco truck stop in Dale, South Carolina, just north of Beaufort. Head down, he thought of his next move, thinking and listening to all the other people most likely going someplace where somebody loved them.

A young Marine walked in on metal crutches, missing his left leg, and sat down next to the now nameless Ishmael.

"Hey, Mack, how you been?" The older red-haired waitress spoke warmly as she poured the Marine a hot cup of coffee.

"Doing well, Lin; thanks for asking. Goin' home tomorrow. Can't wait!"

"That's great, Mack! We're going to miss you."

Nameless looked at the plastic nametag above her pocket. Lin. *Funny name,* he thought, and then it hit him. Mack-Lin. He liked it, putting the two strangers together. "Macklin," he said to himself.

Another sip of coffee, and he noticed the menu. Texaco Gas 'N' Go, Dale, South Carolina. He had a new name now, Macklin Dale. It would do.

The next morning, Macklin Dale walked up to the MPs at the gate to Paris Island. "I want to be a Marine."

It took a lot of talking and several days for the Marine recruiter to sort it all out. No birth certificate, driver's license, or other meaningful ID for one Macklin Dale. Born in New Orleans, parents dead, foster home to foster home, living on the streets for three years. *Sad story,* the Marine recruiter thought, but the Marines were looking for a few good men!

Macklin Dale now had a real name with ID, courtesy of the United States Marine Corps.

Two years passed quickly for Macklin as he used his skills learned long ago in a castle in the middle of snow-covered mountains, a man made to order for the Corps and Vietnam.

Grey had not recovered from her loss, and even Borack, with his unusual gifts, could not break her sadness.

Then one day Turk returned with the mail to the New York penthouse. "Something here for you, Grey," Turk said without any thought to the fact she had never once received one single piece of mail. Her heart jumped.

Turk looked silently for a dark spot, and Grey went to the sunroof.

The letter was postmarked from San Diego, California. She quickly yet carefully opened it. A picture, a picture of her love in dress blues and covered with medals. She flipped it over. "Grey, I will always love you. Someday. Macklin Dale."

"Macklin!" She spoke the name from her heart. "Someday, my love, someday." Grey would die with this secret, or so she hoped.

Although she never mentioned her treasure to Abbadon, he knew exactly where his son was and could care less. What he did not know, however, was that Grey also knew.

POLLY

Trembling like a chicken caught in a rainstorm, Polly placed the phone back on to the receiver. Standing in a public payphone booth thirty feet from the Hikes Point Lounge, he felt as if the whole world was watching him, a million eyes piercing into his soul, seeing his fear, laughing at the front of his pants recently darkened by urine. He hated Abbadon for making him less than human. But for Polly, hate could never outweigh his fear. He was in trouble, and he knew it.

Afraid to leave the security of the public phone, he

pondered his next move. He thought about the past and tried desperately to contemplate the future, if in fact there would be one.

Had not he served the master well? Wasn't he the best student in his covey? Did not Abbadon give him a most sacred name?

For his entire life, all that his father, the master, asked, he'd given his best. Small things, big things, paint this, paint that, kill him, kill them. Whatever was required, Polly knew he did the job and did it well. And now, just because of a small problem, a couple of nobodies snooping around, the father was angry. It just wasn't fair.

Polly believed in his heart that Abbadon never really truly loved him, not as he loved his sister, Grey.

"Big surprise," he snorted with malice. "Wonder why that is!" Polly knew the answer.

What was it Abbadon instructed? "Go to the safe house immediately."

"Yeah right," Polly answered himself. "I'll just go right now. Knock on the door and walk right in. Cheerfully greet fifteen stoned and drunk bikers. Hey, guys, how's it hanging? Hey, Polly, how come your pants are all wet?"

He started walking. "Yeah, I bet I'll do that. Screw you, Abbadon, and screw your pet gorilla, Turk!" False courage grew with each step until he reached his black BMW and drove north to the downtown luxury condo.

This wouldn't be the first time Polly disobeyed his father. Actually, he did so often and never once had he been burnt. "You ain't as smart as you think you are, Father!" There was hurt and growing hatred in his voice.

Abbadon forbade Polly to have any friends or relationships outside the family. "Never get close to anyone, especially a woman," the father warned. And drugs of any kind were off limits; sex and drugs were tools of the master, not vices.

"Oh, I'm so scared," Polly laughed in mock fear.

In the past year, he found great comfort and relaxation with his friend Richie Prunnaire, the manager of the Pussy Cat Club. Although Richie was much older, Polly was the boss, and the club manager treated him with respect.

After a hard day's work herding the Mexicans and preparing for *The Beginning* with perfection, Polly believed a little private social time was good for the soul. After all, it was lonely doing his work, and who was Abbadon to complain? Did the father think Polly was so stupid as to not recognize why Abbadon kept his sister in great luxury and comfort. "Queen Grey," Polly called her in private, jealous moments.

So at the end of the day, what was wrong with visiting his friend Richie? A couple of drinks and a few snorts of coke only served to relax and focus him. And the dancers, the pretty young girls who followed Polly like they might a king. Didn't they love how well he dressed, the car, the fabulous condo, his hard-as-steel body? Mostly, they loved his money.

"To hell with Abbadon," he said in defiance. "You are in New York, I am in Louisville, and I will do as I please, and you don't have a clue!"

"Shut up, you mothers, and turn down the stereo!" Mikey Klanski, decked out in his Hell's Angels best, stepped over several drunk bikers, picking up the phone on the sixth ring. "Klanski's Convent, Mother Theresa speaking." A long pause. "This is Turk. Put Polly on."

Klanski feared little. A thousand fights in prison and very bad clubs and bars across America, all of which he walked away from, making him both mean and dauntless. However, Turk was a different story. During two brief encounters, Klanski quickly realized that the big and thick Iranian was not a barroom drunk or prison sissy. The Turk was bad to the bone.

"Polly?" Klanski answered, a tiny bit of expectation in his voice. "Is he supposed to be here?"

"Yes."

"Well, Turk, he ain't here. Hasn't been all day."

"Okay." The phone went dead.

Polly took his time packing the extra large Hartman suitcase and the matching overnighter, sipping an iced cold Bud, not in any hurry to move from this splendor into the biker dump.

The cell phone buzzed on the bed next to his alligator wallet. The caller ID read, "private number." Only two people had Polly's number, the father and Richie. He prayed for the latter.

His hand was shaking, and his recent bravado went south. "Hello?" Polly's voice almost sounded girlish.

"Polly?" The voice was deep and menacing.

"Turk?"

"Where are you?"

"Turk, uh, I'm at my place. You know, picking up a few things. Just about ready to head to the safe house, you know?"

Thirty seconds of silence felt like thirty minutes to Polly. "Go now and do not leave the safe house!" *Click.*

Klanski kicked, pulled, and pushed the inebriated biker

gang members to their feet in surprise. "Get up, you worthless bunch of drunks! Get out and go to your own dumps. I got company coming."

"Girls?" one of the lesser impaired asked hopefully.

"No, stupid, maybe Turk."

Instant sobriety and exit. Only Willie and Wally, Klanski's lifelong sidekicks, remained.

Thirty minutes later Polly knocked at the door. Willie peeked out the tattered plastic blinds. "Polly," he said as he turned to Klanski.

The lead biker opened the door halfway as his hand gripped the razor sharp bowie knife strapped to his backside.

"Polly, where you been?"

"What do you mean, where've I been? You my daddy now?" Polly attempted to sound like the big man.

"I really could care less, Polly, but the Turk was calling for you, and he didn't sound like he was lonely and needing a shoulder to cry on."

"Screw the Turk! I don't report to that muscle-head either. I'll be downstairs if anyone calls."

"Let me know if you need anything, Polly—cold beer, a little white powder, dancing girls."

"Screw you too, Klanski, and the bike you rode in on!" Polly opened the steel door, hit the light switch, and proceeded down thirteen wooden steps to the basement apartment.

Klanski turned to his pals, Willie and Wally. "Sensitive little girl, ain't she?"

Turk met Sean at the small private airport in south Jersey. Neither spoke as they walked up the gangway, entering the small private jet. Turk carried a canvas overnight bag while Sean hauled a larger duffle bag on board.

NUMBER THREE

Sean MacIntosh relaxed in the front seat of the eighteen-passenger jet. Turk sat quietly in the last seat next to the toilet, eyes closed.

Sean was around the age of Polly, with reddish blond hair shortly cropped, green eyes with specks of brown, like tiny flaws in a cat's eye marble, tanned with a spattering of freckles across his short pug nose, and had white teeth, perfectly straight, giving him a warm, trusting smile. Six feet tall and solidly built, he could be Polly's brother if you did not know better.

Actually, in a way, they were brothers, or at least joined together by their adopted father, Borack Abbadon.

Sean MacIntosh, born to Protestant parents in the heart of Ireland, learned to hate Catholics and soldiers of the crown before he could walk. Parents killed by the "in the pope we hope crowd" when he was five, the boy was bounced from house to house.

At six years old, he went to war by dropping a hand grenade into the gas line intake of a British personnel carrier. None survived, and the child flew thirty feet with the explosion, suffering second and third-degree burns from his tiny shoulders to his shoeless feet.

Borack found the boy the next day, walking the streets black with dust, horribly burned, and suffering from a severe concussion.

Sean, just short of two years older than Polly, was the first to speak to the new boy when Grey and her baby brother arrived at the mountainous castle.

"Hi, my name is Three. You'll probably be called Six."

The boys grew up together in their covey, learning and training side by side. Polly was always smarter, tougher, and meaner than Three.

Three attempted to make friends, but Polly rejected all efforts. He just simply hated everyone, especially the new kid with the scars on his back and his stupid grin.

Borack knew people. It might even be fair to say he could read their souls. He could see that Sean's was blank. Not good, not evil, just empty.

The young man lived a simple life in a one-bedroom basement apartment in a secluded Muslim neighborhood—Muslim school, Muslim temple, Muslim bakery; Muslim everything surrounded Sean's everyday existence.

It was a strange sight to watch this handsome Irish lad walk about in a white tee shirt, jeans, and no brand tennis shoes among a small society of strangely dressed Muslims, they so solemn, while he was always smiling and waving as if part of the family.

However, the boy was respected and treated as someone special. After all, the Muslim leaders knew his father. They knew the man if not by sight, by his gifts to their cause. The boy was to be protected.

Besides that fact, Sean MacIntosh was very good at one thing. Although slow in certain things, the young man was a brilliant bomb maker.

Willie and Wally slept peacefully, spread out on the filthy carpet that could cause the dry heaves or worse for any normal person. One might suspect that their clothing masked the carpet stench.

Klanski sat at the kitchen table taking long pulls from the quart of Jack Daniels Black. He could in fact drink the whole thing and still ride a Fat Boy or fight one.

At 4:30 a.m., a heavy knock on the door brought Mikey, as the boys called him, out of his Jack Daniels snooze. Willie grunted, and Wally passed serious gas.

"Come in." Klanski's voice was harsh from three packs of Camels. "Door's open." He slowly gripped the .357 Magnum loosely secured under the Formica tabletop.

Turk stepped carefully into the filth, surveying each inch of the disgusting rat hole in seconds. He, too, held tightly to a nine mil in his pocket, seventeen rounds, with hammer cocked.

Sean poked his head around the giant, producing a grand Irish smile. "Top of the morning, mate! Nice place you have here."

"Yeah, kinda homey, ain't it," Klanski replied flatly and drained the last of his Jack in one large gulp.

"Polly?" The Turk was tense.

"Sleeping like a baby downstairs. Probably dreaming of going to Disneyland."

Turk's dark eyes peered at Klanski, and the biker knew to shut his mouth.

"Get him, now."

Without hesitation, Mikey stood and went to the metal door, quickly moving down the thirteen steps, where Polly slept and rocked like a baby with his binky.

"Rise and shine, sweet prince; your carriage awaits." Klanski purposely shook Polly hard.

"Huh, what…who is it?" Polly sat up quickly, taking a moment to acclimate himself.

"Mr. Turk is here with his girlfriend. He asked if he might have a moment." He sang the words more than spoke them.

"Turk? Here? What, uh, what does he want?" Fear was obvious and sickening.

"Well, I'm not completely sure, Polly my boy, but I'll lay a hundred to one he ain't taking you to Orlando."

Polly quickly pulled on his tailored slacks, silk shirt buttoned, and slipped on the Italian loafers, all done in record time.

Just as Polly reached the top of the stairs, he heard a low sustained rumble. He stopped again.

Sean looked over toward Willie and Wally. "I do believe one of the boys over there must have swallowed a skunk and the poor thing is trying to crawl out." A rare, quick smile parsed Turk's tight lips.

Polly stepped forward. "God, this place smells like a toilet. Disgusting! Hey, Turk, what's up?" A forced smile attempted to hide the fear, or worse yet, stop him from peeing.

Before Turk could respond, Polly asked Sean, "Who are you?"

"I declare, Turk, the man doesn't even recognize his own brother; I'm hurt to the bone!"

"Brother?" Polly was confused and needed a drink of water to keep from gagging in this cesspool.

"Indeed, mate! Don't you remember the covey? I'm Three! Top of the morning, brother Six!"

"Oh God!" Polly ran to the sink, throwing two Pizza Hut boxes aside and vomiting as though he'd swallowed Wally's skunk.

"What the—" Klanski acted as if this was so disgusting in his model home. "Come on, Polly; puke in the head, not our kitchen sink!"

"Screw you," Polly moaned.

"Clean it up," stated the Iranian matter-of-factly.

"Huh?" Polly acted like a child whose daddy told him to take out the garbage.

"I said, clean it up!"

Polly rinsed the sink, gagging all the while.

Turk turned to Klanski. "Go back down and bring up Polly's stuff. All of it. Leave nothing."

Klanski went to task as Polly asked. "What's the plan?"

"New York," Turk answered flatly.

"Cool, I'm sick of this hillbilly town." Polly felt a moment of relief. If Turk was going to stomp his brains out, he'd do it here and do it now. New York must mean the father had forgiven him. He added, "I'll be back for the grand opening, *The Beginning*, won't I?"

"No clue. Get your crap. We're wasting time."

Turk turned to Klanski. "Later. Stay close." He shut the door and walked to the big black car, with Three and Six behind him.

"Give me the keys." Turk held out his meaty bear paw.

"Keys?" Polly's concern returned.

"Yes, keys! Car. Apartment."

"Yeah, sure. Here, Turk." Polly handed the ring of keys secured by a BMW gold key holder.

Turk tossed the keys to Sean. The shining BMW was several feet away, resting peacefully in the broken concrete driveway. "Here." Turk gave Sean a handwritten note. "Go now."

Sean walked to the grand automobile as Turk opened the passenger door for Polly. "Get in." Sean, now twenty feet away, turned back. "See ya, Turk. Have a good flight home." He smiled stiffly. "See ya, Six. Godspeed, my brother."

The big car squealed as Turk made a U-turn and headed northeast.

Sean started the powerful BMW and listened to the purr of the engine for a moment. Turning on the overhead light, he opened the note.

My son:

Go to this address immediately. It is our condo downtown where Polly has been staying. It will be your home until *The Beginning* has ended. All of Polly's clothes should fit you. They are yours now. He will not need them any longer.

You have earned my blessing and the right to my name as a father's son. All proper identification will arrive by Federal Express tomorrow, along with access to our local bank account, credit cards, and a special cell phone. Stay in the condo until I call.

Do not fail me,

Father

"Your will be done!" Sean smiled, backed out, and hit the radio "Play" button.

Mikey Klanski watched all this through the crack in the blinds as he started on a new bottle of Jack. "Now, they're some seriously weird cats."

He moved toward the back as Wally let a long one go. Mikey kicked him hard. "Go to the bathroom and clean your pants, dirt bag." Wally grunted, turned over, and placed his arm around Willie.

RUN LIKE THE DEVIL'S AFTER YOU

"Where we headed?" Polly asked nervously.

"Airport." Turk stared straight ahead.

The big man pressed the control, and the heavy gate slid open. Signs hung all along the fence. "Private Property," "No Trespassing," "High Voltage."

In the distance, Polly could see the sleek private jet resting just several yards from a metal building with a single-fuel tank to the left. The building was dark, but tiny green and red lights illuminated the jet's cockpit.

Turk parked the car next to the east side fence, some

hundred yards from the jet. "Get out," Turk said without emotion.

"You leaving the car here, Turk?"

"Yes, someone will move it to our garage later." *Audible full sentence from the giant,* Polly mused to himself.

Polly nervously walked two steps in front of the Iranian, hoping with all hope that his father wished him safe in New York. Yes, of course, safe from the snoopers.

Polly saw stars first and then raced in and out of blackness. The powerful blow to the back of his head sent him crashing face-first into the cool black pavement. No chance of breaking the fall, as his nose broke at the base and teeth scattered like dominoes. Fighting to find consciousness, he rolled to his side to see Turk's boot-covered left foot moving down toward his head, a boulder falling on a snail. One stomp, head crushed, bye-bye Polly.

Fear igniting every nerve ending, adrenalin pumping blood to brain and muscle, Polly rolled a fraction of a second before the size-fifteen boot slammed an inch from his bleeding face. Not only could he hear the power of boot to earth, but he actually felt the ground shake.

Another roll, boom, a new stomp. Roll, boom, roll, boom.

With agility that only youth provides, Polly sprang to his feet, circling the giant, thinking of escape. Turk pulled the black pistol from his coat pocket. At that exact same moment Polly swung the switchblade knife with a six-inch blade. *Click.* The stainless metal glistened in the night. *Swoosh!* The blade went in and through the giant's paw.

Turk's gun hit the pavement. The Iranian sneered, slowly pulling the knife back through his bleeding flesh as if it were but a tiny splinter. "I'm going to tear your arms off!" An unholy growl hissed from Turk's lips.

Polly knew he had but one chance to run, and run he did.

Much faster than the giant, Polly raced like a frightened antelope with a grizzly in pursuit. He gained ground, quickly becoming more shadow than man as the grizzly growled and roared.

There, he could see it, the fence, separation, escape. With the agility of a cobra, Polly coiled and shot into the night as if propelled by rocket fuel. Up, close, up, stretch, push. Sparks flew as his silver belt buckle touched the top wire. Up and over he hit hands first, forward roll, to his feet, racing toward the breaking dawn before him.

Charged with blind fury, Turk ran full force into the electric fence, where voltage with sound hummed in the night's mist. The power against power was colossal, yet the fence won the battle.

Thrown thirty feet back, Turk lay convulsing on the pavement, smoldering lines across his long wool coat and the smell of burning flesh as the dark bloody line burned his face.

Fifteen minutes later, Turk stood outside the jet, cell phone in hand.

Two rings and Turk's counterpart, Mosha, answered.

"Turk,"—the grizzly sucked in a huge gulp of air—"Polly's gone."

"Gone?"

"Disappeared."

"Hold." Several minutes passed before Mosha returned to the phone. "Come home."

Turk stood silent for a moment and raised his head, looking out beyond the fence. A red-yellow dawn was awakening.

THE PLAN FOR THE BEGINNING

Just a few days remained until Borack Abbadon would begin the six years of chaos.

After many long years in preparation and racing toward two billion dollars spent, *The Beginning* was a mere 120 hours until show time.

All the details, careful planning, a thousand pieces delicately sculptured to complete the puzzle.

Borack, guided by the master's brilliance, had long ago painted the total picture on the puzzle box. The artistry was done, the puzzle pieces precisely cut, nothing really left to do but the doing, snap each delicate puzzle piece into place.

The Beginning would most likely go unnoticed by a self-absorbed world; it was so planned. But the second year of chaos might raise an eyebrow or two. Then it would build, each chaotic year layered on top of the previous year's turmoil, all moving toward the finality of chaos the world had never seen and would never see again, control of the souls of mankind.

Think it through, the master thought—one god, one perfect angel, one man, and one woman. Six thousand years later, a world divided. The "I'm so holy" robots, of whom most would still go to hell—they just didn't know it—and the free choicers, those who served the clarity of enjoying all the pleasures available if one was not burdened by the shackles of the only begotten son.

From that single beginning, a man, a woman, a simple fruit. Why were they forbidden to enjoy its pleasure and rewards? Did God eat from the tree?

Did he not enjoy the fruit? The master certainly had.

And the world went plural. Cain and Abel, good son, bad son, or so we're supposed to believe. Why was Cain convicted anyway? Who said he must work hard and give the best of his own labor to God? Abel was weak and took advantage of his brother. Cain didn't intend to kill his brother only to gain a little respect. It was an accident!

Then two again, Isaac and Ishmael. Which one was treated like a dog? God's chosen people? Certainly not! Isaac gets it all, and Ishmael is thrown to the desert like a stillborn lamb. You call that fair?

And how about poor old Job. Who screwed him over?

The master? Absolutely not! Look what he did for Job's children! Was it he who killed them?

And poor old Judas. What did he do that was so wrong anyway? Tried to get ahead, build a little financial security. He didn't know what they planned to do to Jesus. Judas made one mistake, attempted to save a little money for a rainy day, and look what that got him! And who hung the poor guy anyway? Was it the master? Absolutely not! It was the Pharisees for God's sake, wasn't it? The sons of Abraham!

Borack felt certain that Judas Iscariot would have a special position in the master's kingdom some day. He hoped his dedication would also bring honor and glory in the new world.

Just a few short days and his real work would begin. Abbadon felt jubilant. *The Beginning*, 666 souls gained in a single moment, the birth of the master's great army building into many millions in six short chaotic years.

"All things start small." Borack breathed in the power given by the master. "All things start small, beginning with ten perfect souls, handpicked and delivered to the Hikes Point Lounge one minute after midnight New Year's Day."

The plan was pure genius in its simplicity. Bars, saloons, and taverns across the world had been selected and purchased by Abbadon in the past ten years.

His children, nearly one hundred, saved by himself from a Godless world. Little innocent babies thrown out like garbage to the trash dump called mankind.

Lovely little ones left by God to be abused, beaten, raped, and tormented. By whom? Certainly not the master or Borack. Absolutely the opposite. Borack saved the innocent little ones, adopted the parentless, and brought them to his home to teach and love.

And now the babies mankind tossed away like dirty dishwater were prepared. They were ready for the master's work. The babies turned warriors would go into battle around the world in a short five days.

From little children to gallant servants of chaos, Borack thought proudly of his work. *All good things start small.*

The invitations were in the mail, twenty countries, all professing their Christian faith. "See where that gets you," Borack proclaimed. His biggest target, of course, was the great Christian basin of the good old US of A, where sixty-six sites were now ready for *The Beginning,* starting with his favorite, the Hikes Point Lounge.

What a joke, he originally thought. *The great family of Irish Catholics, the birthplace of drunks! And the Hikes Point Lounge! Now there's a solid business for a third generation of alcoholics.*

Paddy O'Doul, the Catholic Christian who never missed Mass a day in his life, he always had something brand new and exciting every week to squeal to the priest in confession. And how many Hail Marys had the fool proclaimed? A million?

"And what about fish Friday! Fish sandwiches, why that sure as hell will get you into heaven," Borack had said just before he ordered the good Catholic's murder.

Abbadon wondered if good old Paddy might be serving some cold frosty mugs of draft in the master's new kingdom. "Have a cold beer, mate. Would you like a fish sandwich? Hail Mary and top of the morning to ya!"

From the beginning, the 666 new souls for the master's army had been carefully selected, their lives lived out in front of a watchful eye, never knowing that their every decision was gently guided by the prince of the air.

All had been raised by Christian parents in middle-class homes. Didn't need the really poor or really rich; they mostly took care of themselves. No, only nice middle-class kids would do. The ones who knew "Jesus loves me, this I know, cause the Bible tells me so…"

The little innocents who wore their navy blue uniforms to class and believed all the crap the flying penguins told them. "Now eat your fish, Johnny, or you'll get the ruler on your knuckles!"

And then the really special children, the Christian rock and rollers, imitating Mommy and Daddy speak in gibberish, calling it speaking in tongues, what a joke! Or those who had to go door to door or on mission trips, all in the name of God. Those were the selected ones, all with a solid foundation in the God of fools.

They would be watched as they stumbled into lust, pride, hate, jealousy, and the real biggie, greed!

Yes, greed, that would be the drawing card. That would be the incentive that would bring them to *The Beginning*.

Borack felt most certain that his plan was absolute. Each of the selected ones had been allowed to enjoy the pleasures only money could deliver. The big house, nice car, great vacations, all there. And then the cocaine, the whiskey, the stealing, the lying, the neighbor's wife. They were each and every one, ready for the big show, ready to feed their greed, ready for *The Beginning*.

Each invitation was hand delivered by impressive couriers. They were personally addressed, return receipt requested, and each of the selected were, shall we say, a bit down on their luck.

The invitations were gold embossed on the finest stationery, all sealed by a red wax initialed marking with a striking ribbon. They read: "B.A. Enterprises, the world's largest entertainment provider, has selected you (their name in handwritten script) to participate in a once-in-a-lifetime drawing.

There will be a first-place drawing for $1,000,000 for one lucky winner with a one in ten chance of winning."

The odds were just too tempting; cashing in was a different story altogether.

The invitation explained that their selection was based on a personal deed somewhere and sometime in their life, which, of course, gave way to curiosity and the knowledge that all believe they'd done something special for someone.

A final stipulation stated that they were not to share this invitation with anyone and they must come unescorted. Failure to meet these simple rules would bring disqualification.

All food, drinks, and entertainment would be on the house!

Six hundred and sixty-six excited people around the world signed the RSVP eagerly.

MACKLIN'S WORST DREAM ALIVE AGAIN

Borack sat casually in the high-back leather chair, Grey at his feet. The man, impeccably dressed, looked as if he would at any moment leave for a major meeting with world leaders or men of business renown. Not so, he just always looked like this.

Dark gray suit stitched together by his favorite Hong Kong tailor at five thousand a pop, white shirt with barely visible red striping monogrammed, of course, with his signature B.A., and the red silk tie and matching handkerchief lining the breast pocket. Solid gold Rolex without the diamonds—Borack hated flashy—and the gold ring of gothic appearance with ruby eyes on his left middle finger, a bit flashy, but with very special meaning.

Grey wore one of her many silk robes, hand stitched as well by the Hong Kong tailor's wife, a simple pair of purple satin slippers, and her beautiful thick hair that looked like the mane of a royal lion.

Turk stood solemnly before his master in the same clothes from that morning. The smell of burnt wool and flesh was disgusting to Abbadon. His hand wrapped in a clean white bandage, thanks to Grey, was seeping blood top and bottom.

The Iranian's head was submissively bowed, his voice flat and low. For the first time, Grey felt pity for the giant that seemed to have no purpose, no hope, no love, nothing except total servitude for Borack's demands. Was she really that different? The thought scared her.

"So there, my dear friend." Borack spoke as if he might even care for the giant. "Let me recap. Polly disarmed my greatest warrior, stabbed him, and then flew over an eight-foot fence."

"Yes, sir." As always, a man of few words.

"And then my greatest warrior,"—Borack's voice was a bit more intense—"ran into an electric fence in pursuit and to no avail."

"Yes, sir."

Borack stood, went to the bar, and poured two fingers of twenty-year-old scotch. He'd started drinking scotch of late, in honor of Paddy O'Doul and his contribution to *The Beginning*. He lit a long hand-rolled Cuban cigar sent to him recently by his longtime friend Fidel.

"Well, I must admit, Grey, my precious, that your baby brother certainly surprised me. I'm impressed!"

"I'm sure he's terrified," Grey retorted in a whisper.

"And so he should be! Not many men can put a knife into the flesh of the Turk and live to tell the story!"

Grey lifted her head and now with courage in her voice asked, "Did you tell Turk to kill Polly?"

"My dear one, how can you ask such a horrible question? Do you believe I could take the only living relative away from you? My son?"

Grey turned to Turk, standing motionless. "Turk? Turk, were you going to kill my brother?"

Turk did not answer, and Borack moved to her side, stroking her hair. "My dear one, you must know better than that. I didn't instruct Turk to kill little Polly, did I, Turk?"

A moment's hesitation. "No, no, Grey."

"But, Grey," Abbadon continued, "Polly's been a bad boy, a very bad boy! And he knows the rules, and he knows what failure brings. It brings consequences."

"What has he done? What sin has my brother committed?"

"Oh, it's not all that bad and not worthy of your concern. However, he does indeed need a serious reprimand; it's my law."

Borack watched as Grey seemed to relax and turned his attention back into the giant's shadow. "And you, my friend, you too have a failure to account for, don't you?"

"Yes, sir."

Borack returned to the marble-top bar and refreshed his scotch. "Can I get either of you anything?"

"No thank you, Borack." Grey was carefully watching his face.

"No, sir."

"Well then, here's what we will do." Abbadon was almost cheerful. "Turk, you are to go immediately to Sean's apartment. I will send a doctor to take care of your wounds."

"Thank you."

"Get a good night's sleep and leave for Louisville tomorrow morning. Take the same jet."

"Yes, sir."

"Find Polly—I'm sure that won't be hard—and stay with him. That means not out of your sight until Grey and I arrive. Tell him Father's not angry and his sister will be there soon. Understood?"

"Yes, sir."

"Now, as to your failure. Mosha will replace you as my right-hand man and you will remain in the Muslim community until your sin has been forgiven. Go, and sin no more."

"Thank you."

Macklin, Rusty, and Annie sat around the dining room table once graced by Mrs. O'Doul's fine Irish cooking. Pizza boxes, paper plates, paper towels, and plastic forks adorned the hand-embroidered placemats.

"Okay then, what have we got?" Macklin sounded like an FBI man.

"Well,"—Annie was excited—"the whole strip mall and the Pussy Cat Club belong to B.A. Enterprises."

"Who?" Rusty asked with a mouth full of pepperoni.

"B.A. Enterprise. The best I could determine is one man owns it. The company is huge with massive real estate holdings, jets, ships, small countries; you name it, and one guy controls it all."

"And he is?" Rusty now was with an empty mouth. "My source thinks his name is Borack Abbadon, but they can't be sure."

Macklin whispered, "Dear God in heaven." He turned white as a ghost.

"What?" The narc's instincts at full alert. "You know this guy?"

"I might, and if it's him, he is probably the most dangerous man you'll ever meet."

"Really?" Rusty's signals were going off like firecrackers in his brain.

"Yes, extremely dangerous, rich, powerful, and most likely untouchable."

Both Rusty and Annie could see just how unnerved Macklin had become.

"From this moment forward, Annie is out of the game."

"Now wait just a second, Mack, I believe—"

"Absolutely, positively, no questions asked, *out of the game!* And I mean *out!*"

"Done." Rusty stood and began to pace. "Annie can stay at my place. The neighbors know me, and they're, let's say, protective. I'll put two plains downstairs in the tavern twenty-four-seven. There is only one way in, and it will be watched."

"And where will you be?" Macklin asked.

"Well, I'll be protecting Annie, of course, when I'm not working the case with you."

"Of course," Macklin said sarcastically, and Annie blushed from head to toe.

Rusty then smacked his forehead hard, leaving a reddish palm print. "Oh wow, am I dumber than a rock or what?"

"Go on." Macklin was impatient.

"Abbadon, you said the real bad guy's name is Abbadon, right?"

"Yes, Borack Abbadon," Annie stated flatly, and the hair rose on Macklin's thick neck.

"We might have the missing piece!"

"And?" Macklin was now on his feet.

"Well, you know I've been working for a tie into Annie's and her, uh, boyfriend's murder and working the biker things behind the Hikes Point."

"Okay?" Macklin was pushing.

"We had surveillance on this biker dive, their main hangout, see, and last night this big BMW shows up. A young, well-dressed, tall kid with blond hair I think gets out and disappears into the dump."

"Blond hair?" Annie answered.

"Yeah, blond hair. Anyway, my boys run the plates; owner's name is Polly Abbadon."

Macklin sat back down, feeling sick to his stomach.

"Then a little later a big black Lincoln rolls in with another young guy and this gigantic Arab. Fifteen minutes later, the first kid and the Incredible Hulk leave in the big Lincoln and the second kid hauls butt in the Beamer. No real reason to pop 'em, so we let it ride."

"The blond-headed kid, Polly Abbadon,"—Annie leaned forward—"you think he's related, then, to our guy?"

Macklin got up, went to the fridge, and popped the top to a Foster's. "It's his son."

"His what? How do you know that, Mack?" The Narc was surprised.

"I just do; leave it at that."

"So what's your plan, Macklin?" Rusty gave reverence to his counterpart.

"Take Annie to your place now. Don't get two plainclothes; make it four. Two at the stairs and two at the door, fully armed, bring out the twelve gauges."

"These really are bad guys, huh?" Rusty sensed the danger in Macklin's voice.

"You don't have a clue, my friend. Not in your wildest nightmare."

"Done. What else?"

"Get back to our office as soon as Annie is secure. It's time we go hunting for an acorn, and God help us when we find the tree."

FIND A RABBIT HIDING, FIND A WOLF WATCHING

Polly, scratched, tattered, and muddy, ran from shadow to shadow, hiding in terror from the giant that almost blew his brains all over the dark runway. He heard the jet climb over his head but couldn't be sure Turk was on it.

Tears streamed down his face as he stumbled forward, searching his confused mind for a way out. Nowhere to run, nowhere to hide, no escape from the mysteries of his father. "Father, yeah right!" He spat the words. *What father would kill his son?* Abbadon would.

He must find a safe place. Where? Who? If only he could reach Grey, she could save him. Grey, his sister, his blood. She could stop Abbadon from killing.

He ran southwest back toward all he knew, back toward the Hikes Point Lounge. "Is it safe?" he asked himself. "Is it safe?"

He stopped one mile from the Party Mall, hiding behind the dumpster in back of Hooters. It was too early for his friend Chad Patrick to be there. As manager, he probably wouldn't be there until four o'clock.

And would Chad help him? They were friends, weren't they? Didn't they have some good times? He and Chad and the two Hooters chicks that liked to hurt you. He wasn't into that "beat me, bite me" stuff like Patrick was. He couldn't wait behind the dumpster until four, and what could a crawdad like Chad do anyway?

A half a mile closer, the huge Party Mall sign so high in the air was calling him. *Here Polly, come to us; we'll keep you safe.*

"That's it! That's it!" Polly remembered. Twice he'd left the keys to the Hikes Point Lounge laying on the bar as he exited the self-locking fire door into the alley. And twice he'd called a locksmith to get him in. But being the brainchild, Polly purchased a fake rock at Ace Hardware, the hide-a-key kind. Yes, the spare secret key would get him safely in since Turk or Sean had all of his original keys now. *Get to the rock, Polly! Get to the rock!*

He felt sure that once inside he would have time to sleep, to think, to plan, and to hopefully contact Grey and someday put a bullet in Turk's thick meatball head.

Yes, get to the rock, get inside, set up camp in the basement where the old black man lived. Yeah, that worthless old janitor he killed.

"Thanks for fixing the place up, Mr. Brown!" Polly scoffed as he entered the basement, falling on the bed where the old man had spent many a year before Polly turned out his lights.

Richie, flashing eight gold chains and eight slicked-back hairs atop his balding head, walked through the Pussy Cat Club, glad-handing all his humble employees and the occasional backside pat to his favorite dancers. "Good to see ya! How ya doin'? Ready for a big night?"

Preparing for an evening of Girls, Girls, Girls, the club manager headed for his plush office for a quick snort of the good stuff to get his engine firing, so to speak.

Richie opened the door, reached in for the light switch plate, which happened to be a plastic naked lady, his special decoration, and stopped dead in his tracks. "Hey, what the—"

"Shut the door. Shut your mouth."

Richie knew Turk by sight, but this was the first time up close and personal.

"Where is Polly?"

"Who?"

Thirty minutes later, the Pussy Cat Club's manager lay facedown on his pink shag carpet. Eyes swollen shut, broken nose, jaw, and missing several teeth, gasping for breath through already swollen lips, Richie curled his hands under his battered body, protecting ten twisted fingers sticking out in all directions.

"Please, please,"—a gurgling sound came out as though he was talking under water —"I don't... kno... where... Polly—"

He never saw the massive boot slowly moving down, down to crush his skull like one might crack a Christmas walnut.

The squad of men dressed in helmets with shields, black armor vests, and automatic rifles surrounded the house. It read "Police" across their backs in reflective yellow.

Boom! The front door shattered in rotted wood. Two flash bangs and two explosions. Mikey, Willie, and Wally lay quietly on the stinking carpet, stunned and motionless. Then, through the smoke, the head biker lifted his eyes to stare up as Rusty and Macklin strolled in pretty as you please.

"Miami Vice. I give up," Klanski mocked, and Macklin kicked him in the mouth, making his one-piece denture two.

"Shut up, scumbag! Where's Polly?"

One hour later, safe room no longer safe, a good haul of pot, pills, and something looking like heroin, and for sure three major felony arrests, i.e. long time go bye-bye, the bikers were ready to sell their mothers.

It didn't take long for Macklin and Rusty to determine that the lowlifes knew little and had no clue where Polly was.

Rusty instructed the armor-wearing cops to cuff the thugs and take them downtown for booking.

Just before the cops put the cuffs on the dirty ringleader, Macklin grabbed a handful of long greasy hair and snapped Klanski's head back. He looked at the cop standing next to him. "Book 'em, Danno." He smiled. "Hawaii Five-O, wrong show, Easy Rider."

Rusty laughed. "Say goodbye to sunlight, sweethearts."

Next, the two partners, hunting, would end at the Pussy

Cat Club, watching the coroner zip up one seriously tortured and dead Richie Prunnaire, ex go-go club manager.

The hunters did not know who murdered the manager, nor did they have any prey in their sacks. The hunters didn't know much, and for sure they did not realize they were now the hunted.

MISTAKES YOU CAN'T MAKE

Macklin sat motionless in Annie's Mercedes Benz at the south end of the parking lot in front and to the right of the strip center where he and Annie maintained their office.

Utilizing extremely high-tech binoculars, hands resting on the black leather steering wheel, Macklin peered across four lanes of steady traffic, fixating both sight and mind on the security-barred door to the Hikes Point Lounge.

He glanced at his Timex—7:15 p.m. and approximately one hour until he'd switch to night vision. Macklin was getting restless. The surveillance began at noon after he and

Rusty left the Louisville police station, where their investigation of the biker boys had produced absolutely zero. They didn't know in what country Abbadon might be and did not have a clue where Polly was, but both were eager to implicate him in the murders of Paddy and Josh. As to Polly's whereabouts, "Hey, man, we told you already!" Mikey was humble and attempting sincerity. "The last we saw of the punk, he was riding off in a big black Lincoln with the giant camel jockey."

Macklin knew Rusty would be with Annie at his crap apartment, waiting for a fresh foursome of undercovers. Rusty would arrive shortly to search the Hikes Point, minus a warrant, with Macklin.

Macklin lived by gut feel. All his life that sixth sense, that thing deep down in his belly, that *moment* feeling he would get, had saved his life more times than he could remember. And now there it was, strong as ever.

"Polly, you little weasel, I know you're in there. Scumbag murderer, hiding, scared, trapped like the rat you are. Well, find a good hole, you diseased little mouse, because the big bad cat is coming."

Then, out of nowhere, a black Lincoln pulled right up to the front door of the Hikes Point Lounge.

Macklin pushed the binoculars tight around his eyes and adjusted the vision slightly as his forehead broke out in tiny beads of sweat.

The driver's door opened. "That's one gigantic Arab," Macklin whispered and quickly wiped the sweat from his forehead with a flick of his left hand.

The driver, or bodyguard, or killer, or all of the above, opened the back door on the driver's side slowly and cautiously. A tall man in a long cashmere coat stood and looked around quickly yet carefully as he turned his head north. Macklin stopped breathing. "Oh dear God, it's him."

The man who brought real terror to Macklin's inner being reached out his hand, gently lifting Grey from the car.

"Grey," Macklin spoke softly. "My dear Grey."

The big Arab unlocked the heavy padlock chain, turned a brass key in two separate deadbolts, and opened the door for Borack Abbadon and Grey. In an instant, all three disappeared as Macklin remained frozen in the past, surrounded by a memory thick as Arctic ice. Thoughts of terror, fear, hate, and yes, love. Macklin's *moment* feeling kicked hard in his belly, bringing him back to action.

"Mack, what's up?" Rusty looked at the Caller ID on his cell phone, answering on the second ring.

"Rusty, they're here."

"Who, Mack? Who's there?"

"The big Arab, probably the Turk, Abbadon,"—a moment's hesitation—"and Grey."

"Holy... who's Grey?"

Again hesitation. "An old friend; I'll explain later. How soon can you get here?"

"Maybe fifteen, ten if I plug in the blue light. But, Mack, we'll need a warrant. I can call Judge—"

Macklin cut him off. "I've got one already. It's black and holds seventeen rounds. Now move your butt!"

"Hang tight, buddy. The cavalry is on the way."

Rusty quickly instructed his undercover team, putting two inside the tiny apartment with Annie. "The rats are in the trap, sweetheart!" He kissed her once full on the lips and ran out the back door of Turner's Tavern.

"Polly, Polly, are you here? Answer me, brother! It's your sister!"

Polly jumped from the bed and quickly ran a couple of circles around the room like a mouse caught in a corner. He stopped and listened.

"Polly, it's Grey! Are you here? I've come to get you!"

"Grey?" a tiny, girlish voice whispered as if ready to cry. "Grey, is that you?"

"Yes, Polly, it's me! Come out! Everything is going to be okay."

Polly crawled up the stairs like a baby still afraid to take his first step. "Grey, is it safe?" He whimpered like a spoiled child.

"Yes, baby brother. I promise."

At the top of the steps from the basement, his face skimming the cold floor, he cracked the door and took a mousy peek. There was Grey, as beautiful as ever, here to save him. And then he saw his father, Borack Abbadon. He was smiling. His father was concerned. Yes, he might have screwed a few things up, made a mistake along the way, but here was his loving sister and his adopted father. They were here to love and forgive.

Polly, secure in his reasoning, started to stand when he saw movement ten feet to the right in the shadows. He peed himself. "Is that Turk over there? Did you bring Turk to finish the job?" He was sobbing.

"No, Son, we did not. It is Mosha with us. Now please come out so we can all go away safely and finish plans for *The Beginning*."

"You're not mad at me, Father?"

"Mad? My son, I love you!" Abbadon's suave, persuasive voice filled the air with love. His sing-song left your heart rejoicing. "Now, come to your father."

"But, Father, Turk tried to kill me!"

"Oh yes, I am so sorry and disappointed in my faithful servant. But, Polly, you know Turk is not that bright. He just got carried away. But your father has punished him, and he is ever so repentant."

"Am I forgiven, Father? Really forgiven?"

"Of course you are, my boy. Would I bring your sister, Grey, if I wished to do you harm?"

That was true, Polly finally surmised. He stood and stepped into the light, displaying the dark wet stain on his wrinkled dirty pants.

"Oh, look at me," Polly stuttered. "When you came in I fell over a stinking mop bucket...got my pants all wet!"

"Sure you did, Son." Borack knew he'd peed himself like a baby. What a weakling and a coward. At the right time, and away from Grey, Turk would finish the job, but it would look as though Macklin killed her brother.

"Come, brother. Come to Grey. Let's go get you cleaned up."

Rusty squealed the unmarked to a stop beside the Benz, where Macklin continued to intently watch the Hikes Point front door. He grabbed a twelve gauge from the trunk and jumped in beside Mack.

"What kept you?" Macklin was gruff.

"Say what? I got here in eleven minutes."

"Okay, here's the deal... oh crap, someone's opened the front door."

Macklin, in his excitement and desire to catch the murderers of Annie's father and boyfriend, made a profound mistake, so uncharacteristic of a man trained to expect the unexpected. Maybe it was the sight of Grey disappearing through the front door or maybe his hatred for Abbadon that caused him to focus and rivet his full attention to the front door. In any case, Macklin screwed up.

"Who's covering the back alley?" Rusty asked matter-of-factly.

"Huh?" Macklin's stomach turned over. "The big guy's coming out!"

"Move it, Mack! Move it! Now!"

Macklin pushed the gas pedal to the floor, jumping the curb through the grass and into traffic, causing pileups in both lanes.

Several minutes earlier, Turk pulled the white plain Chevrolet Impala to the back door of the Hikes Point Lounge. Sean MacIntosh got out of the passenger side as Abbadon pushed Polly in beside the Turk. He and Grey hurriedly slid into the backseat as Sean entered the bar, locking the door to the alley. Within three minutes the Impala cruised toward the downtown condo at sixty-six miles per hour.

Macklin slid the Mercedes with badly damaged front tires in front of the Lincoln. Both men flew from the car with guns in hand, pointing first at the big man and then to the front door and back again.

"On the ground, scumbag! *Now!*" Rusty quickly patted the giant for weapons.

Macklin grabbed a handful of the man's collar and pulled his face close. "Where's the man and the girl?" He hissed the question.

"No English! No English!" the big man screamed.

"Move!" Macklin shouted over his shoulder to Rusty. "I'll cover!"

Rusty went in low, pistol sweeping back and forth, up and down, hammer back. Macklin did the same, towering over the narc's shoulder.

The place was bright with florescent lights illuminating the entire area, reflecting back from the bar's thirty-foot long mirror. The jukebox was playing *"Midnight Train to Georgia."*

No shadows, wide open, no place to hide, and no Abbadon or Grey. Only Sean MacIntosh, smiling as he wiped and stacked whiskey glasses with a white bar towel.

"Top of the morning, gentlemen!" Sean spoke in a heavy Irish brogue. "If it's a holdup you be after, you're a bit out of luck! You see, we won't be opening for a couple of days more, and, fellas, there ain't a nickel in the old till yet!"

Macklin's mind raced as he quickly surveyed the bar area, peering over and under the red-checkered freshly laundered tablecloths. They did have a solid description of Polly, and although this smiling Irishman could be his brother, it wasn't the punk they were after.

Rusty turned and mumbled something obscene as he heard a car door shut and the car engines sound fade away. "No English!"

"I'm proud to say my loving parents blessed me with a fine Irish name!" He had a wide sincere grin and raised both arms out proudly. "I was baptized Sean MacIntosh, the son of a famous Irish clan if ever was!"

"Cut the crap, Sean whatever it is. ID!"

"Can I ask you gentlemen what is going about here?"

"Shut your Irish mouth. We're cops! ID now!"

"Well, of course, officers! Always willing to respect the law, you know." He pulled out his wallet, producing a Kentucky driver's license. "My uncle Billy was a copper back in the homeland. Took a bullet for God and country, don't you know."

"Shut up," Rusty stated flatly as he searched the young man's wallet.

"Can I get you boys a draft or a shot of Irish whiskey now?"

"The man said shut up!" Macklin snapped.

"Who were the man and woman come in here twenty minutes ago?"

"Who were they?" Sean looked genuinely confused yet humorous at the same time.

"Did I stutter?" Macklin grabbed a fistful of his shirt and nearly pulled Sean across the bar. "Let me try again. Who were the man and the woman?"

"Oh, you mean Mr. A and his girlfriend, don't ya?"

"That's a start. What's Mr. A's full name?"

"Don't have a clue. Only met him today. The gentleman just said to call him Mr. A. Didn't introduce me to the fine lass he had on his arm."

Macklin wanted to smash his face in.

Rusty could see that Macklin was near explosion and jumped in. "Okay, kid, Sean, what are you doing here?"

"First day on the job, and a fine job it be!"

Rusty smiled between tight lips. "And that job is?"

"I'm the manager! I'm here to open the Hikes Point

Lounge New Year's Eve! It's as if the blessed Mother herself is looking out for Sean MacIntosh."

"So all you know is Mister A?" Macklin back now and focused. "And you're the manager?"

"That about totals it up," Sean shot back with his big grin.

"Then who exactly do you work for, mate?" Rusty asked sarcastically.

"Oh, here, mate." Sean, a bit sarcastic himself, pulled a single typed paper from his shirt pocket. "It's all right there, mate, in black and white."

Both men read a short and simple employment contract. The letterhead proclaimed "B.A. Properties."

"How did you get the job?" Macklin was growing weary.

"From a pal, you know. A mate I got to know at the Pussy Cat Club. Helped me out when I was feeling a bit of a pinch. Been like a brother to me, he has."

"And what is this mate been like a brother to you called?" Rusty asked.

"Polly." Sean smiled a big grin wide.

"Polly what?"

"Just Polly. Like the parrot." Sean started laughing at that one.

"And Polly, your mate, gave you this job?"

"Oh no, just told me to come take a look. Said he had some pull. Told me to be here today, knock on the back door, and the job was mine. Luck of the Irish, mate!"

Macklin thought this kid was really innocent or a really good actor. Either way, they were getting nowhere fast. "And what happened to, uh, Mister A and the woman?"

"Gave me my employment agreement, shook my hand, and left same way I came in."

"Did you see what kind of car?" Rusty perked up.

"Yes, as a matter-of-fact, couldn't help but notice such a fine carriage."

"What was it?" Both men were hoping for a solid clue.

"It was silver, I believe, or maybe gray. Big as a potato truck."

"Potato truck?" Rusty's brow curled.

"Oh, sorry, mate. It was a long limo, one of those with more doors than a public toilet."

"Let's go, Mack. APB the limo."

Both men headed quickly for the door. Macklin turned, looking sharply at the Irish kid, the new manager of the Hikes Point Lounge. "We'll be watching you, mate!"

"A comfort to know!" Sean shot back, smiling. "Always nice to know the coppers are watching the pub. Top of the evening, mate!"

TWENTY-FOUR HOURS

When Macklin and Rusty walked from the Hikes Point, they were greeted by six police cars, one being that of Captain Mullins.

After five hours downtown at headquarters, the captain released Rusty and Macklin on a short leash. Fortunately, no one received serious injury in the pileup, and with a signed promissory note from Macklin to pay all damages to civilian vehicles, they returned to Turner's Tavern.

Two undercovers sat at either side of the front door

and two more at the bar. Thirty minutes until closing, only three locals remained, all known by Rusty.

Macklin, Annie, and Rusty sat quietly and very disappointed at the back table, drinking cold drafts.

"Mack," Rusty said in a low voice, "who is Grey?"

Macklin remained quiet for a long moment, as if going back into a dark past, quite hesitant to relive it.

Annie held tightly to Rusty's hand, feeling his strength, as she also wished to reach out to her friend, who wore his apparent agony like never before.

Marked by intense emotion yet contained, Macklin began, "A very long time ago, when I was but a child…"

Macklin relayed his story from the time of Abbadon's rescue to his departure at age nineteen. He did so in obvious anguish, struggling with each word and proclamation.

It was mental surgery without painkillers. But even in his agonizing recall, Macklin visibly changed at the end of the story. Color returned to his face, and a smile crossed his lips for a moment. He explained slowly as his eyes glistened with beginning tears and ended the thirty-minute narrative. "And you ask, who is Grey?"

Neither Rusty nor Annie could respond. Both were in a state of shock.

"Grey," Macklin stated the name as if it was a holy untouchable goddess, someone or something to worship, and obviously he did just that. "Grey, the most beautiful person in the world and the only woman I love or ever will love."

"Wow," was all Rusty could muster, and Annie couldn't even find a worthy response to this most incredible story. She even thought that Stephen King or Spielberg couldn't dream this up. The three remained quiet for a long time until Rusty looked over his shoulder toward the bar. "Scotch; bring us a bottle of J.W. Black."

After both men downed a healthy gulp, Rusty reached out, placing his hand on Macklin's shoulder. "Geez, Mack, that is the most extraordinary thing I've ever been told. I just don't know what to say."

Macklin forced a smile. "Nothing to say, my friend. That's how I lived and who I am. Taught to hate, trained to kill, brainwashed to feel nothing except complete servitude. And it almost worked; most likely would have if I hadn't known Grey and experienced love for the first time in my young life."

Annie said timidly, "And you haven't seen or talked to her for all these years? Since you were nineteen?"

"Not until today."

"Today?" Annie asked, confused.

"Was it Grey at the Hikes Point? Was it her with Abbadon?"

"Yes, Rusty, it was Grey and that evil maniac that controls her every waking moment."

"Mack, there has got to be a way! You know, a way to find her, to rescue her, to put an end to the freak that controls her."

"Yeah, well, Rusty, easier said than done. Believe me, for most of my life, I have tried, with the resources of the FBI and the CIA. Nothing. I've done everything and gotten nowhere."

"I understand, Mack, or at least think I do, but this is still just a man. Yeah, he's got money and power, but, Mack, he is still just a man!"

"You think so, Rusty? You think he's just a man?"

"Well yeah, I guess. What else can he be?"

"Protected!"

"By who and what, Mack?" Annie interjected.

"By evil." Macklin lowered his head. "Pure undiluted wickedness with a guided focus and purpose."

"Purpose?" Annie stood in defiance. "Purpose? Purpose to do what? Snatch innocent children? Brainwash babies to become slaves?"

Macklin shook his head slowly and grimly smiled. "It is oh so much bigger than that, sweetheart. Much, much bigger."

"How so, Mack?" Rusty gently guided Annie back to her chair.

"He wants to destroy the world, or at least what good remains."

"In Louisville, Kentucky?" Rusty thought Mack's proclamation a bit overboard.

"No, no, my friend, not just Louisville. I said the world! East, west, north, south—Louisville, New York, L.A., London, New Zealand, Podunk, Africa. The world! Anywhere and everywhere anything good exists! What aren't you understanding?"

"Can he?" Annie added, this time with real fear in her voice.

"Maybe, I can't say." Macklin seemed to be thinking. "But I believe Louisville is important to Abbadon. It's the starting place, and the Hikes Point Lounge will be his kick-off party."

"Unbelievable!" Rusty was beginning to believe Macklin's nightmare.

"You see, this thing has been in the planning stages for

years. Maybe fifty, maybe a hundred, maybe since Adam and Eve. I just can't say. Louisville is nothing but a tiny cloud on the coast of Africa. The Hikes Point a single raindrop. But it will grow, it will strengthen, it will develop into a category-five hurricane that will leave devastation like never before!"

"But how do you stop such a thing?" Annie was now dancing in the terror.

"You probably can't." Macklin was now back to FBI, CIA mode. "But we can try, and try we will. The first battle will be fought at the Hikes Point Lounge and soon. I am sure of this."

Rusty asked, "Do you think Abbadon is here because of you?"

"No, I'm sure not. We were a major surprise, and this man, this thing, is not accustomed to surprises."

Rusty rubbed his hands together. "Okay, partner, what's the plan?"

"I don't have a plan, and sometimes that's the best way to attack. Just like in the Marine Corps; cammo-up, lay low, wait, and then in that all-important second, aim and fire. One shot, one kill!"

"Wait until?" Rusty, trained to move, asked.

"Twenty-four hours, my friend. New Year's Eve, at the Hikes Point Lounge."

After stopping at Polly's condo to gather his clothing, the group moved to a penthouse suite in the Hyatt.

The Turk and Mosha remained in the kitchen area drinking thick high-octane Columbian coffee, chain-smoking Turkish cigarettes.

Grey moved nervously in the high-back chair as Polly paced back and forth in front of her.

Borack Abbadon stood motionless, puffing a Cuban cigar in deep thought. He began to sway. "Luc a od, luc a od, luc a od..."

This only made Polly more nervous, and his pacing quickened.

Abbadon slowly stopped and turned. "Polly, you make me nervous as hell!"

This surprised Grey. She'd seen Abbadon mad, angry, and evil many times before, but never agitated. Never in all their time together had she once heard him say he was nervous. Now she sensed something was wrong, very wrong indeed. She could feel Abbadon worry as if he wore it like a heavy coat on a hot sunny day. She liked what she felt.

"What's wrong?" Her voice still held a simple innocence.

"Macklin!"

Grey's eyes flashed, and her cheeks blushed. Abbadon did not notice the change.

"Macklin?" Polly sounded as stupid as he actually was.

Borack looked at him as one might look at a cockroach crawling across the floor.

"Have you seen him?" Grey tried her level best to hide the excitement in her voice.

"No, but I felt him today. He was close; he was watching us at the Hikes Point Lounge. A father senses his children," he said with sarcasm.

"Leave him to me, Father!" Polly boasted. "Trust me, please. I'll kill him for you!"

Abbadon moved in an instant as if in one spot and in a second twenty feet across the room, glaring down at his weakest son. "Leave him to me? I'll kill him?"

"Yes, Father, I can—"

Abbadon picked him up off his feet with one hand and put his face close to Polly's trembling lips. "You'd have to face him, boy, face to face, *mano a mano*. The rabbit and the wolf. You'd pee your pants, and he'd swallow you whole!" Abbadon threw him back in the chair as Grey covered her mouth, hiding hope.

Borack was now back to business. "Here's the plan, the way, *The Beginning,* and no one will stop it. No one! Especially Macklin." Abbadon continued, "At precisely 12:01 tonight..."

NEW YEAR'S EVE: THE *BEGINNING*

8:59 P.M. DECEMBER 31

Borack Abbadon paced the floor like a caged tiger, an animal hungry, angry, looking for one small opening to run through and devour.

Fifteen of his finest servants from the castle were there. Covey Ravens and teachers of the arts—all had participated in the development of Borack Abbadon's large family of adopted children.

They were ready, after so many years of servitude to the master. Now, finally, *The Beginning* would in fact begin, start slow, unnoticed, and build layer upon layer of evil until the six years of chaos reached out and captured every living soul in its wake, a massive ship sailing upon the sea of life, deep in the waters of mankind, sailing silently.

Millions would be drowning in their own greed, lust, and hatred for each other. They would surely see the great ship approaching, rescue on the horizon. "Help us! Save me! Pull me aboard! Oh God, don't let us drown!" But it would be too late; the time has arrived...your sins have found you.

There would be no God, no holy child to pull the miserable wretches from the deep they had gladly swum into. No lifelines, life boats, or brave swimmers to the rescue. Only the wake of the colossal craft moving through the waters of the lost, sucking each man and woman into its mighty tow. Down, down, into a swirling whirlpool of terror and hopelessness. Deep like never before. Spinning without control in utter blackness. Down, down, down, they would travel until they reached their eternal destination and become soldiers for the master, servants of the prince.

One hundred locations, 666 souls, captured in moments, destined to receive their due reward. All good things start small.

Borack was building a mighty kingdom. In six years, the world would be lost as it now existed and re-created to serve the master. He would be the mighty ship's captain, he would be the navigator, and he would sit at the right hand.

Borack thought, *Yes, every great thing ever created started small. The pyramids, one cornerstone. The mighty Nile, one tiny mountain brook. Ruler of all the earth...one lonely, fallen angel.*

Now, in the next few hours, it would finally start. The cornerstone, the tiny brook, the Hikes Point Lounge, *The Beginning.*

9:00 P.M. NEW YEAR'S EVE
HIKES POINT LOUNGE—*THE BEGINNING*

The vinyl, six-foot sign flapped in the winter breeze as the snow began to fall. The WHAS weather girl predicted six inches before morning.

"Hikes Point Lounge—Grand Opening New Year's Eve—By Invitation Only."

The rotating motorized floodlight turned slowly in sweeping circles. The white beam illuminated skyward as if racing beyond the heavens. The large glistening snowflakes danced as they softly fell to earth in the brilliance of the inviting glow.

A glorious sight indeed! The floodlight bringing the lost sheep home. The bright red paint that covered the exterior of the Hikes Point seemed to be alive as a thousand neon lights encircled the establishment. Music played out into the snowy night, calling, welcoming. A dazzling gold limo waited in front for the winner of the grand-opening night million-dollar lotto. Just one quick look around and each special invitee would know his or her ship had finally come in.

Just inside the front door hung a red velvet rope clipped to silver poles with gold crowns. Mosha loomed large beside the rope, standing behind a small podium.

The giant wore a black tuxedo, white shirt, black tie, suspenders, and shiny size-eighteen plastic slip-on shoes gave Mosha the appearance of a sophisticated genie.

His only job that night would be to collect the special invitations, check the IDs of the fortunate ten guests, and lock the front door when all had arrived.

Sean MacIntosh stood confidently behind the bar, awaiting the special guests of B.A. Enterprises. He wore a heavy starched white tuxedo shirt, red cummerbund, red bowtie, and red suspenders. His pants were white with a satin stripe down each leg. The red canvas Converse tennis shoes seemed to fit well with his Irish persona and short blond spiked hairdo.

They were in place; they were ready to rumble. Mosha and Sean were ready for *The Beginning*.

Borack Abbadon continued to pace nervously. His fifteen faithful sat quietly around the dining table in his presidential suite. Each looked down at his highly sophisticated satellite phone before him, awaiting the first calls, calls from his children reporting in, bringing the good news of victory from around the world. In twenty-four hours, hundreds of souls gained, a few here, a few there. *The Beginning,* and no one would be the wiser.

Grey watched Abbadon's every move. *Why is he so nervous, even distraught,* she wondered. *Is it* The Beginning? *It can't be, can it? This is nothing compared to what he's planned for the future.*

Grey looked up to find Abbadon staring at her. No, not staring, more like glaring. Seeing deep into her, reading every thought, as if Grey was nothing more than a children's book. He turned away and continued to pace. *Something is very wrong,* Grey thought.

She silently rose from the high-back chair, her throne as Borack called it, and walked to the bathroom.

Inside she splashed cold water on her face and looked into the mirror. Grey never considered herself beautiful, although she certainly was. She hated mirrors and the reflection of who was looking back. Grey felt dirty and empty. For her there was no purpose, no plan, no reason for living. Borack had his *Beginning,* followed by five years of chaos. His purpose, his plan was total evil. An entire life dedicated to wickedness.

And now Grey for the first time accepted her role as queen to darkness. Abbadon had *The Beginning;* Grey began to pray for the end.

A single tear rolled down her ivory cheek, falling to the tile floor without sound. Yet the tear came back like the roar of a tidal wave to her. Emotions began to rise from a deep place within. Feelings suppressed for year after year. She had been dead for so long.

Grey whispered, "God, dear God, help me. Oh, God, stop this evil. I beg you, stop this wicked man."

She dropped slowly to her knees, not by her own accord it seemed, but as if guided by a power she could not see, yet felt deep within. It felt good; it felt clean.

She began to cry without any sound, and she prayed. "Oh, God, I know you exist. This great evil must have an opposite. This hate must have love on the other side. Save me, God, and forgive me."

An inner peace slowly enveloped her. The air in the room tasted sweet, the light soft and warm. In a tiny voice, one like a child's, Grey whispered, "Jesus loves me, this I know…"

Annie, too, paced the floor like a nervous cat inside Rusty's tiny bedroom above the tavern. Guarded now by six undercover cops, she swallowed anxiety like a camel drinking water, waiting for Rusty or Mack to call, hoping with all hope they would catch the murderer of her father and Josh, praying that both men would survive the night.

Macklin poured yet another cup of black coffee into the Styrofoam cup from his ancient thermos. Parked at the far east edge of the parking lot to the Pussy Cat Club, he could see the front door to the Hikes Point. Rusty provided the brown two-door Honda from the narc's fleet. "Just the kind of ride some fat pervert would drive to the Pussycat Club with a pocket full of dollar bills," Macklin mused.

Macklin keyed his two-way. "Anything?"

"Nope," Rusty responded back. "All quiet on the western front, buddy, but I'm freezing my butt off."

Rusty dressed for the occasion but was still very cold as he hid alongside the dumpster behind the Hikes Point, starting to resemble an alleyway snowman for wino's.

"Mack, call Annie. Tell her all is cool. Make sure she's okay."

"Done."

> **THOU SHALT HAVE NO OTHER GODS BEFORE ME**

Jimmy Ryan was the first invitee to arrive at the Hikes Point Lounge. It was 9:05 p.m.

"Good evening. May I see your invitation, please?" Mosha sounded as though he might have worked with Lon Cheney in a black and white horror picture.

"Yeah, sure! Man, this is great stuff! Look at the place! Wow! Think I got a chance at winning the million?" Jimmy pulled the invitation from his overcoat pocket, handing it to the grizzly.

Mosha shrugged his shoulders, smiling down at the little guy. "Who knows? Do you feel lucky?"

"That's my middle name!"

"Here." Mosha gave the man a small glossy white card with a raised red number. "Don't lose it, Mr. Lucky."

Jimmy Ryan took the card with the red number one, smiled up at the Frankenstein look-alike, and headed to the bar.

"Top of the evening, mate!" Sean did have a killer smile. "What'll it be?"

"Scotch. Tall glass, lots of ice, water. Make it Chevis."

"A man who knows his whiskey! So I guess you be one of the lucky ones, I'd say?" Sean inquired.

"Let's hope so," Jimmy replied, a bit sullen. "God knows I could use the money."

"My name is Sean, Sean MacIntosh! A pure Irishman from the top of my head to my dancing feet."

"Jimmy Ryan, nice to meet you, Sean. Cool place. You own it?"

"Nah, just the manager, but it is indeed a fine place to earn a living."

"You know, I was really surprised to get the invitation. I mean, like, out of nowhere. This special delivery inviting me! I still don't understand it!"

"Nothin' to understand, mate. Mr. B.A., the owner of this establishment and hundreds more just like it around the world, is just a swell fella!"

"Really?"

"Yeah, like I say, this bloke has more money than God and likes to help people out. He looks for poor souls, you know, the kind in a pinch, and gives them a new start, a new beginning, so to speak. Found me when I was a small tike, homeless and nearly dead. Raised me like I was one of the family. Gave me a good education and put me here as the manager. I'm making two large a week and all the scotch whiskey a mate could dream for!"

"Wow, sounds like one hell of a guy!"

Sean laughed. "You got that right, mate!"

"What do you think the odds are, Sean? You know, of winning anything tonight?"

The smiling Irishman turned serious and leaned close to Jimmy Ryan. "I got it solid, mate, that someone tonight is going to be really surprised, maybe more than just one of ya!"

"Really?"

"Send my soul to hell if I'm lying!" Sean refilled Jimmy's drink. "Now tell me about yourself, lad. I'd like to know all I can about a future millionaire."

"Well, Sean, not much to tell really, pretty boring life."

"Aw, now come on, Jimmy Boy, we all been to the crossroad sometime or another."

"Crossroad? Yeah, I guess that's a good way to put it, Sean. I've been to the crossroad."

Sean poured the third drink. "So then, mate, you've been to the crossroad, you say?"

"You see, my dad was a painter. You know, houses, small stuff like that, a hard worker. My mom was a teacher's aide at the Catholic parish elementary. Both good Catholics, always going to Mass, cramming religion down our throats."

"Yeah, I get it, Jimmy. In the pope we hope!"

"Exactly! I have two older brothers, much older. I was

the baby of the family. Both my brothers were real good in sports and went to college on scholarship. I on the other hand made straight A's and got beat up a lot."

"In Catholic school?"

"Yep, good, old Catholic school. If the other boys weren't picking on me, the nuns were!"

"Aw geez, mate, I know what you mean. Ain't much fond of the old penguins myself!"

"So anyway, being an altar boy made Mom and Dad happy, and I didn't see much future in being a painter like the old man, so I became a priest."

"You did, did you? Well Hail Mary, let's take communion!"

Jimmy laughed. "So after ten years moving from parish to parish, I settled down in a small church as Father Ryan. I was only thirty-two."

"Another scotch, Father?"

"Yeah right, Sean. Ex-Father Ryan."

"What happened?" Sean appeared to really care.

"Well, I met a man you see. We met one evening at the neighborhood pub where most of my flock indulged. He was a strange man, very deep in his thought and words. I felt something strong and wonderful in his presence."

"What was his name, Jimmy?"

"That's the weird part, Sean. I spent a great deal of time with this man, many nights at the pub, suppers together, long walks, always talking about God and the true meaning of life. I can tell you exactly what he looked like—tall, very strong, handsome, with deep dark eyes and always impeccably dressed."

"He wasn't a queer now was he, Jimmy Boy?"

"No, absolutely not. He was a man's man. You could feel his power, sense his wisdom. But I'll be damned, I can't remember his name!"

"So what did you and this strange man talk about?"

"Many things, Sean. Important stuff, like is there really a God? And if there is, why is there so much suffering?"

"The man had a good point, mate."

"Exactly, Sean. I began to see things anew. My whole life had been a giant hoax! I guess it was then, you know, when I came to the crossroad."

"The crossroad. Yes, Jimmy, I understand, the crossroad."

"Yes, he asked me once to list all that God had done for me and to match that to all I'd done for myself. He explained that I was God, he was God, every man was his own god, and that is how we should live our life, serving the only true god, ourselves."

"I like the message, Jimmy! Look around; see God anywhere? You think God's going to give you a million bucks tonight?"

Jimmy Ryan became stoic, reflective, as if trying to go back, back to the crossroads. "No, Sean, I guess not. Tonight a man, a stranger, might give me a million dollars, and I plan to worship me with it. Me, Jimmy Ryan, ex-priest and new god of the Hikes Point Lounge!"

"That's the spirit, Jimmy Boy! Take care of yourself first, mate, and the rest can go to hell!"

> **THOU SHALT NOT MAKE UNTO THEE ANY GRAVEN IMAGES**

Tommy Johns was the second invitee to enter the Hikes Point.

"Good evening. May I see your invitation?"

"Holy Moses! You're big as a mountain! I could use a guy like you to carry cripples for me. Here's my card. Tommy Johns is the name, healing the lame is my game!"

Mosha looked at the man as if he were watching his favorite TV program, "The Flintstones." The big man fought the urge to reply, "Yabba dabba doo!"

"Your number, Mr. Johns; do not lose it."

The Reverend Johns looked down at the big red number two, and Mosha threw the good preacher's card into the trash.

Two steps into the bar, Mr. Johns gave a quick yet careful look-see around the place. He could sense the excitement, feel an unseen presence, taste the show about to begin. The electricity was palpable, so similar to what he felt before each healing revival where thousands waited to see his healing power. *Screw the miracles,* he thought. *Tonight I'm here to raise a million George Washington's to life. Now that's a miracle!*

The good reverend stood tall, which was harder than you think at five feet six inches. Hands on his hips, head high and mighty, legs apart, Moses ready to lead the Israelites to the promised land.

The miracle worker dressed in solid white, head to toe, not necessarily cool in the dead of winter, but no matter, white was his trademark. It spoke to simplicity, to cleanliness, to holiness, to the color of angels, to his being the light in a dark world.

He shot his arms in the air, flashing two gold pinkie rings with fake rubies and a large Rolex that ticked with each second. "My brothers, stand aside and watch Almighty God at work. Look and wonder! Stand in awe as the number two transforms into one million!"

Sean looked at Jimmy Ryan. "Hail Mary, Father, if it ain't an angel of the Lord!"

Jimmy laughed. "Now you know why I was Catholic."

The holiness healer approached the bar.

"Top of the evening, Rev. What'll it be?"

"Well, my fine young deliverer of inebriation, I rarely

indulge, communion aside, but tonight I wish to celebrate. God has once again chosen to bless this humble southern preacher. Rum and Coke if you please! Make it a double!"

"Coming right up, Pastor!" Sean filled the tall glass with Rum and a splash of Coke.

The Reverend drained the twelve-ounce glass in one quick gulp. "Now that's how you fix a real man's drink! Hit me again, boy, and get the bar a round!" He pulled a wad of bills from his pocket big enough to choke a horse, secured by a gold money clip with the sign of the cross engraved in its surface.

"No need to pay, mate. Your money is no good here; everything is on the house."

"Like Sunday dinner at the widow's home!" His smile now displayed a gold tooth right of center.

The man in white turned to Jimmy Ryan. If he'd worn a mask, Jimmy might have asked where Tonto was. "Allow me to properly introduce myself. My name is Tommy Johns, the Reverend Johns of Worldwide Ministries. You might have heard or seen one of the thousands of my TV healing services."

"Can't say that I have, Preacher." The ex-priest felt a sudden need to vomit. "Excuse me, gentlemen. Mother Nature is calling."

Jimmy returned after several minutes of dry heaving. "How 'bout a draft, Sean. I think I'll play the pinballs."

Sean handed him a frosty mug. "By the way, the machines pay cash … Father."

"Father?" Tommy Johns asked quizzically.

"Yeah, ex-priest, Catholic, pope we hope, you know, mate."

"Father, ha!" Pastor Johns' face became cruel and condescending. "No man is to be called father except the Almighty!" A long pause. "But then again, I have been given many children. I have a flock of little ones around the world!"

Sean was really starting to enjoy this. "You know, Reverend—"

Johns cut him off. "Now, now, son, not so formal. Call me Tommy; all my friends do! Freshen her up, sonny. Make it a double."

"You know, Tommy, I've seen your show, I mean your healing service, a couple of times. I think on that Christian channel."

Reverend Johns perked up. "Really? Was I good, uh, I mean, did you see God at work?"

"Yeah, for real! Awesome, Tommy! But I don't recall seeing it on the tube for the past couple of years. What's up?" Sean expressed concern.

The good rev sucked on his fourth drink.

"Well, my boy, it was the devil!"

"Nah, the devil? Are you serious?"

"Absolutely!" The pastor's voice rose two octaves.

"You see, Sean, Sean's the name, right?"

"Right as rain, mate. Sean MacIntosh, a Christian boy saved, sanctified, and baptized in the Holy Ghost!"

"Good, boy, good. So anyway, I grew up on a small farm just outside Jonesboro, Arkansas. My mommy and daddy were hardworking country folk. Read the Bible nearly every night. Why, by the time I turned thirteen, I could nearly quote the entire Bible! Momma called it *the gift*."

"Good churchgoing people, I'd bet." Sean leaned in closer.

"The best, boy! God-fearing people! My daddy was a deacon, and Mamma taught Sunday school. They were pillars of the New Bethel Missionary Baptist church. Hardworking, Bible-believing people of faith."

"Yeah, just plain ole God-fearing parents. You were lucky, Tommy. Lucky to be raised by Christians, I mean."

"Yes, I've always been lucky, especially with my gift, and earned a good living serving the Lord."

"That's the truth, mate, if ever I heard it. Why, you pretty well became famous preaching and healing. That's a fact!"

"Too famous, I suppose. Brought my good works to the devil's attention."

"The devil, really?" Sean could get a man to tell his darkest secrets and want to.

"That's right, boy, Satan himself! You know what his second name is, Sean, the devil?"

"Well, I've heard several—"

"I tell you, boy!" Spittle sprayed from his twisted mouth like it did during a hot August tent meeting. "The old wily devil does indeed have an earthly given name. He's called the IRS! That's right boy, the Internal Revenue Service! Fix me a drink."

"Wow, amazing story, Tommy, but what happened in between? You know, between thirteen memorizing the Bible and now. Was there like a crossroad?"

Tommy Johns laughed in disgust. "Crossroad? Good way to put it, Sean, crossroad. I guess you can say it was exactly that, one wide and dark crossroad."

"What happened?"

"Well, Sean, when I was about fifteen, Daddy and I

were baling hay on the back ten acres. Something went wrong with the baler, still ain't sure what, and Pop was trying to fix it I guess I might have hit something, but I still think my daddy did it, and the machine kicked on. Within seconds, before I could figure out what happened, the baler nearly ate his arm off clean up to his shoulder."

"That's horrible, Tommy, but it was an accident!"

"Yeah right. I thought so, Mamma thought so, but not my dad. From that point on, he wouldn't even look at me. Then he started to drink, all day, every day. Ain't much else to do if you're a one-armed farmer, I guess."

Jimmy shouted from the pinball machines, "Hey, Sean, I'm up a thousand points. Pour me another cold one, please."

"Coming right up, Mr. Lucky!" Sean delivered the cold mug of draft and returned to the bar. "Go on, Tommy. What happened next? The crossroad."

"So, feeling hopeless, I went to praying. I prayed hours every day. When it was sunny, in the cornfield, or down by the creek. When it rained, I'd be on my knees in the barn. Praying day after day. Then one day I felt the power, the power of healing! I ran so fast into that old house and grabbed hold of my mamma, screaming, 'God gave me a new gift, Mamma! I can heal!'"

"Glory," Sean replied mockingly. Reverend Johns was too drunk now to know any better.

"Mamma was crying and praising the Lord up a storm. We ran into the living room to lay hands on Pop, to heal him."

"Did you? Heal your dad?"

"Not a chance. He told me to get the hell away from

him and hit me with a whiskey bottle. The healing feeling left as quickly as it had come."

"Was that your crossroad, Tommy?"

"Nah, that happened the next spring. You see, this evangelist came to town with his big white tent, called it the Holy Ghost Traveling Show. Well, they were saving souls, healing people right and left, speaking in tongues."

"Speaking in tongues? What's that, mate?"

"Oh, I'm not really sure. Supposed to be about getting filled with the Holy Ghost and speaking in an unknown language."

"Did you speak in tongues?"

"I tried! Honest to God, I tried. But all I could do was imitate the boys with the traveling show. I still can remember one phrase they'd shout over and over: "Luc a od, luc a od, luc a od. Pretty stupid, huh?"

"Not really," Sean said on a serious note. "So this preacher, the traveling show, that was your crossroad?"

"Could have been, I guess. But for sure it put me in the fork in the road."

"Hit me again, Sean." The rev was starting to slur his words. "So Mamma up and falls in love with the evangelist, just like that!"

"What was his name?"

"You know, Sean, that is the really strange part!"

"How so?"

"Well, I spent two years off and on with the man. He taught me how to preach, to heal people, to speak in the unknown tongue. But mostly he taught me how to make money. Lots of it! All that, and I just can't for the life of me remember his name!"

Tommy Johns took off his coat and continued. "Then one day after he returned from one of his many revival trips, he sat me down for what he called my most important lesson."

"Did he still live with your ma?"

"No, oh no. He dumped her right after we moved to Texas. Me and Mom lived in a shack way down the hill from his big mansion. My mother was broken. She aged ten years in our first ten months. I didn't really care, though. I knew my mother was a whore, but I loved the preacher! I guess you could say he became my god. But why can't I remember his name? Hey, Sean, I think I'll call him Mr. Crossroad!"

"I like it! Got a nice ring to it, mate. Mr. Crossroad."

Reverend Johns finished his drink and slid the glass forward for a refill. "So anyhow, the man, Mr. Crossroads, sits me down like a father would a son. It was then I got the last lesson."

Sean was now clearly interested in the Mr. Crossroads lesson. "Go on, Tommy!"

"He said, he being Father Crossroad,"—a childish giggle—"'Son, you've been taught to worship a God of pain and suffering. All for him, nothing for you. Remember the Second Commandment, boy?' Of course I did: 'Thou shalt not make unto thee any graven images,' but I don't know if I understood it."

"What did he mean?" Sean was so into the story now.

"It was the graven image part I think. Here's what you should worship, Crossroads told me, and pulled a fancy leather wallet from his coat pocket and opened it, flashing a lot of money. 'Here's your graven image, son, here are the people you should worship: Washington, Jefferson, Franklin, especially Franklin! Burn those images into your brain, live for them, worship them, and all the pleasures of the world will be yours!'"

"I like it!" Sean stated with enthusiasm. "You can put these graven images in the bank!"

"Exactly, and so I did. When he left, Mr. Crossroads that is, I never saw him again, although it always feels like he's close. I got his tent, truck, and all the assets of the Holy Ghost Traveling Show!"

"So that's how you got in the preaching business?"

"You guessed it. And preach I did all across America in every cow town you could imagine. But then I remembered the healing part, and that was where the real money was made! Plant a few cripples in the crowd, smack them in the head, watch them flop around a bit and then run out screaming, 'I've been healed!'"

"Big money in that, is there?"

"Oh yeah! Sean, we went from simple offering plates to five gallon buckets overnight. Suckers ready to give you their last dime for a moment of glory, and I could bring 'em glory!"

"So I guess you're a rich man, mate, a millionaire?"

"Was until the devil showed up in a dark gray suit!"

"IRS?"

"Yep. Took the cars, the houses, the racehorses, the furniture, everything but the clothes on my back. Back taxes! Why, I was doing the Lord's work! Tax free, you know."

> **THOU SHALT NOT TAKE THE NAME OF THY LORD GOD IN VAIN**

Katie Zanderfield entered the Hikes Point Lounge shortly after the good Reverend Tommy Johns.

She was a striking woman indeed. Long thick black hair covered her shoulders, flowing down over the raincoat draped loosely around her. Deep pacific blue eyes flashed angrily, screaming, "Beware—attack dog."

"That's fine, just leave me here at the table." Her voice was flat and hollow.

Mosha pushed her wheelchair in place at the first table

to the right, some ten feet from his post at the front door. He said nothing.

Katie quickly surveyed the territory her eyes glistening like a panther ready to pounce.

Jimmy Ryan continued to pound and shake the pinball machine. "Two thousand," he shouted, whatever that was supposed to mean. And the Reverend Tommy Johns rested his head on folded arms at the far table next to the men's room. Almost unconscious, he whispered, "Luc a od, luc a od, luc a od."

Sean approached the young woman, displaying his warmest smile. "Top of the evening, my young, fair lass! My name is Sean, Sean MacIntosh."

"Are you really Irish or just attempting to impress me with your lucky charms? Well, don't bother! I can spot a phony a mile away. Most likely you're some country hick who has a CD of greatest Irish hits!"

Sean took two steps back. "Just a sec there, missy; didn't mean to offend or anything. But to answer your inquiry, I'm as Irish as they come. Born proudly in a bed of clover, all with four glorious leaves, you know? And I don't have any Irish CDs; don't really like their music much."

"Well, excuse me, Mr. MacIntosh. I guess I should be oh-so-thankful to be served by a leprechaun. I'll bet my wheelchair you have a shamrock tattooed on your lily-white butt!"

"Now how in the green earth did you guess that, lassie?" An even bigger smile. "Care for some bubbly, darling? Dom? In a silver slipper?"

"Cut the crap, elf boy." Her persona changed from wicked stepmother to Cinderella in a flash. "Yes, Sean, champagne, lightly chilled, would be nice. Thank you so very much. Now run along, boy."

Sean turned, grinning broadly. "This one is going to be fun to watch!"

Katie glanced over her right shoulder to see Mosha sadly looking at her. "Take a picture, you big freak! What's the matter? You never seen a cripple before?"

Mosha slowly turned his head toward the door, not really understanding all of what she'd said.

Sean returned to her table with an ice bucket, a cold bottle of Dom, and a crystal champagne flute. "Can I get the princess anything else?" His smile was awesome, she had to admit.

"Yes, Sean, you may."

"I am at my lady's beck and call."

"Well then, Sean MacIntosh, see if you can pull a million dollars for me out of your tattooed tushie!"

"You'll have to wait until midnight, my princess, but for you, hold on to this." Sean actually pulled a small golden four-leaf clover from his pocket and placed it in her hand, closing her slender soft fingers around the lucky charm. "Luck of the Irish, princess!"

Katie was forced to smile.

Sean pulled another cold draft for the hot pinball player then walked over to the good preacher. He shook the man gently. "You Bible thumpers just can't hold your liquor, can ya?"

"Good evening, may I see your invitation please?" Mosha handed the older gentleman his card, number four. Taking off his gray wool coat and felt hat, the new arrival headed straight to the bar.

"Whiskey please. Jack Daniels."

Jimmy Ryan had stopped playing pinball. He was now watching the beautiful woman with the gleaming hair. She reminded him of the only girl he'd ever loved. The one who did not know he did. After all, a twenty-eight-year-old priest could never love a seventeen-year-old virgin. But he did, before the crossroad.

He moved without knowing why, moving silently to the defiant sullen woman with head high, sipping champagne. "Can I join you, miss?"

"Are you serious?" There was a nasty *get away* tone to her voice. "What do you think? An easy target? A pick up? Let's go hit on the cripple?"

"No ma'am. Nothing like that. I was just lonely, nervous I guess, waiting for the midnight drawing."

"Ain't we all," she snapped.

"I'm really quite harmless, miss. I mean, I'm a priest, or at least I was."

"Oh God, please save me," Katie moaned. "Well, sit down; you make me nervous standing there like a dog begging for a bone."

"Thank you. My name is Jimmy Ryan."

"Okay, Jimmy boy, I'm Katie Zanderfield, cripple extraordinaire."

"Zanderfield?" There was tension in Jimmy's voice. "The girl in the terrible tragic accident a year ago? I followed that story."

"Well, aren't we lucky!" Katie snapped.

"I'm so sorry, I mean, well, there aren't really words, Katie, but I remember praying for you."

"Oh, that's really rich! Praying for me? Get your prayers

answered, Father Jimmy? Guess not! Guess you weren't much of a priest, huh?"

"Guess not."

"Well, don't feel so bad, Jimmy boy. God stopped listening to me too. As a matter-of-fact, my ex-man of the cloth, I don't really believe there is a God to hear our stupid prayers! And if there is, damn him, damn him, damn him for what he didn't do!" Venom was now rising in her throat, so strong a sensation the woman could taste the poison. "Now leave me alone before I really tell you about the God you serve, Father Ryan."

Jimmy rose quietly. "I am truly sorry, Ms. Zanderfield."

"Yeah right, sorry, you and God. Well, you can both go to hell!"

Jimmy went back to playing pinball, wishing he wasn't there, million dollars or not. Katie lit a long brown thin cigarette and drew the smoke in hard. Sean picked up the sweet aroma of very good weed.

Several minutes later the smoke rolled into her lungs, into her bloodstream, and stopped in her brain, bringing relief to her soul and the constant pain caused by the spinal injury that had left her paralyzed from the waist down.

She closed her eyes, letting the weed take her back, back to the moment when all she knew and loved came to an end.

Just a nice Sunday drive in the country. Autumn leaves and a warm Indian summer day. A family picnic. She recalled her mother singing hymns in the backseat, holding hands with Katie's father. "Look, honey, look, see what a glorious day God has given us!"

Katie tried to forget, but her thoughts would not give

way. Mommy and Daddy, good Methodist Christians. Both worked at the post office and did their best for their only child, Katherine. And Peter, handsome Peter, childhood sweethearts, engaged just that night at her parents' humble home. All riding along in Peter's Jeep Cherokee. Riding along in the country, celebrating in fall's masterpiece of color. Just riding along listening to mother's sweet voice singing "Down by the River." Riding along, going on a picnic, one big happy family.

Katie's eyes were closed as she relived the moment. Peter was driving and looked over at her so lovingly. He didn't see the truck, but she had, racing through the intersection at ninety miles per hour. The red truck exploded, guided blindly by a drunk driver. No more picnic!

A country road far out into the Indiana farmland. Only the occasional farmhouse sitting peacefully off the road surrounded by yellow-topped corn or green fields of soybeans as far as you could see. No one saw the accident; no one heard the explosion. No one heard Katie's mother or her love, Peter, scream out as the flames devoured them. But Katie heard them, and she still could.

The young girl had been thrown from the Jeep some fifty feet, broken, battered, and bloody. She felt the heat, she could smell their bodies burning, she had heard her mother scream, "Dear God, help us!" Then the lights went out.

She didn't know how long she lay in the corn, maybe minutes, maybe hours, but when she awoke, a tall man stood over her. The sun directly over his shoulders left him shrouded in shadows. His voice was low and sweet. It sounded like beautiful music. Was she dead? Was this God?

"'Dear God, help us.' Was that not your mother's last

dying wish? God help us from what? From dying? Where is your mother's God, Katie?"

"Who are you," Katie moaned. "Where am I?"

"I am here to save you, child. I am your only hope. You are at the crossroad."

"Mommy, Daddy, Peter!" All pleas went unanswered.

"Mommy? Daddy? Peter? They're all dead, Katie, gone. Tortured in a fiery grave. Left to die a horrible death. Left here, Katie, at the crossroad."

"Oh God," she cried out.

"God? You're calling for God now? Like your mother? God, please save us? Where was God when your mother screamed in agony? Where was he, Katie?"

"I don't—"

"Yes," he whispered. "Yes, my precious child. You don't know because he left you here to die. Now damn him, Katie! Say it! Say it, child. Damn your God!"

"Damn you, damn you, damn you!" she screamed, and blackness returned.

No one saw the stranger come or go and really didn't believe a word of Katie's bizarre encounter with the mystery man. There was no place called Crossroads around there, not even a road. But then again, no one could explain the long white satin coat that covered her at the scene.

Katie opened her eyes, refocused, and raised her glass to Sean. "Hey, Irish, the princess is dry! Chop chop!"

A million dollars, she thought. *The new surgery in Germany. It won't be God who helps me. No, not God. It will be the luck of the Irish maybe.*

REMEMBER THE SABBATH DAY TO KEEP IT HOLY

Mosha advised the old man that he was early by fifteen minutes. "Sir, your invitation said 9:50 p.m., not 9:35, correct?"

Leon Schwartz looked up to the huge man in a tuxedo as if surprised. "Early? Am I early? I'm sorry, force of habit you see, never been late to anything in my life. Early bird gets the worm. Never late, never sorry. Save a minute, make a dollar!"

Mosha motioned the man forward toward the bar. He murmured, "Filthy Jew."

Leon now sat nervously at the bar, sipping a Jack Daniels whiskey. "So, Sean, you own this place?"

"Not even close, mate. But I am the manager; best job I ever had."

"I like this place." The old man slowly turned around, surveying the establishment with an eagle eye. "I might buy it! Would you stay on if I did? Manage the place for me? I'd need a good man I could trust."

Sean looked the man over carefully. Maybe late sixties, short, nearly bald, and overweight. His clothes were old yet expensive. Sean reckoned Mr. Leon Schwartz had a little money, a long time ago.

"You ever own a pub, Mr. Schwartz?"

"Oh heavens no, son! Didn't start drinking until I was almost sixty, except maybe a glass of wine here and there, mostly to celebrate Hanukkah way back in the day. But I'm a real shrewd businessman. A lot of people surely know that!"

"A shrewd businessman? Tough to compete with that, sir!"

"Yes, well, I am Jewish by birth and did attend synagogue before I switched my faith, became born again."

"Born again? You know, Mr. Schwartz, I'm an Irish Jew myself! Not many of my kind running about."

The old man laughed heartily. "I should say not, young man. Can't say I ever met an Irish Jew before!"

Sean went back to his question. "So you were—what'd you call it—born again?"

"Yes, that's the Christian terminology, born again, you know, accepting Christ as Savior."

"Big move, Mr. Schwartz, for a Jew I mean."

"I'll say it was a very big move." Leon turned sad.

"So why go from Jew to Christian, Mr. Schwartz?"

"Well, son, I had some help then, a lot of help you might say."

"Who?"

"The most beautiful girl in all the world, that's who."

"Gets you every time, mate!"

"You have no idea, son. No idea." Leon Schwartz seemed to travel back over mountains of desire and happiness and through valleys of loss and respect. Sean just watched and waited.

"I think I'd like another whiskey, Sean." The bartender filled his glass with Jack.

"So, there was this beautiful girl?"

"Yes, Sean, very beautiful. You see, I'd worked hard all my life, sixteen hours a day, except Saturday, you know, the Sabbath."

"Yeah, right, the Sabbath."

"I'd started my business back then, Leon's Deli, had four locations in New Jersey! All were doing well. Then I took the big leap, went to New York. This time I got fancy, called the new place Leon's New York Deli!"

"Got a nice ring to it, Leon."

"Yes, well, it was hard back then, finding good help you know, minimum wage, no benefits. But, Sean, I always let my girls keep 50 percent of the tips!"

"Well, that was good of ya, mate." Sean thought, *Penny pinching Jew.*

"Yes, I guess so. Anyway, I needed help, so I ran an ad in *The Times*—expensive! Help wanted, ten-hour shift. Good hourly wage, tips, and 20 percent off personal food. Keep 'em from stealing, you know?"

"Of course."

"So one day in walks this real beauty, fresh off the Greyhound bus. Patsy Pierce, a West Virginia beauty queen and devout Nazarene. A gift from God I used to say."

"So this is the girl who got you born again?"

"The one and only. Why, she worked six days a week and four hours each day off the clock just for tips! I liked that. I've always admired hard work. Well, even though I was thirty years older than Patsy, we fell in love. I started staying in New York more and more, much to the dismay of my wife and sons in Jersey. But I was building something. It was all for them!"

"And you fell for the beautiful country girl, the Nazarene?"

"It was as if God himself had sent her." Leon wiped a tear from his fat face. "Whiskey please."

A long pause. "Then, after six months, I asked Patsy to marry me. Funny, she didn't act surprised as I recall."

"So why would she, mate? You're a handsome gent, hardworking, a businessman! I'd bet my lucky charms the girl looked up to you, respected you, needed you!" Now the Irishman sounded like a rabbi.

"Yes she did. I'm sure she did." Again, quiet reflection. "But she said we'd talk about it if I did two things. Divorce my wife of twenty-five years immediately and become born again."

"And?"

"I did both. But it was hard, Sean, really hard. My wife took all my deli operations in New Jersey, and my boys disowned me. I haven't seen or talked to them in eighteen years."

"Did you marry the girl, Patsy?"

"Not for a year. First I had to be born again. So I went to church every Sunday morning, Sunday evening, Wednesday prayer meeting, and I read the Bible, the New Testament part, faithfully every night, sometimes with Patsy after we closed the deli. Then one Sunday it hit me, so I ran to the altar. I was born again. Sean, I guess I cried for a solid week. I felt like a new man!"

"Some might say it was your crossroad, mate."

"Crossroad? Maybe, or maybe my crossroad came a little farther down the road."

"How so?"

"Well, Patsy insisted that we live to the letter of the Nazarene law. Things like she wouldn't cut her hair, always wore long sleeves and floor-length skirts at work, and God forbid you even walk the dog on Sunday!"

"Sunday?" Sean acted stupid.

"Yes, son, Sunday! The Sabbath! Remember it and keep it holy!"

"Right."

"Well, Leon's New York Deli was dead in the middle of a large Jewish community, and they love their deli come Sunday. Plus, some of my best Hebrew customers found out I was born again. No Jews on Saturday, their choice; no Jews on Sunday, my choice. Anyhow, my business started to suffer, and I was nearly broke."

"Terrible, Leon, just terrible!" Sean poured the old Jewish born again a fresh whiskey.

"But then it happened. Patsy believed it might even be a miracle. Maybe it was."

Sean leaned in close. "A miracle, the crossroad?"

"Yes, I guess you're right, Sean! It was my crossroad!"

"Wow! Go on, Leon. Go on!"

"Well, at church, Broadway Nazarene, Patsy attended the young adult's Sunday-school class and I was with the seniors—age difference thing and I didn't really care. So one day Patsy tells me about this new man in her class, an accountant. She felt sure he could help us save the business!"

"Did he? Did he save your business?"

"You bet he did! The man was brilliant! Very handsome and extremely smart, you know. He was a planner. He said, 'Leon, let's start over. Let's call it *The Beginning*.'"

"Yes, so we joined forces. The plan Mr. ... uh, holy Moses, I can't remember his name! Anyway, the accountant said we were going to open Leon's New York Delis in every mall across America. First year, seven new openings. Second year, twenty! In five years there were sixty-six Leon's in thirty states!"

"You still own all that?"

"No, Sean, not anymore. Just after the fourth year, the accountant, whatever his name is, and Patsy came to me with a plan to open on Sundays. At first I argued. What about Sunday, the Sabbath? We're supposed to keep it holy! Pasty said, 'Screw that, Leon! It's the biggest shopping day of the week. Are you stupid?' It was two against one, and everything was in Patsy's name."

"What? You put everything, sixty-six delis, in her name?"

"Yes, on the advice of the accountant. We were trying to save money on alimony."

"Did you?"

"I guess I did. When you got nothing, you pay nothing."

"So what happened to the business?"

"Ha! You want to talk crossroads? I came to my office one morning—it was raining like the day after Noah boarded the ark as I remember—and there's this man, an attorney, waiting to see me. 'Mr. Schwartz,' he says as he hands me two thick envelopes and tells me I'm being served."

"Served?"

"Yes, an order of eviction from my office building, which I also owned, or thought I did, and divorce papers."

"Holy moly!" Sean wished he could laugh out loud, although he was having a pretty good time inside. "Could they do that?"

"I guess so; they did! Remember, son, it was all in Patsy's name. Patsy, the innocent little Nazarene from West Virginia. Remember the Sabbath and keep it holy. She's found her crossroads too, I imagine!"

HONOR THY FATHER AND THY MOTHER

Candy attacked rather than chewed the enormous wad of pink bubble gum inside her red-lipped small mouth, waiting for the junk heap car to stop spitting and sputtering. The young girl hit the dashboard with her fist. "Stop! Damn you, you piece of crap!" One last shake and the motor died. "Cool!"

Candy Sweet, her legitimate legal name, changed two years ago, with proof tattooed on obvious selected parts of her body, stepped from the black Firebird, gold eagle flaking across the hood. "Cool place, man! Private party, a million buckaroos calling, 'Candy, Candy Sweet, come to daddy, darling.'" She giggled like she always did when nervous, excited, happy, or afraid. Tonight Candy Sweet was all of the above.

The go-go queen walked in the door as if she owned the place. "Hey, sweetie pie, been waiting long for baby-Candy?"

She ran her long Walgreen glued-on nails tenderly across Mosha's face. He blushed, although hard to see through his dark skin. "Nice suit, big boy!"

"Thank you." Mosha almost smiled. "Your invitation, please."

"Well, of course, you big hunk of man. Let me see now, I know I brought it!" Fumbling around in her red sequined purse, Candy managed to drop its entire contents on Mosha's greeting podium.

She giggled. "Well, here it is! Are you a football player?"

"No ma'am," Mosha stuttered. "I'm just a personal bodyguard."

"Well, I guess so. Maybe you can guard my body sometime… big boy!"

"Yes ma'am."

Mosha collected her stuff, placing it carefully back into the sparkling bag—red lipstick, eyeliner, Virginia Slims cigarettes, Bic lighter, glass tube filled with white powder, small bottle of painkillers, and five neatly rolled joints.

Candy pulled one of the joints back out, sliding it into Mosha's coat pocket. "Maybe later, bodyguard." She blew the giant a kiss and stepped forward. All eyes now focused on the new show, number five.

"Buckle up, boys and girls,"—her best Marilyn Monroe voice. "Are you ready for a little Candy?"

Leon swung the bar stool south and gave a low whistle. "Would you look at that, Sean! Just take a look at that!"

"Settle down, Pop. Settle down," Sean responded. "You can bet your deli she ain't from West Virginia or ever been born again."

Candy stood confident, if only outwardly, legs apart, hands on hips, head tilted upward. Everything was red with a million sparkling sequins—red fake fur top with puffy shoulders, short, really short, red plastic skirt, six-inch red heels, and a pink angora boa.

She was hot, and she knew it! Everything was red as if the devil had dressed her tonight. Red eyeliner, very red lips, all red except her bleached-out spiked hair.

Ex-Father Jimmy stopped his game, smiling, staring like a high-school kid in a cathouse. Candy looked him up and down, tilted her head, and blew him a seductive, wet kiss.

Candy looked to the left two feet away at Katie Zanderfield. "Say, hey, sister, what be happening?"

Katie snarled and turned ugly. "Now just who do you think you are, Miss Mardi Gras? Get moving; your sparkles hurt my eyes! Go hit on the drunk in the white suit by the men's room; looks like your type."

Candy, somewhat surprised by the greeting and not all that articulate, said, "Well, pardon moi, Ms. Fancy Dancy, didn't mean to offend the queen, so to speak!"

Candy Sweet started to move toward the bar when Katie hit her with a handful of wet ice. "Slut," she hissed.

Candy, now red from neck to hairline, completing her scarlet look, slowly turned back. "Maybe, Ice Princess. Maybe. ButI guess you won't be dancing tonight either!"

The Reverend Johns, awakened by the catfight, looked across the room at the devil doll, smiled, saw a fresh drink before him, took a long pull, and went back to healing dreams.

Candy moved slowly to the bar, hips swinging like a willow tree in a summer breeze.

"Top of the morning, lass. A splash of an entrance, darling, if ever there was! Candy is it?"

"Mmm, I love that voice, fella. You from England or something?"

"Getting close! My name is Sean, Sean MacIntosh, proud Irishman of noble birth!"

"No doubt, Sean the Irishman, whisper my name, all of it." She didn't speak; she purred.

"Candy. Candy Sweet." He did in fact whisper.

"Like a taste?" She stuck her pinkie finger to his lips.

Leon let out an uncontrolled grunt, instantly embarrassed. "I think I'll go shoot some pool." A game most Jewish lads were good at, Sean knew.

"See ya in a bit, mate."

"Hurry back, sailor." Candy was back to Monroe speak.

"What can I pour you, Candy Sweet?"

"I'll have whatever the ice queen is drinking."

"Champagne it is! The drink of royalty!" Sean poured a glass of Dom for her.

"Yuck!" Candy puckered. "What is this crap?"

"Champagne, Dom, the best!"

"Why, of course it is, my Irish sweetheart. Throw some ice in there, will ya?"

"Hey, this stuff ain't half bad, Sean!" Candy started to like it after her third glass. "Kinda tastes like ginger ale. Hey, that's it, fix me a ginger and vodka!"

"Coming right up, your sweetness."

"Say, what's up with the cripple anyhow?"

"Ah, a sad story, sad indeed. The girl lost her dear mother and father just a year ago. Also lost her childhood sweetheart as well!"

"Oh really, like how?"

"Well, you see, they were all out for a nice Sunday drive, and out of nowhere a truck hits 'em. Poor fellow, he nearly bought the farm too! Anyhow, all dead, except Miss Katie. That's her name, Katie Zanderfield. You know, Candy, met her crossroad, changed everything. Left the poor lass crippled. That's why she's hoping to win the grand prize tonight. For surgery in Germany."

"Well, sometimes you just run out of luck. What'd you say, hit the crossroad?"

"Yeah, you walk right up to the crossroad, the moment of truth, Candy. Do I go right or move left? The crossroad. Mostly just happens once in a lifetime. Ever been there?"

"You bet your sweet Irish butt I've been there! Took a hard left, and I'm still rocking and rolling! Strolling down the crossroad of easy come, easy go."

"Tell me about it, Candy girl, your crossroad."

"Ha, the ice queen thinks she had it bad. I know what bad really tastes like."

"How so?"

"Well, when I was twelve, I was even hot back then. All the boys liked me...a lot! And my daddy, 'good old time, go to church Daddy,' was a stinking janitor at my school! Can you imagine the embarrassment! Well, I figured if the old man was going to pick up the trash at school, I'd be the trash!" Her girlish voice was now cold and hard.

203

"Were you poor, Candy?"

"I guess, but I'd sell a little pot here and there, enough to buy hot clothes, makeup, cigarettes, you know, hanging cool."

Sean fixed a fresh drink—tall glass, ice, vodka, and a splash of ginger ale.

"So my old man the janitor up and dies, heart attack or something, and now my mom is working in the school's cafeteria. And of course, to make ends meet, she starts cleaning houses in the neighborhood. God, I wanted to die!"

"Wow, bet that was tough."

"Tough? Are you kidding? I was the laughing stock for my entire junior year!"

She took a long sip of her drink. "Yummy!"

"So one night my old lady and I get into a major fight, big time. She starts spouting off some crap about honoring your parents. 'Read the Bible,' she says."

"And…"

"Well, she grabbed me by the arm, and ain't nobody going to do that, so I hit her and told her to go to hell. Her and Daddy were failures, and I wasn't going to grow up no bum like them!"

"And then?"

"I called my man, Billy. He'd dropped out of school in the tenth, was doing good. Selling a little weed, some snort, a lot of crack. He was rolling in it big time. So Billy and me, we decide to head to Vegas, my dream, you know?"

"Vegas?"

"Yeah, Vegas… duh! I'm a dancer! Professional!"

"I can see that! I swear it fits you!"

"Thanks. So anyway, we get to Vegas and I'm doing

really good. Then wild Bill gets popped, six months in lockup. Now my boy has a record in Sin City, so we decide to cut it back home to Louisville."

"You still with, uh, wild Bill?"

"Duh, don't think so. He's doing five to ten in LaGrange, and this girl ain't got time to wait."

"So you still dance, Candy?"

"Where have you been lately, Ireland? I'm the late show at the Pussy Cat Club, duh!"

"Cool, maybe I can catch your act tonight."

"Maybe, unless of course Miss Candy Sweet wins a million smackers. Then bye-bye Pussy Cat and hello Hollywood. Now that's what you call a crossroad!"

ON THE MOVE

TEN P.M., NEW YEAR'S EVE

Macklin clicked the walkie-talkie. "You frozen yet?"

"Thanks, Mack! I bet you're nice and warm in the Honda, huh?"

"Toasty, like a bug in a rug. Want to switch places?"

"Nah, I'm good now. I had one of my narc buddies make a quick pass through the alley, drop off a thick blanket and a thermos of coffee."

"Nice to have friends."

"Oh yeah. Plus, he brought a bag with a can of Spam, crackers, and a double-decker strawberry Moon Pie!"

"Living large, ain't we?"

"Anything happening out front, Mack?"

"So far five people have gone in, three guys, two girls. One of the chicks is in a wheelchair, and the other looks like she could put you in one! It's strange, though, it's like they're on a timetable, I think—about every ten minutes."

"What do you think is going on, Mack?" Rusty was also confused.

"Not sure, pal, but I'll bet my old FBI badge something big is going to happen, and my gut says around midnight. How about you?"

"Peaceful, just me and several small dog-size rats. I think the evil little creatures are after my Moon Pie. Twas the night before Christmas and all through the dumpster, not a creature was stirring, not even a mouse."

"Hey, maybe the rats ate the mouse."

"You're sick, Mack, really sick."

"Enjoy the Moon Pie. I'll check back shortly. Out."

Rusty unwrapped his strawberry Moon Pie, throwing it as far down the alley as possible, praying the big rats would follow.

Annie watched the two undercovers. "Say, boys, I need a cold beer. How 'bout you?"

"Oh yeah," they sang in unison.

"Okay, I'll run down to the bar; be right back."

"Hey, Annie, Rusty says for you to stay put and—"

She cut the narc off. "Give me a break, Charlie. You've

got two of Louisville's finest downstairs. Don't trust your buddies?"

"Three minutes, Annie."

"You got it. Miller Lite, boys?"

"Make it Bud," Charlie replied.

"Hey, Charlie, Raymond's brother reminds me of our captain, don't he?" Both men laughed, returning to episode twelve, second season of *Everybody Loves Raymond*.

The second two undercovers sat at the bar sipping drafts while watching ESPN classics. Neither saw Annie silently exit the back door.

She walked down the street toward the drycleaners to Ma Bell and called a cab. Ten minutes later she instructed the cabbie, "Hikes Point, please." It was 11:00 p.m.

Grey seemed to have a strange peacefulness, Abbadon thought. "Feeling better, my precious?" he asked in his musical voice, albeit tension filled.

"Like never before," Grey stated sweetly.

"Good."

Borack turned to Turk. "Now listen carefully!"

"Yes sir," the repenting giant replied.

"Be at the back alley door at precisely 11:55. Go in and get Sean out." Borack lowered his voice so Grey could not hear, but she did. "Polly should be inside at the back door. Take him downstairs and tie and gag him. I think it's time for Polly to go home to hell."

THOU SHALT NOT KILL

Perry Yancey could have easily been stereotyped as a typical African American male, ghetto born and raised.

His father, Jackson, had been a complete heroin addict at the tender age of seventeen. Jack, as his friends called him, spent most of his early adult years in and out of prisons as he attempted to feed the devil within that controlled every waking moment of his life.

Two days after his twenty-ninth birthday, Jackson was paroled for the second time. He fully intended to stay away from the devil drug and make something of himself.

Ethington Linen, owned and operated by Ambrose of the same name, supplied over two hundred jobs to the west-end community of African Americans. Mr. Ethington was a true believer in giving a man a second chance and often a third if they tried to make a better life for themselves and their families.

Jackson's younger sister, Lorna, nicknamed Smoky because of her silky brown skin, worked for Ambrose Ethington as stockroom manager. Through her persuasive ability, Mr. Ethington agreed to give Jackson a job upon release from prison.

Jackson Yancey's first day on the job started in the laundry's washroom, where for ten hours you would load and pull your guts out, moving on wet, slick floors, operating a bank of eight six-hundred pound washers.

After three months of hard work and clean living, Jack decided to ask the cute white girl who fed napkins through the high-speed ironer to have a beer after work. She accepted.

Within thirty days, Jack and Tina were living together. Two months later, Tina Brown was pregnant.

Their fast-moving romance deteriorated rapidly from tolerate to hate. Jackson Yancey moved in with his mother, and Tina Brown returned to the trailer park in redneck Fairdale, Kentucky, where her mother and father lived.

When the baby was born, her hillbilly daddy went berserk. Tina failed to mention during her pregnancy that the father of the child was a black man.

Two weeks prior to the baby seeing first light, his father, Jackson Yancey, was shot and killed by the owner of Quick Way Liquors in a botched armed robbery.

Tina, not allowed to move back into the redneck's trailer as long a she "held on to that half breed," as her Old Milwaukee drinking daddy put it, was alone, broke and afraid.

The young mother left the hospital with her two-day-old son in search of the boy's father. Mabel Yancey, Jackson's sixty-five-year-old mother, opened the door to her one-bedroom apartment dead center in the Thirty-Second Street projects.

Mabel stood silently, giving the chunky white girl with the tiny baby a careful look and see. "Can I help you, girl?"

"Yes, uh, well, I'm looking for Jackson. Is he here?"

"Jack? Now what's you want with Jackson?"

Tina was almost ready to bolt, but there really was nowhere to run. End of the line.

"Well, ma'am, this is … are you Jackson's mamma?"

"I might be."

"Well, you see, this is Jackson's baby son."

"Oh Lord, child! Lord, Lord, good Lord, child! Come inside."

Mamma Mabel told the girl that Jackson Yancey was with the Lord now; his sins had found him out.

Tina didn't react to the news of Jack's death. The girl was numb and sleepwalking in this never-ending tragedy.

Tina was very silent for a long while before she found the courage to speak to the large motherly woman with silver and black hair. "I can't keep the baby."

"Why's that, child?"

"I don't have no place to live, 'cept my daddy's, and he said…" Tina struggled for words that were not purebred redneck speak.

"Where's your daddy live, girl?"

"Fairdale."

"Mmm, mmm, mmm." Ma Mabel shook her head slowly in acknowledgment. "So what's your hillbilly redneck daddy tell you? 'Ain't no half-breed baby gonna live in my house'?"

"He lives in a trailer, ma'am."

"Ha! Figures, white trash! Let me see my grandson."

Mabel touched the light brown skin of the baby boy, smiling. "Now don't you worry, little fella. Mamma Mabel take good care of you."

The old woman stood up, baby in arms. "Now you go on, child. Start over if you can. Mamma Mabel take care of this child. But, girl, don't you ever, I mean ever, come back looking for this boy. You hear me?"

Tina did and never returned.

Mabel rocked the big baby, ten pounds, eight ounces at birth, in her arms. "Now what we gonna call you, son? It's got to be a good name."

The old woman held tightly to the newborn child and slowly walked across the room to a very old record player, carefully placing a seventy-eight on the silver spindle. She returned to her large oak rocking chair, settling in with her new responsibility, and quietly sang along to the record "Moon River."

Mabel Yancey was for sure the only human being who listened to Perry Como in the Thirty-Second Street projects. "Well now, you're a handsome little guy. Got that olive skin. Maybe you grow up to be a big singer. I think we'll call you Perry."

The kindly grandmother died of a massive stroke when Perry was yet to reach his sixth birthday.

Passed from relative to relative, he was abused, mistreated, and very unwanted. Perry Yancey was half-white living in a black world.

At the age of fifteen, with an eighth-grade education, the courts placed Perry in a teenage detention center, where he continued to be abused in his half-breed status.

By his twenty-second birthday, Perry Yancey was a confirmed alcoholic, and yes, he worked for Ethington Linen, in the washroom like his daddy.

Perry Yancey was not a bad man; he was just an ordinary drunk. A hard worker and leader of the washroom crew. That is, when he could stay sober. He'd be good for several months, go on a three- or four-day binge, get fired, come back, and be rehired and start the process all over.

Sherry Burns, the daughter of a West Virginia coal miner who married her second cousin, was mildly retarded. After two abortions before the age of sixteen, the mentally handicapped girl was shipped from Huntington, West Virginia to live with her grandparents in Louisville, Kentucky.

Grandpa Wayne worked as head cook for Standard Country Club, and Peg, his wife and third cousin, worked there as well, waitressing.

Standard Country Club was a big customer of Ethington Linen, so good old Grandpa Wayne "pulled a few strings" as he told Sherry, getting her a job at the laundry counting and folding kitchen towels.

The girl really did not understand how she became pregnant previously. With an IQ just below eighty, all she knew was she lived to be touched, kissed, and yes, loved, the things neither her parents nor her grandparents provided.

So it wasn't unreasonable to see why the lonely handicapped girl and the lonely, abused Perry would find their destiny in each other's miserable lives.

The tragic couple set up house, where else but the Thirty-Second Street projects. A mixed-blood man with a retarded white girl did not make a lot of friends in the hood.

They would ride the first bus of the morning at 5:00 a.m. together, twenty-two blocks, then walk three more to Ethington Linen.

Sherry's shift started two hours later than Perry's, so she'd sit quietly in the lunchroom, thinking about little girl things. Perry, finishing his job two hours before Sherry clocked out, never waited for her. Instead, he would immediately walk twelve blocks to the Red Slipper Bar, where he would get drunk and stumble home to have sex with the girl from West Virginal who wanted a Barbie doll for Christmas.

The cycle of hopelessness continued, both living in alcohol and little girl dreams.

Sherry gave birth to a son eighteen months after their love blossomed like a garden of tangled weeds.

The big man and top loan shark in the projects was known by all as Mango, pronounced Mon-go. Perry thought it wise to name his son after the project's king. However, for once in her childish life, Sherry refused the request of a man. The boy would be called Freddy, after her half-brother who probably got her pregnant the first time.

Thus, the baby boy with the big head left the hospital one-third black and two-thirds white, legally addressed as Freddy Mango Yancey.

As the boy grew, you could tell something just wasn't

right. He always had this silly grin on his face and did not seem afraid of anything.

At the age of six, the child's father would be at the Red Slipper if he had money or in the alley drinking wine if he did not. Sherry played with her dollhouse, and the small, skinny, almost-white boy looked for action in the ghetto.

The young child would just simply walk out the door while his mother rearranged doll furniture. Down the street he'd go looking for a hot dice game. Most nights he'd find the action. It was as if the boy could smell it.

Mango, project king, loan shark, and expert gambler who would cut you in a heartbeat, took a real liking to the child.

Mango would tell the brothers, "Hey now, watch this, Freddy. What's ten plus forty-one? Eight plus one hundred and six? Seventeen plus nine?" Bingo, every time the kid got it right.

"This little white boy got a thing for numbers, man! I'm telling you now the little man is a cal-cu-la-tor!"

Freddy would always stand right beside Mango in a dice game. Project King would have him blow the dice before a roll, and the child always knew what to say. "Easy comes a seven! Hard eight, hard eight! Snake eyes, you're popped, man!"

After each dice game, Mango would give his "good luck Freddy" four or five bucks.

One night the King asked the kid what he did with the money he gave him. "Hey, little Mango, what's you done with all that cash I gave you?"

"My dad always borrows it."

"Say what? Does he pay you back, boy, with a little juice?"

"Nah, Mango. But he said he would... someday."

The next night, payday Friday, Mango walked into the Red Slipper. He pulled Perry off the bar stool, ripped off his Dickies work pants pockets, and took exactly $150 from the drunk. He then nearly beat him to death.

When Perry Yancey left General Hospital twelve days later, he borrowed one of his drinking buddy's cars and drove Sherry and Freddy to her grandparents' home. Without saying a word, he threw what little possessions the mother and child owned onto the wet grass and drove away.

Two days later, Perry Yancey was pronounced dead in the small playground area behind the Thirty-Second Street Projects. There was a large kitchen knife implanted in his chest.

"Good evening. May I see your invitation, mister?"

"You can call me Fred, or Mango, or Friendly Fred. That's the name, Friendly Fred Yancey!"

Mosha handed Friendly Fred Mango Yancey his card with the red number.

"Ah baby! Gotta love it, just gotta love it! Number six, come to Daddy! Hard six, come to Papa, hard six for one million! I'm giving odds!"

Freddy did his best 360 and moon walked to the bar. Facing Candy Sweet, he clutched his heart with both hands, exclaiming in his best Jack Nicolson voice, "Here's Johnny!"

Candy giggled. "You're crazy, or you're drunk."

"Oh, darling,"—now sounding like John Wayne—"a little of both, girlfriend. Been riding the range, pushing them little doggies hard. I'm mighty parched."

Candy flipped back. "You're mighty something, I guess, for sure."

"Can a cowpoke buy the lady a cool drink?"

"Only if you have a million dollars."

"Oh, baby, come to Daddy." Quick turn to W.C. Fields, wiggling the fingers on both hands. "In a matter of moments I will be, with the luck of the draw, buying you diamonds and raccoon coats."

"Hey, Irishman,"—Candy giggled again—"this guy is crazy! With a capital K."

"Top of the evening, mate. Sorry, I didn't quite catch your name."

"Friendly Fred's the name, gambling's the game. Soon to be widely known as Millionaire Mango!"

"Okay, Friendly Fred, what's your drink?"

"Vodka, Danny boy, a gentlemen's drink! Straight up, tall glass, three ice cubes, hold the olive."

"The name's Sean, mate." The bartender extended his hand.

Freddy shook the Irish bartender's hand and began to bellow out "Oh Danny Boy" in his best Irish brogue, finishing the tune with a tap dance.

"Who you supposed to be now, Freddy, the lucky charm's midget?" Candy said sarcastically.

"I'm hurt, my beautiful lass!" Freddy frowned. "That was my best Dennis O'Connor."

Sean chimed in, "Candy, the lucky charm's character is a leprechaun, not a midget."

"Midget, leprechaun, Dennis, whatever, who cares? This is bor-ing! I think I'll freshen my face." Candy walked to the ladies' room.

Freddy drained the tall vodka in two large gulps. "Ah, now that's a drink, Danny boy. I'll have another. Do you think she's married?"

Sean laughed, shaking his head. "Ten to one she ain't."

"There is a God!" Friendly slammed his second Vodka.

"So, you feeling lucky tonight, Freddy? Ready to win one million dollars?"

"Lucky? Dare say, you ask do I feel lucky tonight? My fine Irish pub master, call me Mr. Lucky!"

Sean laughed as he prepared Friendly Fred a fresh, tall Vodka. "So then, Mr. Lucky it is!"

"Indeed, Sean my boy, lucky since the day I was born."

"Tell me about it, Freddy. Tell me about your good fortune."

Friendly Fred turned gray and sullen. "Well, let's see, Sean. My daddy was a black man. He was a drunk who got himself stabbed to death. And my dear mother was retarded. How's that for a lucky start in life?"

"Hmmm." Sean looked saddened. "Had a rough start myself, lad, back there in the motherland."

"Yes, well, my good luck continued as I was shipped from foster home to foster home. Learned how to make people like me. A gift from God! Here comes Friendly Fred."

"And what do you do, Fred? I mean what kind of work?"

"I am a salesman, brother Sean! I can sell ice to Eskimos, water to fish, rocks to a mountain, sand to a beach. Just give me the holy book of the Yellow Pages and watch Brother Fred heal the masses!"

"So what are you selling now, mate?"

Freddy laughed, but it was a bitter effort. "Currently, I seem to be in-between opportunities. However, at the stroke of midnight, Mr. Lucky will be catching the red-eye to Vegas with his lucky million!"

"You like to gamble, do ya?"

"Like? Love's a better word, Irish!"

"Are you any good at it?"

"Does a cat have nine lives? Here, Sean, let me show you." Fred pulled a silver dollar from his pants pocket. One coin and three one-dollar bills in his wallet, along with a two-dollar scratch-off, were all that staved off vagrancy. "Call it in the air, Irish!"

"Heads!"

"Best two out of three," Fred fired back.

After losing five tosses in a row, Freddy returned the silver dollar to his dirty pants pocket. "Better save my luck for the million."

"So, have you ever been married, Freddy?"

"Once, a beautiful girl from the hills of West Virginy!"

"Divorced?"

"Nah, she died. A horrible accident."

"I'm sorry, Freddy." Sean feigned sincerity. "I guess that was a stroke of bad luck, huh? Like when a man reaches his crossroad in life, ya know what I mean?"

"Crossroad? Yeah, I suppose it was, Sean. My crossroad."

"Excuse me a second, Freddy; looks like the reverend needs some healing." Sean fixed a drink and carried it toward the TV evangelist by the men's room door.

"Crossroad…" Freddy allowed his mind to reach back to the place he didn't like to go.

Friendly Fred Yancey had been selling Yellow Page advertising in the West Virginia area just across the Kentucky state line, northeast of Ashland. He'd been staying at the Holiday Inn, corporate rate, and by now known as the best pool player in town. It was there he met Estelle Tingle.

Estelle was a cute girl, short, and a size below Lane Bryant shopping. A great smile attached to hillbilly speak, it was love at first sight.

Six months later and with Freddy's luck, the couple married in the Good Hope Baptist Church. Before the year was out, Fred Yancey was promoted to assistant manager of Tom's Hardware and Feed Store. The owner, Tom Tingle, was Freddy's father-in-law.

One year almost to the day of the couple's marriage, Freddy came home in his normal depression-loaded mood. Twelve pack, three removed, under his arm, he opened the door to the single-wide trailer that he paid a hundred bucks a month rent on, check made payable to his father-in-law.

Fred, just after a year, hated his life in total. Twelve hours a day at Tom's Hardware, six days a week. No one worked on Sundays, being the Sabbath and all. Then church, dinner with the hillbillies, and start the struggle all over again. Without his nightly twelve pack, Friendly Fred felt sure he'd go nuts and kill the entire Tingle family.

He opened the trailer door slowly, not wanting to ever see or hear his young bride who had put on an unneeded thirty pounds in twelve months.

"Freddy," his roly poly wife squealed. "Freddy, my handsome hubby! I've fixed you a special meal tonight—fried pork chops, fried potatoes, fried squash, and fried corn fritters!"

Freddy wondered how much lard it would take to fry up his fat wife. Probably a fifty-five-gallon drum of the pork fat to fry the pork fat.

He popped the top of a fresh beer and flopped down in the easy chair that really didn't feel easy.

"Honey," squealed the piglet, as Freddy thought of her, "honey, you'll never guess what happened!"

"What, Estelle?" Zero enthusiasm from Freddy.

"I missed my period!" Freddy's young bride jumped for joy, and the trailer actually moved.

"You missed what?" Terror struck deep as he contemplated another Tingle hillbilly.

"My period, silly! We're going to have a baby, Freddy!"

He wanted to vomit, to run and never stop, to disappear off the face of the earth.

"Aren't you happy, sweet face?" She gave a quizzical squeal.

"Oh yeah, I'm real happy."

Estelle jumped into his lap, almost taking his breath away and snapping one of the support boards to the underneath side of the chair.

"Geez, Estelle! You nearly broke my legs!"

"Aren't you excited, Freddy? Aren't you happy? What do ya want? A boy? A girl? One of each?" Her voice made the hair on his neck stand.

"Who knows, kiddo, maybe you'll have a litter."

"Oh, silly, girls can't have litters! Only animals, like dogs and pigs."

And fat hillbillies, he thought.

Estelle skipped to the kitchen, where she flipped, stirred, and munched fried stuff.

Freddy, still in shock, choked on the pungent odor of smoky grease that filled the twenty-year-old trailer sitting on concrete blocks. He got up, went to the tiny bedroom, and changed into his hunting clothes.

Several minutes later, he placed four beers in the pockets of his hunting vest, grabbing the twelve gauge from the small pantry. "The coons been getting in the trash. I'm going to take Jaws for a look around." Jaws was his coonhound and most likely the only thing he really loved.

"Oh, honey,"—more screech than talk—"dinner in half an hour. Don't be late! I'm so hungry I could eat a cow!"

"I'll lay ten to one on that," he murmured as he left the greasy, smoke-filled kitchen.

Freddy walked close to a half a mile straight up the wooded hills behind the trailer. Jaws sniffed and huffed in search of the ever-elusive coon. As if he carried the weight of the world on his shoulders, he sat down upon a damp, moss-covered, rotting log to contemplate his predicament. Looking at the twelve-gauge shotgun, suicide became a real issue for considerable consideration.

"Having any luck?" The voice was deep yet musical and came from within inches, although it could have been miles away.

"Geez-o-pete, man!" Freddy nearly wet his hunting britches. "Where did you come from?"

The man was tall and extremely handsome in the full moon. "Oh, I'm just out walking. I love to walk in the dark."

"Yeah, well, you sure do it quietly! Man, you scared the livin' crap out of me."

"I'm sorry. I've been watching you a while. It looked like you were doing more thinking than hunting, however." His smile was soothing, Fred thought.

"Sound observation, friend. The thinking part."

"Ah, soul searching. It's what real men must do, I think. Especially if you're at a crossroad. Are you, my friend? At a crossroad?"

"Crossroad? Let's see, I hate my job, my life, the stinkin' trailer, and my wife is pregnant! You tell me. Am I at a crossroad?"

"Sounds like it." There was a long pause, and Freddy felt safe and strong next to this man dressed as though he could narrate *Wild Kingdom*. "You see, there are moments, maybe several, but mostly just one, a moment when a man has to make a critical decision. Something hard, tough, a decision most men would not ever wish to consider. But the decision will not go away on its own. It's a defining moment. It is your crossroad."

"That is exactly where I'm at now!" Fred sounded like a pleading child.

"At your crossroad?" the strong confident voice inquired.

"Yes, I am. I'm at one gigantic crossroad, and I don't know which way to turn."

"Hmm." The voice was so soothing. "Let me give you some sound advice, young man, a tidbit of wisdom that will serve you well."

"I'm all ears. God knows I need some help!"

The handsome man laughed warmly. "God? Yes, God. The question is not if he knows you need help; the question is can he provide any help? And the answer is no."

"I'm not much of a praying man anyway."

"Good." The word rolled off his lips like honey on a hot biscuit. "Good. Real wisdom comes from within. This is the only life you will ever have. Always think me first because no one else will care for you. And when you reach the crossroad, look down the road that brings you freedom! Select the path that brings you happiness, and to hell with everyone else!"

"I understand. It makes total sense." Freddy spoke as if in a mental fog. "Me first; to hell with the rest."

"Exactly, son." The man laid his strong hands on Freddy's shoulder, and they provided warmth and strength. "You must do what you must do."

"Well, I should be going now. I have a lot of walking to do."

The man stood. "What's that smell anyway? Coming from that trailer down the hill?"

Freddy had to think for a minute. "Oh that, that smell! It's my wife frying everything but the cat."

"Ah, I see. Best be careful with hot grease. Very dangerous indeed. Gets close to a flame and *boom!* The fire will spread in seconds, especially in an old trailer like that one."

Red and blue lights flashed up the gravel road to the trailer. Freddy stood shaking in the light drizzle beside Sheriff Davey's cruiser.

"Looks like a grease fire, Mr. Tingle," the volunteer fire chief informed Estelle's father. "Fred said he was coon hunting and saw the trailer explode from a mile up the hill. By the time he got here, it was too late. We're real sorry, Tom."

Freddy stood all alone, wet, and cold. He had reached his crossroad. He looked away from the smoldering remains of his home, the twenty-year-old trailer. The red-hot embers glowed among yellow and red-looking flames, consuming all that was left of his life. It looked like hell, and his wife and unborn son laid in its heat.

No longer able to look at the hellish glow, he turned to see a man standing in the shadows beside Tommy Tingle's pick up, the man he'd met in the woods, the same man who'd told him about the crossroads in life. The man smiled at Freddy. Moving his lips silently, he said, "Thou shalt not kill."

AND THE PARTY NEVER ENDS

Sean returned to the bar after providing the Reverend Tommy Johns with a fresher-upper, the fresher being ninety proof, and the upper a spoonful of high-quality speed. The preacher needed a little pick-me-up, the bartender thought.

"Sorry, Freddy, got to take care of my invited guests, don't you know? The good old rev needed a bit of a boost. So where were we then, mate? Your wife and the crossroad?"

Freddy ignored the question; he needed action, a little gambling and a whole lot of vodka. Just what the doctor ordered to bring him back to reality. The reality of self.

The truth of me first. He'd leave the horror of that fiery night, that crossroad, his murder, for later, later for his enchanted nightmares, the kind that drunken sleep couldn't eliminate.

"Sean," he asked, feeling better, considering a little action, "who's that Jew over at the pool table?"

"Leon, Leon Schwartz."

"He's shooting pool by himself. Any good?"

"I've watched him a bit. Not half bad I'd say. Might even get better if you throw out a little cash bait. You know what they say, Freddy."

"No, Sean, what?"

"Jews are good at two things—making you money and taking your money!"

"Not today, my Irish mate, not today."

Freddy ambled over to the pool table. "Care if I join you?"

"Delighted! Please. My name is Leon."

"Glad to meet you, Leon. I'm Fred, Friendly Fred!"

"What's your game, Freddy? Eight ball? Nine ball?"

"Oh gosh, Leon, I don't play that much. You call it."

Leon knew a hustler when he saw one, and Friendly Fred had pool chalk in his veins. "Nine ball it is! Go ahead and break 'em, Fred."

"You want to make it a bit more fun, Leon? Say a couple bucks?"

"Ah sure, Friendly Fred! How about we make it twenty?"

"Are you a hustler?" Freddy asked as if hurt.

"Me?" Now Leon sounded hurt. "A hustler? I'm just an old bagel pusher."

"Well, okay, partner, but I ain't played but one time this

whole year." Freddy chalked the cue, leaned low over his stick, and let it slide forward with power. "Nine ball, side pocket," Freddy yelled. "Call me Mr. Lucky!"

He collected Leon's twenty, thankful he'd won the first game since all he had were three one-dollar bills in his wallet.

Ex-priest Father Jimmy Ryan returned from the bar with a Chevis on the rocks for himself and a vodka ginger for his new friend, Candy Sweet.

"So tell me, Father Jimmy, what's it like being a man of God?"

"Candy, I keep telling you, I'm neither priest, father, nor man of God. I'm just a man looking for hope in all the wrong places."

"Wrong places? Well I declare, Fa- I mean, Jimmy Ryan, wrong place, you say? Let me tell ya, honey, Candy Sweet knows all about wrong places, and this ain't one of them!"

"You think?" Jimmy was nothing if not infatuated with the young stripper.

"Ain't no way, Jimmy; add it up! The place is clean, nice bar, Sean is an honest to God Irish bartender, ain't that special, and the drinks are strong and free!"

"I guess when you put it that way, well—"

"Ain't no well to it, darling!" Candy blew a big pink bubble. "Plus, we got some really special people here with us."

"Special? I'm not so sure. Maybe unusual fits better."

"Jimmy, Jimmy, Jimmy. You got to go outside to feel the sunshine."

"Please explain that one." The ex-priest was naïve.

"Where you been, Father, sorry, Jimmy? Look around us, darling; add it up!"

"Add it up?"

"Yeah, sweet face." Another pink bubble popped. "Add it up! Look around! Let's see now, we have you, ex-priest. Then there's the famous world television preacher. Did you ever see his show, healing people, flopping around like big fish on stage? Weird, Jimmy, totally freaking weird!"

"I think it was an act." Jimmy looked sad.

"Duh! Ya think?" Candy looked toward the bar, raising her glass for a refill.

"And then we have the little old Jewish fella. Baptist, Catholic, Jew. All in one place, a bar no less, and hoping to win one million dollars! Does that sound normal to you? And who the hell picked all of us anyway?"

"Good question, Candy. I see the irony—Jew, preacher, priest—but what about you and the others?"

"Oh, that's easy, sweetie. You got me, a dancer, the cripple who wishes she was one, and Friendly Fred. That's a bunch of people rolled up in one gigantic crazy person!"

"So what's that tell you, Candy?"

"Tell me? Come on now, my cute ex-priest. It tells me we all came from the planter planet!"

"Planter...planet?"

"Yeah, darling, we're all a bunch of nuts!" Candy Sweet howled with childish laughter.

Jimmy gave the proclamation serious thought. "Hmm, a bunch of nuts? All rejects brought together on New Year's Eve. All looking for the impossible, one winner, maybe, the rest losers. So goes life."

"Hold the offering plate there, Father. I ain't no loser!"

"Sorry, Candy, I didn't mean you were a loser. I think you are a remarkable and very beautiful woman."

"That's okay, Jimmy boy, I know what you're saying. We are a crazy bunch of nuts!" Candy grabbed Father Ryan's face with both hands and kissed him flush upon his surprised lips. "All better, baby boy?"

Jimmy Ryan blushed. He'd never in his life been kissed like that, and the ex-priest liked it.

"You know, sweet face,"—Candy seemed serious now—"maybe it's like Sean said."

"Sean?"

"Yeah, silly, maybe it's like he said. We are all here at the crossroad!"

Freddy lost the next nine-ball game because he couldn't keep his eyes off Candy Sweet. He'd planned to leave the bar with the dancer that night, and now she was kissing the weasel in the corner! "Didn't someone say he was a priest?" Well, he would get to that business after he took every last penny-pinching dollar from the pool-hustling Jew!

"Rack 'em, Friendly Fred." Leon's smile was forced. "Got to give a poor, old Jew a chance to cross the Jordan!"

Sean watched Jimmy Ryan walk toward the men's room but couldn't see him enter from where he stood behind the bar. A few moments later, Candy placed her empty glass on the bar. "Fill 'er up, Irish. I'll be back shortly."

Candy wiggled and swayed her hips as only a professional dancer could as she too walked toward the restrooms.

Sean again could not be sure if she entered the boys' or girls' room. He looked over toward Mosha, who had a clear shot at the restrooms. The big gatekeeper smiled and gave Sean the thumbs-up sign.

"And the party never ends." Sean chuckled.

THOU SHALT NOT COMMIT ADULTERY

"Good evening." Mosha's voice was flat and monotone. "Your invitation, please."

June Swift, flashing a quick smile without supporting emotion, took her lucky number from the giant. "Seven," she whispered. "Seven." *It has been seven years,* the tall, well-dressed woman thought. Seven long years since her life crumbled from solid rock to mere particles of dust.

June Swift stopped momentarily beside the table where Katie Zanderfield was slumped over in her wheelchair, well on her way to drunk and high on weed. "Good evening."

Ms. Swift's voice maintained the sound of good manners and pride long gone.

Katie raised her head with bloodshot eyes and looked up with an empty smile. She attempted a weak smile then lowered her head back to the safety of self-pity.

"Welcome, missy! Welcome to the Hikes Point! My name is Sean MacIntosh, the proud son of Irish royalty. What might I serve ya?"

June forced the weak smile as empty as Katie's. "Wine please. Chardonnay, chilled."

"Coming right up, my fine lady; chilled as ordered!"

"Fine lady," she mused. "Yes, once upon a time. A very long once upon a time ago."

"I didn't quite catch the name when you came in."

Again, the empty smile. "June, June Swift. Ms. June Swift." She sipped her wine as if at a state dinner.

"So, may I call you June, ma'am?"

"Yes, of course, Sean."

"Well, June, do you feel lucky tonight? Ready to take home a million big ones? Hit the jackpot?"

"Quite honestly, Sean, I haven't really given it much thought. Luck, I mean. My luck ran out a long time ago."

"Like to talk about it?"

She looked Sean directly in his eyes as tears filled the outer edges of her own. "Not really. If you don't mind, I think I would prefer to sit quietly until the drawing. I usually don't frequent bars. Sorry."

"Quite all right, missy! Find a comfortable place, and I'll freshen up that chardonnay."

"Thank you, Sean." Her voice was as shallow as the wine glass. June Swift moved to a table between the girl in the wheelchair and the rowdy man talking like Groucho Marx as he circled the pool table like a tiger on the hunt.

"Here ya go, missy!" Sean placed the silver ice bucket in the middle of the table with a freshly opened bottle of very good and expensive chardonnay. "Compliments of the house!"

"Thank you, Sean."

June Swift placed her cashmere coat across the chair to her left. Dressed in a light-gray wool suit and white silk blouse tight to her neck, she looked the picture of class. Too classy for the Hikes Point, Sean thought.

Ms. Swift would turn fifty in just a matter of days. She felt much older. At first, she'd thought the entire Hikes Point thing was a prank, a trick to embarrass her even more, if that were possible. But after careful consideration, she believed that it might be a way out, the end of her misery and suffering. Send five hundred thousand to each of her sons now attending university and living with their father, Dr. Scotty Swift. Once done, she would find Erik, who was responsible for her life going straight to hell, and put a bullet in his head from the snub nose .38 she carried in her Gucci purse.

June Swift pulled a Marlboro from a newly opened box and flicked her Bic. A long sip of wine and a hard pull from her cigarette took her back, back to her unimaginable sin.

It had started so innocently. A chance encounter in the mall, of all places. Was it boredom? Maybe a bit of loneliness? No, she knew those excuses would never fit the crime. June Swift knew what she had done. Lust put her out of the perfect life. Secret sex, plain and simple. And now there was a great price to pay for her sins.

June gave up the perfect marriage, a lifestyle few could only dream of. And in doing so, she lost it all.

Scotty Swift, Dr. Swift, was a well-respected heart surgeon. He worked long hours and was seldom home. The motive she reasoned for her adultery.

They had the perfect home with manicured lawn, four full baths, and nearly eight thousand square feet in total. She drove a new Range Rover to the club, the hair salon, and the almost daily trips to the mall. And yes, Scotty Swift, the awesome doctor, loved her very much.

And now Scotty lived in their home, the one she meticulously decorated, with his new wife, an operating room nurse twenty years his junior. And just yesterday her so-called friend Angie phoned. "June Bug, you'll never guess what I heard at the club! The good doctor and his teenage bride just bought this big house in Maui!" What are friends for?

But the real hurt, the agony that could bring on instant vomiting, was delivered when Scotty took the boys, her sons, away. In seven years not a single phone call, Mother's Day card, nothing. All that was left for her to remember was that cloudy day as they walked out of divorce court. Scotty led the boys to his dark blue 560 SEL Mercedes. Scotty Jr. turned with tears streaming down his flushed cheeks and said for all the world to hear, "I hate you, Mother! You're a whore!" The last words spoken by her oldest son. Little Stevie did not even look back.

It had been like any other mall day. Do a little shopping, maybe some new jogging sneakers. Stop by the Mandarin for Chinese and return home to the comforts and safety that millionaires enjoy. Just another day.

"I'm looking for a pair of comfortable running shoes."

June wore a pink, expensive jogging outfit that displayed her long, slender, muscular body. She looked much younger than forty-three, as her husband often told her.

The shoe salesman was pushing thirty with the body of an athlete. "Hey, you're in luck! We just got in the newest thing in running shoes, Earthotonics! But I better warn you, these bad boys ain't cheap."

June smiled. "Do I look like I'm worried about paying too much for shoes, Erik?" She read the young man's nametag.

Erik gently pulled up her half sock, white with pink trim and a little fuzz ball at the back. His fingers were long and slender. He placed his right hand softly around her tight calf muscle as he slid the new everything running shoe on her foot. It was at that moment that lust filled her soul. Erik's slender body, long, black, shoulder-length curly hair, a killer smile with a soothing persuasiveness in every word uttered.

"Now how's that feel, Mrs..." He touched her leg once more.

"June, Erik. Call me June."

"All right then, June, feel good?"

"Very." She blushed, and Erik the shoe salesman read her loud and clear.

In the next thirty days, June Swift purchased seventeen pairs of shoes from the handsome keeper of feet. On the thirty-first day, Erik's day off, she crawled beneath the sheets with the young lad.

She could not be sure by whom or how Scotty found out about her adultery, although she suspected her best friend and confidant let it slip at the club. In any case, she was caught.

After spending the day with sweet Erik in his one-room efficiency apartment, she'd returned home to the mansion, as Scotty, Jr. called it, to find the big Mercedes in the circular driveway. Unusual for a Wednesday, she thought.

The front door was locked, also extremely unusual. Panic started slowly as her house key did not work the deadbolt and the locks looked new. Then the door opened, and Dr. Swift stood stiffly before her.

"Here." Scotty handed her a large brown envelope. "Inside you will find a new checkbook with ten thousand dollars deposited today. There is a Visa card, five thousand-dollar limit, and keys to your new apartment with directions. You can keep the Range Rover. Now get off my porch!"

"Scotty, wait. Scotty, what's this all about? Let me explain, darling!"

"Darling? You dare to call me that? It's real simple, June. You wish to be a whore, be a whore. But not in my house, in my life, or with my sons!"

"Wait... please tell me... I don't understand."

"Don't understand?" Scotty laughed cruelly. "I'll get the pictures, darling!"

Scotty handed her several black-and-white photos of her in bed with a young man.

Head lowered, the guilty wife whispered, "Where did you get these?"

"Get them? Where did I get them, darling? Well, your boyfriend, Erik, sold them to me for a mere five thousand dollars."

"Oh my God." June almost fainted.

"Little late for that... darling!" Scotty slammed the door in her face.

The adulteress stood silently frozen in the moment, hoping to awaken from this horrible dream. *Erik had it all set up!* She slowly moved in a dream state toward the Range Rover. Lost. Forever lost.

The next morning she received divorce papers at her new apartment. She called the first attorney she found in the Yellow Pages. The Yellow Page ad was a full two-color page, *Specializing in Divorce Proceedings*. She scheduled an appointment for later that day.

The next order of the day was to visit the mall and kill Erik!

"I'm sorry, miss, but Erik quit yesterday. Didn't even give us a week's notice. Said he was moving to Florida."

She would not find him at the apartment either.

The next several weeks were nothing but a blur for June Swift. Alcohol and cigarettes, both new vices for the adulteress.

Her new attorney, handsome and with a smooth, musical way of talking, helped her to maintain some sanity, if even in a drunken state. "Don't worry, Mrs. Swift; we will get you what's due! Yes, yes, joint custody is automatic." She trusted the well-dressed attorney.

June tried her best to focus as she sat next to her attorney and across from Scotty, with his three lawyers smiling back.

She blinked her eyes and shook her head back and forth, attempting to fight through the fog, the mental mist created by the pills her attorney had given her earlier.

She looked to the left at the first row of seats behind Scotty and his expensive legal team. Scotty's parents were there, there with her sons, Scotty, Jr. and Stevie, in-between, all looking at her as if she were a witch ready to be tied to the stake. June unconsciously touched her chest, as if expecting to find a scarlet letter sewn to her jacket.

The judge, a member of the club and weekly golf partner of her husband, brought the proceedings to order.

"I have read the summations of both legal representatives. As Mrs. Swift has forfeited all property and monetary rights to any existing commingled assets, and with the signed prenuptial agreement legally binding, this court, based on the request of Dr. Swift, awards Mrs. Swift one hundred thousand dollars and clear title to a Range Rover automobile."

June looked left and right. Confusion wrinkled her face. "What did he just say?"

"Quiet, June." Her grand attorney patted her hand as if she were a young child in church.

"And furthermore, this court awards full custody of Scott Swift, Jr. and Stephen Swift to their father, Dr. Scott Swift. Case dismissed."

The judge hurriedly left the bench. Dr. Swift stood before the table, where his wife slumped in disbelief. "Good luck and good riddance."

June lifted her head to see her husband and boys exit the courtroom. "What just happened?" she asked her attorney. "I mean, there isn't any prenuptial agreement. A hundred thousand? Full custody? What just happened?" Her voice was shrill and frightened.

"Well, June, it's like this, you see. There are times in every living soul's life that he or she must face the unknown. It is part of the journey, that walk along the highway of mankind, the path that leads to the crossroad. You are now there. Goodbye and good luck."

AND THE PARTY ...

Former priest Jimmy Ryan walked into the men's room a virgin. He walked out in love.

Candy giggled, stumbling on her not-so-stable high heels as she clung to the ex-priest as he attempted to wipe the red lipstick from his mouth with the paper towel carried from the men's room.

"Well, there you be," Sean exhorted. "I thought we'd lost you."

"Lost us? Contraire, my Irish cutie! We was just discussing nature, wasn't we, Jimmy?"

"Nature?" Sean knew full well what she meant.

"Yeah, nature. You know, the birds and the bees!"

"Well, here ya go, mates!" Sean handed the couple fresh drinks. "Watch out for those bees."

"You're such a silly boy, Irish!" The same silly giggle. "We're not talkin' old stinging bees; we're talkin' honey bees!"

"Love, ain't it grand," Sean fired back as the love bees buzzed back to their table.

"Where you been?" Freddy asked in an accusatory voice.

"Say what?" Candy now talking as if she had a mouth full of marbles. "Did you just ask me where I've been?" Candy was moving in on belligerent.

"Yeah! I was, you know, worried." Freddy was toning down his anger.

"Chill out, hot dog." Jimmy was not as drunk as the others and didn't want Freddy to question his whereabouts.

"What'd you call me? What'd you say, pope pusher?" Freddy felt his back pocket for his knife.

Jimmy stood facing Freddy.

"Why, you cracker eating—" Freddy threw a wild roundhouse punch that missed Jimmy by a mile.

Jimmy Ryan, an expert boxer in days gone by, hit Freddy flush on the jaw with a solid left hook, sending him backward into the table. Pool balls scattered.

"Well, I guess we're done shooting pool," Leon stated matter-of-factly.

Freddy stuck his hand in his pocket and in a flash produced a gleaming blade. "Now who's the hot dog, Father Peanuts?"

Mosha moved quickly, twisting Freddy's hand backward. The knife fell to the floor, and with a powerful push, Mosha flung Freddy into the red leather booth five feet away. "*Sit,*" he said, and Freddy did just that.

"Come on, Candy!" Jimmy pulled the girl to her feet. "Let's move to the other side, where we don't have to smell hot dogs!"

Leon sat across from Fred. "Come on now, Freddy. It ain't worth all this now, is it? Let's get another drink and shoot some more pool, okay?"

"I'm gonna get that puke, Leon. Get him good!"

"Okay, Freddy, okay. You'll get him. But stay cool. What do you want to drink?"

"Vodka, Leon. Tall glass. Thanks."

"Hey, Rev, you back among the living I see."

"Yeah, Sean, I think I might have popped off for a minute or two. Hey, that last drink you poured was outstanding. What'd you do?"

"Not a thing, mate. Just rum and Coke. That's your drink, right?"

"Yes, of course, rum and Coke. But wow, that last one gave me life. It was like I'd been healed!"

"Good," Sean replied. "I'll fix you a fresher upper." This time the Irish bartender filled the tall glass with Coke, a splash of rum, and a double portion of high-octane speed.

"Man,"—the rev smacked his lips—"that drink could start me preachin'!"

Candy Sweet no longer sat on the other side of Jimmy Ryan in their new placement across the room from the hot dog. They were side-by-side, thighs pressed together. Jimmy could feel the heat.

"That's it, Freddy, my last twenty; you cleaned me out.

Story of my life!" Leon was down $220 to Friendly, now doing his best Jackie Gleason.

"I guess I just got lucky, Leon. Here's twenty; maybe you can get one of the girls in the game. You might have better luck with the wheelchair lady." Freddy's mirth was laced with scorn. "See ya in a sec."

"Say, Sean, what's up with the cripple anyway?"

"Well, Rev, 'bout a year ago the lass had this terrible automobile crash. Read about it. Her parents and boyfriend got all burned up. Left her in the wheelchair. She's hoping to win the million for some special spine operation in Germany or France, I think."

"Interesting." The previous former faith healer, enemy of the IRS, started the wheels of heaven rolling in his scheming little brain. *Maybe she just thinks she can't walk. Lord knows I've seen that before,* he thought to himself. *If I can just get her to believe, give faith a chance, just maybe…*

Stoked by a double spoonful of white powder, the good reverend considered healing the girl. If successful and if she won the million bucks, no doubt she'd share her blessings with the man sent by God!

Tommy Johns smiled wickedly. "Hey, Sean, watch this. It's show time!"

The good reverend slithered across the floor, rubbing his healing hands together rapidly, needing to feel the healing heat. Down on one knee beside Katie's wheelchair, the show began.

Mumbling a whole bunch of jibber jabber stuff the tent revival preacher taught him years ago, Tommy Johns got everyone's attention.

"By the power of the Holy Ghost and the gift of casting out demons, I command you, Satan, to come out. *Come out! Come out!* I command you, devil! *Come out!*"

Reverend Johns threw one arm toward the heavens and slapped Katie Zanderfield hard on her forehead, leaving his reddish handprint. "Be healed! I command you, be healed!"

This for sure brought the young incapacitated girl from her drink and pot-induced slumber. "Heal this!" Katie screamed and hit the faith healer flush between the eyes with the half-empty bottle of Dom.

Freddy Yancey stopped dead in his tracks. "Holy moly," he said, taking two steps back.

Mosha rushed to the table, grabbed the faith healer by the collar, and turned to Katie Zanderfield. "Sorry. Do you want I kill him?"

Katie didn't understand that Mosha sincerely meant it. "No, don't kill him. Just bring the piece of trash to the toilet, where he belongs."

"Okay." Mosha opened the men's room door and threw the healer under the bank of urinals.

Moments passed, and all went back to normal at the Hikes Point, Ladies Invited, Happy Hour Never Ends.

Friendly Fred, still rubbing his jaw and not forgetting the ex-priest's insult, approached June Swift. "Would you like to dance?"

"Would you like for me to shoot you?" she stated with all sincerity.

"Well, excuse me!" Steve Martin's voice responded.

"Get away from me, dirt bag!" June spit the words and turned away from Freddy.

"What a night!" Freddy murmured as he pushed the men's room door open. "Hot Dog? Dirt bag?" They wouldn't be calling him names when he won the million dollars. "Nah, not them, not when Mr. Lucky is rich! You da man! Have a drink, come over to the house, meet the family." They'd love him then, and he'd tell them to go straight to hell, all of them. All except Candy Sweet. They'd be on the red-eye to Vegas.

Freddy walked toward the middle urinal, struggling to unzip his pants. The zipper always seemed to catch halfway down and halfway up.

And there, just under the place of relief, rested the preacher, out cold with a trickle of blood running from his nose.

"Opportunity!" Freddy laughed and commenced to relieve himself upon and all over the preacher. "You've been healed." He laughed and cursed as his zipper pull came off in his fingers.

Freddy left the men's room, fly open.

Macklin keyed the walkie-talkie. "Finish your Moon Pie yet, copper?"

Rusty, snuggling in his blanket by the dumpster, fired back, "No, my warm friend, but the rats are gone!"

"Good." Macklin chuckled. "Anything going on in the alley?"

"Nope. All calm on the western front. Quiet as a church rat. You?"

"Same ole, same ole. Wait. You need to see this!"

"What?"

"This low-rider Chevy Impala just pulled up with a Mexican dressed in red, head to toe. Our eighth visitor of the evening."

"What in the hell is going on, Mack?"

"Don't know, partner, but I'm betting we'll know come midnight. Stay warm, buddy."

"Too cold to know what warm is. Out."

THOU SHALT NOT STEAL

Mosha gave the short man a glaring look as the red chili pepper with legs entered. "Your invitation, please."

"What's up, bro? Man, you bigger than a fifty-two Oldsmobile. I need to recruit you to my troops, you know, hang out with my gang. You know, man, get into the Mexican connection."

"No thank you." Mosha handed the scarlet gangster wannabe his number.

"Say, man, what's up with the eight? I ain't no eight! I be a one or a ten, man. Eight? Are you pullin' my chain?" The

Mexican looked around to realize he was being watched by the Hikes Point misfits in total.

Standing as if on stage, he modeled his flaming attire: floor-length red overcoat, extra-wide red fedora with a black band, ruffled red shirt, red pants with matching red silk stripes down each leg, and shining red shoes that could pass for plastic.

"What's happenin,' my people!"

The Mexican that dressed for Halloween hip-hopped to the bar. "Eight is great, be lookin' for his mate. Don't be late for running with the eight. Got a date, give the million to the eight!"

Freddy was the first to greet eight at the bar. "Far out, man! What an entrance. This place could use a little class!"

The Mexican gave Freddy the once-over. "What's up, brother man? We all cool, you know. Just a villain with the chillin.'" He gave Freddy the chili pepper's handshake, which got lost in translation.

"You be happening, my brother!" Fred was now Richard Pryor.

"Hey, my brother, check out your trousers, man! You be all up on me exposing yourself!"

"Oh that, my zipper broke."

"Zipper broke?" The Mexican laughed, throwing his head back, displaying several gold teeth. "Man, you white boys are some funny dudes, man. Like here I am now rappin' with a clown!"

"Now I'm a clown?" Freddy let it ride because deep down, blacks and Mexicans scared him.

"I'm Fred, Fred Yancey. But all my boys call me Mango."

"Mango?" The Mexican took a step back, laughing even harder. "Mango? Like the fruit, bro?"

Freddy turned almost as red as the Mexican's clothes and wished his fly wasn't open. "Nah, man! Not some stinkin' fruit. I was named after a drug dealer, you know, man, a real bad dude!"

"That's cool, man. That's cool! Mango. Heavy name for a white boy, that's all, man. I'm Peppie. And all my troops call me Little Honcho, man. Honcho, 'cause I be the man, bro! Honcho say, go steal me a car; it's at my place, man! Steal me a Rolex; it be on my arm, brother. Steal me some cash, and the liquor store is closed up with yellow police tape, man!"

"Cool!" Freddy responded as he held his pants shut with his right hand.

"What's you doing, bro? Keepin' something in or something out?" Peppie howled, and Sean joined in.

"The zipper, remember?"

"Oh yeah, bro, the zipper done broke. You a funny freakin' white boy!"

"Peppie, Sean MacIntosh. It is a pleasure to have you, mate. What's your drink?"

Peppie looked at Fred, astonished. "What'd he say? Did he say, 'What's your drink?' Did he ask Senor Honcho Peppie, 'What's your drink?'"

Sean looked confused, and Freddy just shook his head up and down in confirmation.

Peppie turned his attention back to the bartender. "What's my drink? Well, bro, I'll give you three guesses—Kool-Aid, Bud, or tequila. What you think be Honcho's drink?"

"Tequila it is, mate!"

All three laughed long and loud.

"Come on, Freddy, do a shot with Peppie! You afraid of tequila, white boy?"

"Honcho, so I'm a white boy, but this senor have pure African blood running in his hot veins! Mango do shots with Peppie!"

Both men threw down tequila shots with beer chasers.

"Irishman, you no like to drink with Peppie and Mango?"

"No thanks, Honcho. First of all, I'm an Irish whiskey lad, and secondly, if I drink on the job, it'd be like stealing from the owner!"

"Stealing from the owner? Are you crazy man? That's the game, bro! You supposed to steal from the owner? They don't steal in England?"

"Ireland, I'm from Ireland."

"Mucho sorry, bro, but stealing is a gift, brother, not a crime! Right, Mango?"

"Well, Peppie." Freddy was talking like Jack Webb, which Peppie didn't get. "The Bible says you shall not steal."

Peppie flashed his gold teeth in a wide grin. "Okay, Freddy, the Bible also says don't name your son after some fruit!"

"Really?" Sean seemed sincere.

"Yeah, man, and it also says you supposed to have things!"

Freddy liked where this was going. "So, Honcho, if I want a new car and don't have any money, I steal it?"

"Steal? We ain't talking 'bout stealing, bro! It's called borrow!"

"So how long you been borrowing stuff, mate?"

The flashy smile. "Man, since I quit wettin' my pants, bro. When I was six my mother would send me to the store. She'd say, 'Here's fifty pesos, Peppie. Get what's on the list, and you can have a nickel.' A nickel? Peppie can have a nickel? No way, man. Peppie filled his big coat pockets with all the list and kept the money!"

"Did you ever get caught, Honcho?"

"Sure, Freddy! I was young. But they would always let me go, and I'd go to a new store! You got to use your brain, Mango! I stole my first bike when I was six. A hot red Chevy when I was twelve!"

"Ever get popped?"

"Mango, what you think, bro? It's the odds, and Peppie wins most of the time. So I spent a little time in reform, a couple years in county. And now they trying to pin an armed robbery rap on Honcho Peppie!"

"If you go to prison, mate, would that be like you reached the crossroad?"

"Mango, what's that mean? Crossroad? Ain't gonna be no crossroad for Honcho Peppie. Peppie be at the crossroad between here and Tijuana! I just cross the border, borrow some rich people's SUV, and sell it to a needy Mexican. It's like in the history books, man—Honcho be a chili pepper Robin Hood!"

THOU SHALT NOT BEAR FALSE WITNESS AGAINST THY NEIGHBOR

Rusty stood shaking the heavy snow from his blanket and returned to his hiding place beside the dumpster. He eyed several empty beer kegs outside the Hikes Point, pushed up against a big piece of plywood from the remodel.

"Bingo!" Rusty carefully reconned the alleyway then quickly moved the two kegs and the plywood. "Now that's more like it, the perfect wino mansion with a view!"

Macklin's walkie-talkie squealed. "Hey, buddy, how you doing guarding the alleyway?"

"Snug as a bug in a rug, partner. Built a house," Rusty responded proudly. "I'll give you a tour later."

"How many bathrooms?"

"Two, very large. One front of the house and one back of the house." Both men snickered like ten-year-olds.

"You nice and warm, Mack?"

"Like a hound dog in front of the fireplace!"

"Lucky you. Anything cookin' out front?"

"Yeah, number nine just walked in. Looked like a Steve McQueen wannabe. Came via the city bus. Keep on your toes, copper. My guts screaming that it will hit the fan soon."

"Mack, have you checked on Annie?"

"Not in a while. I'll call now. Over and out."

"Your invitation, please," the ever-stoic Mosha requested and handed the man with the short hair and mean expression his card. Number nine in red.

The good Reverend Tommy Johns stirred under the urinals, his head throbbing for reasons he could not remember, due to a slight concussion. As the TV preacher regained his wits, he wondered why the front of his clothes were all wet. Lifting his shirt to his nose, it became apparent. "Ah man, somebody peed on me. I'm gonna kill..." The rev attempted to jump up, hitting his forehead square on the porcelain urinal base. *Bam!* Back to tent revival dreams.

Jimmy and Candy continued to coo like love pigeons in the back booth as *You've Got A Friend* played softly on the jukebox.

June Swift, now on her second bottle of chardonnay, felt the false bravado that alcohol delivers as she contemplated suicide and felt sure her ex-husband and sons would be sorry.

Close to the front, the attractive Katie Zanderfield leaned her head forward, resting on her slim arms. Katie dreamt that she ran through the white sand, touching the coral green waves of a faraway island. It was her honeymoon, which had been stopped at her crossroad.

Leon had returned to the bar, where he discussed the possibilities of franchising the Hikes Point with Sean. The Irishman bartender pretended to be interested in the Jewish man's dreams never again to be realized.

Freddy followed Honcho Peppie into the men's room before a new game of pool, twenty bucks a pop.

"What the hell?" Peppie looked down at the little man under the receptacle for male relief. "Man, look at the egg on this dude's forehead! How'd he get here, bro?"

Freddy chuckled. "The chick in the wheelchair smacked him with a champagne bottle. Knocked him out cold. Then the giant rolled his butt in here."

"Man, this lizard's all wet!" Peppie attempted to reason that one out.

"Yeah," Freddy said matter-of-factly, "I peed on him."

"Say what? Bro, that's cold, man. I mean, that ain't right, brother man."

Freddy justified his actions. "Ain't right? Honcho, what you see lying there before you is a bona fide television healing preacher!"

"No way, bro."

"Indeedie, Honcho, in every way. He was trying to heal

the cripple out front when she popped him alongside his stupid head."

"TV preacher, bro?"

"In the flesh."

"Whoa, brother. My mamma used to send those clowns money, money we didn't have. She died of cancer while she prayed, watching channel forty-two, listening to one of those faith-healin' maggots!"

Peppie unzipped his red trousers and followed Freddy's prior insult. Freddy, of course, didn't have to pull down any zipper.

Shelby Gaffney walked straight to the bar. An old and well-worn leather bomber jacket with a wool collar covered a clean white mock turtleneck. Equally worn Levi jeans and scoffed black combat boots did in fact meet the specific image of Steve McQueen from *The Great Escape* movie.

"Welcome, mate, what'll it be?"

"Budweiser." A man of few words, Sean surmised.

"I'm Sean MacIntosh, mate, Irish through and through! And you are?"

The rugged-looking ex-con stared at the bartender long and hard before replying. "Shelby. Nothing through and through."

The silence was broken when Friendly Fred proclaimed for the outside world to hear, "Just call me Mr. Lucky! Mango the magnificent!" Freddy collected the crisp twenty from his new Mexican sucker.

Shelby lit a non-filter cigarette and spit a piece of tobacco aside. "When's the drawing?"

"When's the drawing?" Sean responded. "Soon, mate, real soon!"

Leon chimed in, "Shelby is it? I'm Leon Schwartz. You might have heard of my delis. Had 'em all across the country. Leon's New York Deli. Ever eat there?"

A cold stare was the answer. Shelby Gaffney hated all blacks, Mexicans and Jews, especially Jews.

The Steve McQueen look-alike spent eight hard years in military prison after cold cocking the black officer who he thought liked to single him out. Dishonorably discharged from the army, the only job available was at a Texas carwash, and it was there that he would learn to hate Mexicans.

When the owner, an honest, hardworking sort, found the cash register empty at close one Saturday, the busiest day of the week, all clues pointed to Shelby Gaffney. However, the owner really liked Shelby and recently had promoted him to assistant manager.

On the other hand, Shelby hated the carwash, the owner, and every stinking Mexican in the state of Texas. He sure as hell wasn't going to do three to five for a lousy 666 bucks.

Shelby appeared in court and testified as to seeing Fernando, the handicapped Mexican who worked inside, take the money and give it to another Mexican.

Fernando received eighteen months in jail and possession of a felony record. Shelby left for Alabama the next day after bearing false witness against his Mexican carwash neighbor.

Six months later, as Shelby drove the stolen Mustang through Dothan, Alabama, he was arrested and convicted of robbing the White Way Laundry Drycleaners, pistol in hand and face all over the hidden cameras.

Shelby Gaffney, inmate 40229, was not happy when Johnny Wills, African American, became his cellmate.

The black man with a wife and three young children did not have a criminal record. In fact, he was a Christian and a Sunday-school teacher at the First Baptist Church of Selma. Thus, everyone was shocked when the fat white girl testified that he, Johnny Wills, raped her in the parking lot at the Dew Point beer joint.

Unfortunately for the falsely accused black man, he was of the same height, weight, and skin color of the "walking the streets" serial rapist.

Shelby knew the court system in good old Alabama. If white girls were being raped, any black man would do for a land of Dixie hanging. With that knowledge and ample time to watch the local news and Court TV in his cell, the white convict lined up his freedom.

He wrote down the facts on a yellow legal pad in his cell, the legal facts that any ten-year-old knew from watching all the news on the night stalker.

A request to see the warden, return to the witness chair to once again bear false witness, and Shelby Gaffney walked out of federal prison free as a bird. Johnny Wills received a life sentence without the possibility of parole.

Leon, as generally the case, felt talkative even if his conversationalist barstool partner didn't seem to share the same enthusiasm.

"So, Mr. Gaffney," Leon said cheerfully, "Sean and I have been discussing the crossroad of life." He waited for a response and got none. Shelby tapped his beer bottle on the bar, giving silent instruction that a fresh brew had been ordered.

Leon, not known to keep quiet, continued, "You know, the point in one's life where an event, the most important decision or thing, happens. That moment when all the world changes for you, be it good or be it bad. That split second. That journey-changing happening, the crossroad."

This almost seemed to perk Steve McQueen up a bit. "Crossroad? A defining moment? No such thing. Life is predestined. Start to finish. And maybe you get a little luck along the way, like tonight when I walk out of here a millionaire."

Shelby stood, straightened his bomber jacket, and motioned for a fresh beer. "Crossroad, Schwartz? Not for me, but I know a stupid Mexican and an innocent black man who might agree with you."

Shelby turned and walked toward June Swift. Reaching her table, the false witness professional turned the chair backward and sat down abruptly, folding his arms across the back support.

June slowly raised her eyes to meet him. "Well I declare, look what the cat drug in, Steve McQueen in person!" Shelby heard the comparison often.

"So what's your name, honey?"

"Honey? How charming! Why, I'm Loretta Lynn. Would you like I sing you a country love song?"

"Sure, why not?"

"Oh dear now, honey. I guess I won't because you see, I'm not really Loretta Lynn. But then I suppose you're really not Steve McQueen, are you? I'm guessing you wish you were but just can't pull it off. You know, being a loser and all."

"Oh yeah! Well you can kiss my—"

Shelby's ready-to-proclaim insult was cut short as the Reverend Tommy Johns exited the men's room looking quite the mess. "Who in the hell peed on me? I'll kill you! I swear I'll send you to hell!"

June turned in her chair and looked back as Katie lifted her head with a smirk. Slurring her words, she exhorted, "Hey, preacher, I guess you really are a puissant now!"

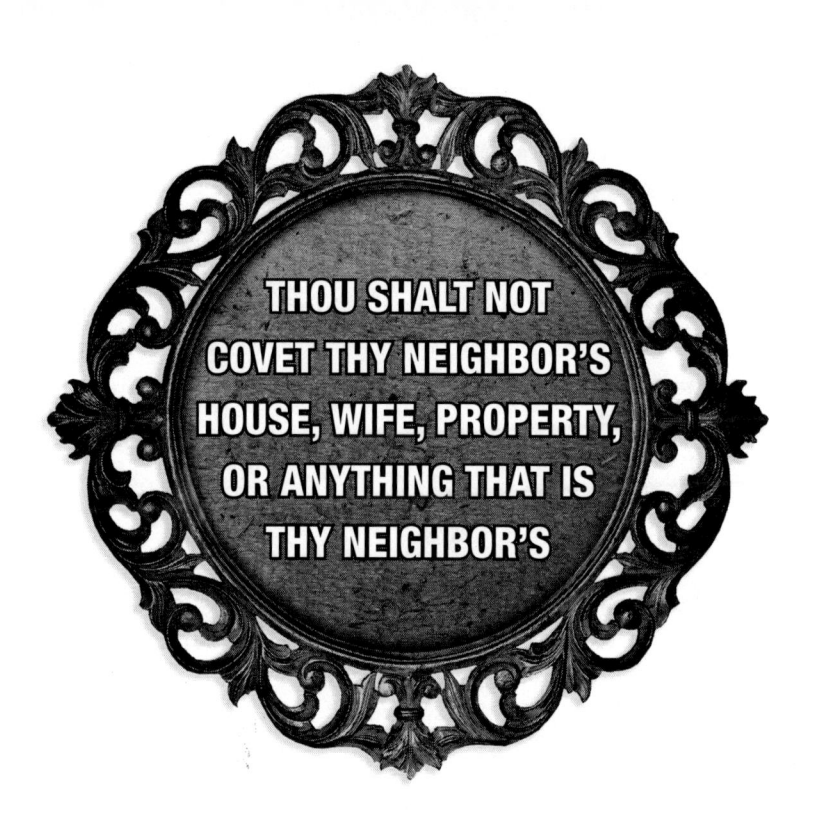

THOU SHALT NOT COVET THY NEIGHBOR'S HOUSE, WIFE, PROPERTY, OR ANYTHING THAT IS THY NEIGHBOR'S

"Bad news, Rusty."

The cop keyed the walkie-talkie. "What, Mack, what?" Fear was rising in his voice.

"Annie's gone."

"Annie's what?" Rusty threw off his blanket and stepped anxiously from his wino mansion.

"She slipped out of your place. Told the narcs she was going down to the bar to get them some beer. Best guess says she's headed this way, to the Hikes Point."

"Mack, we've got to do something!"

"Calm down, calm down, buddy. Give me two minutes. I'll pick you up in the alley. I want to catch these murderer thugs, but Annie's safety comes first. I'm moving now."

Macklin watched the silver Lincoln Town Car through the heavy snow pull up in front of the Hikes Point. A tall young man walked inside.

J. Andrew Crawford III took his card with the red number ten from Mosha. "Thank you, sir. Ten, good number. All we need is five more zeroes."

J. Andrew needed the money as desperately as the rest of the Hikes Point misfits. In thirty days he would appear in circuit court to face felony fraud charges. A million bucks just might be enough to save him from serious prison time. He would need at least half of that to retain the law firm of Henthorn, Haddad, and Wildman, the best attorneys in town.

He still couldn't believe that the real estate empire he'd worked so hard to build had fallen like a deck of cards around his feet. Why? More importantly, why him? Was being the third a curse?

J. Andrew Crawford, the soon-to-be indicted real estate mogul's grandfather, had once been a somewhat famous local builder back in the day. The old man built hundreds of shotgun houses in the west end and several motels across the river. But unfortunately he joined a group of friends at the track on sunny spring days. "The ponies got your grandpa, boy." The third heard the stories a thousand times. Exactas, trifectas, daily doubles. Get rich quick while you just sat back with a big cigar and mint julep. All of grandpa's horses were still on the track. Once a millionaire, the old man was now dead broke. The ponies got him.

And then there was his father, J. Andrew Crawford II, a financial wizard, a genius when it came to the world of money. Andy, as his mother called him, lived the good life growing up. His father, a self-made millionaire four times, just didn't know when to walk away, just like good old Grandpa! But Daddy dearest was not foolish enough to be coerced by exacta's or twenty-to-one odds, no not dear old Dad. His game was IPOs, puts and calls, all of which he succeeded in winning the guessing game known as investments. But the big bucks were to be made in commodities futures. Yes, the things people needed. Corn, wheat, oil, pork bellies. J. Andrew III scoffed in recollection. Pork bellies! His genius father lost a fortune on freaking pig parts—bacon to be more precise.

But J. Andrew knew better than to take such risks. He'd learned the good and the bad from good old Papa and Granddaddy. Take the best of what they did was the plan. Match real estate with investing, and so he did.

At the age of twenty-seven, Andy was the top realtor with the firm. Too good to be giving old boys half his take. Thus, Crawford Real Estate Investments gave birth.

Before his thirtieth birthday, Mr. Real Estate had married the beautiful Nancy Thomas. Two young children, the big house, boat on the lake, and the Lincoln Town Car. Crawfords always drove Lincoln Town Cars. Yes, J. Andrew did in fact have it all. All, including debt clear up to his eyeballs.

Now Andy's next-door neighbors, who owned the biggest home in the subdivision, were quite another story. Peter was a lowly elementary school teacher, and Wanda, his chunky, plain wife, stood to inherit two million dollars from her late father. Through backyard barbecues and chit-chats, Andy knew sweet Wanda got the trust in full on her thirtieth birthday, just twelve short months away.

Andy really struggled to sleep at night as he schemed his plot to help Wanda turn two million into ten. However, he knew that her penny-pinching wimp husband, the schoolteacher, would never let go of the money. Penny earned, penny saved sort of fella. Therefore, Plan B.

Plan B actually took shape in Sunday church service. J. Andrew hated going to church. He considered all worshipers to be a bunch of fake do-gooders. Three hundred hypocrites singing, praying, and shaking hands, giving you the phony smile and "So good to see you. Wasn't that a terrific sermon?" He knew it was a ton of bull. But that Sunday, the preacher hit a homerun, the greatest sermon ever pronounced, "Thou shalt not covet thy neighbor's stuff," or something along those lines.

Andy's family and Petey, as his short, thick, millionaire wife called him, were for all outsiders to think, the perfect neighbors. There were cookouts, Sunday school, PTA, bridge. Why, Andy and Petey even shared a riding mower.

But J. Andrew knew that wobbling Wanda had the hots for him. She was always giving him the look—the one that said, "Motel love!" She made it quite easy to stop coveting thy neighbor's stuff and move right into owning thy neighbor's house, wife, and two million smackers.

It started so innocently. Little skinny Peter with his

shiny bald head busy writing the ABCs on the blackboard while Andy's wife went to Florida with her parents and the rug rats. He'd been too busy to go, "Real estate, honey, real estate!"

"Hey, Wanda, hate to bother you, but I'm out of cream, batching it you know, wife out of town."

"Oh, Andy, you poor thing! I'd never go to Florida and leave a handsome man like you all alone."

Bada bing! Next day, "Sorry, Wanda, do you have any orange juice? You see, I have this big bottle of vodka and…"

In six months both couples were divorced. Twelve months and the handsome young J. Andrew Crawford III moved in with the Weight Watcher's Wanda and began to invest her two million dollars.

J. Andrew still didn't clearly understand just how it all fell apart. He had secret info, inside knowledge from the planning commission. The governor would get a bill through the state legislature without a problem. Soon they would legalize casino gambling, and J. Andrew Crawford would own the only hundred-acre plot anywhere close to the race track. Sure, five million seemed steep to the average Joe blow idiot, but not the third generation of real estate financial wizards. What was five million anyway? He stood to be worth a hundred million. Give Petula Pig back her two million, and he'd be off as the southern version of Donald Trump! But the governor lost his casino plan and the next election. Now Andrew owned a five million-dollar cow pasture.

Then the local politicians started to look at why this nobody was so eager to buy a chunk of worthless land, except for corn. And how did he borrow five million dollars? Well of course, Wanda gave him two, and his fraudulent list of bogus real estate holdings looked good to a banker when the borrower already had two million cash!

Current status: no wife, no big house, no casino, no two million, and no Wanda. Nothing but the potential for spending ten years in prison and his eight-year-old Lincoln Town Car. He really needed to win the million dollars.

Leon continued to map out his franchising plan on bar napkins as J. Andrew Crawford III approached the bar. Before Sean could offer his Irish greeting, Andy asked for a double scotch on the rocks.

"Now here's a man who knows how to dress!" Leon was impressed with the three-piece suit and highly polished shoes. Andy still looked the part.

"Thank you, sir."

"Leon Schwartz at your service."

"I'm Andy." All pretenses long gone.

"Say, Andy,"—Leon pulled the barstool closer—"have you ever thought about the crossroads of life?"

Shelby moved in front of the good reverend, blocking his way to the bar. "Man, what happened to you?"

Tommy Johns shot fiery glances around the room. "Not sure. Woke up in the bathroom, lying on the stinking floor. Some pervert peed on me, I think. I'll kill him!"

"Hold on there, cowboy. Don't go off half-cocked. Go get you a wet towel and a drink. Clean yourself up before you go kill somebody."

"Yeah, right. I smell like the toilet." Continuing to give all around the evil eye, the pee-stained preacher headed to the bar.

"Hey," Shelby spoke, "bring me back a Budweiser."

Tommy Johns approached the bar. "Oh wow, preacher, you smell like the bathroom," Leon stated without malice.

"Yeah? Well you smell like carp balls, Jew boy!"

"Hold up there, mate." Sean handed the rev several warm, wet towels. "Clean yourself up a bit, lad."

"What happened?" Leon again was sincere.

"Some son of the devil peed all over me, that's what happened! Any ideas as to who, rabbi?"

"Certainly not, sir!"

"Rum and Coke, Sean. Make it stiff, and a bottle of Bud."

"You got it, mate."

Tommy Johns returned to the table where Shelby waited, wiping urine stains as he walked.

Shelby leaned forward, as if the holder of a great secret. "I can't swear to it, but I overhead a couple of the boys talking, and one of them was laughing. Said the Mexican peed all over you!"

"I'll kill that Satan worshiper!"

Shelby pulled the rev back to his chair. "Calm down there, buddy boy. Surprise is the best method of attack here." The ex-con slid a buck knife under the table to the preacher.

"Put that in your pocket before you go after that pimp-dressing Mexican. Make it an even fight 'cause you know that tomato picker is carrying a blade."

J. Andrew Crawford III looked around at this menagerie, smiling in disbelief. "Nice place you got here, Sean. Kind of a hometown feel."

Sean gave a wicked smile back. "Just wait, mate. The party is just getting started."

ALL GREAT BEGINNINGS MUST END

Polly leaned against the passenger side door as far as he could possibly get from the driver. Although Abbadon promised, father to son, that Turk would not harm him in any way, his skin still crawled sitting inside the van with the Iranian monster.

"Polly, don't be a baby. I will not be bad for you. I am sorry. I was crazy. You are safe with me. We team." Turk, sounding sincere, did little to comfort the young Polly, although in his own way, he was every bit the psycho Turk could be.

"Here. Proof. You trust, I trust." Turk handed Polly a big gun, a Smith and Wesson .357 Magnum. "I lie, you shoot me."

Polly took a deep breath as he moved the gun back and forth between his hands. "If you get crazy on me, Turk, I swear to God I'll shoot you! Understand?"

Turk did not look at Polly, but a slight smile broke his dark and brooding face. "Yes, we good friends now?"

"Well, okay, Turk. you know I've always really liked you. You're like, well, my brother, okay?"

"Okay then." Turk's eyes said friendship, but his heart said break the little weasel's neck.

Both Polly and Turk slumped in the front seats of the van as they watched the alley. Rusty, busy with building his beer keg and plywood shelter, did not see the Walker Heating and Plumbing van pull in and park some fifty feet east of Rusty's hiding place.

"Look," Polly whispered as Macklin slowly pulled the beat-up Honda to a stop. Rusty immediately jumped in the passenger side door.

"We have to move, Rusty!" Macklin's voice was unusually strained. "Annie just pulled in the parking lot as I left my lookout spot."

"Go, go, go!" Rusty shivered from the fear of losing the girl he loved as much as from the sudden heat hitting his nearly frozen face and hands.

"Lock and load, partner. It's party time!" Macklin's adrenaline put all his senses at peak dispatch.

The little Honda slid sideways as Macklin and Rusty exited the alley. It was time to save Annie and kill anyone who tried to hurt her.

"Okay, Turk. I'm going in to wrap it up with Sean. Watch my back."

"Okay, Polly, do good." Turk patted Abbadon's adopted son with his right paw.

"*The Beginning.*" Polly attempted to sound like a crusader.

"Yes, *The Beginning*, for the master." Turk was much too stupid to even understand anything.

Grey cowered in shock and horror as Borack Abbadon raged like the actual son of Satan in the flesh.

Great howls of torturous anger filled the room. He turned in dizzying circles. Round and round he went, growling like a wolf caught in a steel trap, the unknown language flying from his lips as Abbadon foamed from the mouth like a skunk with rabies.

For the past hour, Borack answered the pool of satellite phones, each time smashing the expensive telecommunication devices as the news from across the world spewed forth. A rainstorm, a heavy snow, a quick response from volunteers, the efficient fire departments, all were subverting his plans! All were extinguishing the flames of *The Beginning*.

Borack, exhausted by disappointment and realization that *The Beginning* was in fact beginning to look like a total failure, slumped like a defeated warrior.

"How? How can this be happening? To me?" Borack's once powerful musical voice now sounded like the pleas of a spoiled child, Grey thought. The beautiful woman, slave to Abbadon, just watched and searched for pity. She could find none.

Forty years in planning, several billion dollars expended, and one hundred children rescued from the gutters of the world. His children, trained, taught incredible talents and skills, developed for this day, this moment, prepared for *The Beginning*.

What could all this mean? Without *The Beginning*, without the first important act, could there even be six years of chaos?

Where was the master at this critical moment? Abbadon did not feel his presence, the strength of his power, the ever-present evil. Was the master gone? Was *The Beginning* a failure? Would Borack suffer the consequences of failing his lord?

The old, hunchbacked woman, once the head mistress of the Covey Castle School, approached Borack cautiously. She didn't really walk in her floor-length hooded black cape; she appeared to float just inches off the floor. In a high-pitched scratchy voice, the dark figure, more demon than woman, whispered in Borack's ear, "Mostly gone, Master."

Borack lifted his head from the distant terror he'd been contemplating. "What, what did you say, Raven? Mostly gone?"

"Yes, Master, mostly gone."

He quickly looked to Grey. His expression was blank, confused, and helpless. Grey remained motionless as she planned her escape. Borack turned his attention back to the old Raven witch. "Gone? Who is gone?"

"Your children, Master. Thirty-two have failed. Sixty-six have disappeared. Only two remain, Master, Sean and Polly, at the Hikes Point Lounge." The black hunchback figure floated backward as rage filled the room, raw hatred that Grey could taste.

"Disappeared?" Borack drug the word from deep within a very dark and evil place.

"Yes, Master." The witch spoke as if in a cave. "All contact lost. It is if they have vanished."

Instead of the usual unholy explosion, Abbadon sunk deep into the large chair across from Grey. A trickle of blood ran from his nose.

"Maybe he is human," Grey considered.

In all her years with the man, or whatever he truly was, never had she seen a weakness. Not a tear, a sneeze, a cough. Not a headache or a scratch. He seemed super human. But now, blood—red human liquid—circulated from within. Maybe even flowing from his heart.

Abbadon was indeed an extraordinarily handsome man. Perfect features head to toe and the strength of ten men. Now Grey watched him age right before her eyes. He seemed to grow smaller. The temple of his thick black hair became gray. His eyes grew dim, and his strong hands began to shake.

"I feel sick." Borack sounded very old and weak. He stumbled to the bathroom.

Grey rushed to the closet and slung her coat over her shoulders. Moving to the door, she felt a light inside her brighten. Strength like never before, a reason to hope, to dream, to live!

The old black raven flew from across the room. Arms outstretched like a large bat, she hissed. "You're not going anywhere. You're not going to disappear like the others!"

The wicked old woman raised her head, and Grey gasped as she looked into the eyes of hell. The raven's smile was without lips, just an open hole with black pointed teeth. Her tongue flickered like a sensing snake tasting the air. The face of fleshy wrinkles looked centuries old and eyes filled with horror. Grey saw flames reflecting in their blackness.

"Now, go to the master, girl. Go now!" The old woman hissed and swayed like a raised cobra.

Grey closed her eyes and prayed. The light inside quickened and grew brighter. "In the name of Christ Jesus, I command you to move, demon!"

Grey placed her hands over her ears as the sound of a thousand people dying poured out of the old woman's soul. The black raven dropped to the floor in a dark heap, spewing out a foul odor like rotting flesh.

Grey stepped over the demon carcass and out the door. "Macklin," she whispered, "I'm coming."

THE HIKES POINT LOUNGE

"Stupid girl!" Rusty said as the Honda skidded to a stop, and they watched the auburn curls tucked under a white wool cap bounce as Annie O'Doul walked into the shadows of the Hikes Point.

"I'm going in, Mack," Rusty stated flatly. "Cover the back, partner."

Macklin placed his hand on the narc's arm as he started to exit the small car. "Careful, Rusty. These aren't your everyday hoodlums. You are about to meet true evil."

"I'm good, Mack. Like you say, it's time to rock and roll!" Rusty jumped out and ran toward the door.

"Your invitation, please." Mosha was somewhat confused with the eleventh guest.

"I don't need a stinking invitation, sir!" Annie was indignant. "My father used to own this place, before someone murdered him!"

Sean was around the bar in seconds, standing next to a very confused Mosha. "Sorry, lass, this is a private party, don't you know? Invitation only."

Polly appeared out of nowhere. "Just a minute, Sean, it is New Year's Eve, after all. What's one more to the party! Give the lady one for the road!"

Crossroad, Sean thought to himself as he escorted the young beauty forward.

Annie attempted to give the appearance of bravado. Just underneath her coat she shook like a wet dog on a December day.

"What would the lady like to drink?" Polly was smooth and confident.

Annie looked him squarely in the eyes, knowing full well this was most likely the murderer of her father and Josh. "Irish whiskey! Make it a double."

"Well, Sean, take care of the lady! I have a few things to do downstairs. I'll be back in a minute or two."

Mosha's confusion turned to irritation as Rusty entered the bar. "And who are you?"

Rusty gave the giant his best smile. "Who am I? Let's see now. I am a cop. I have a badge." He flashed it. "And I have a big gun. Now move aside, big guy, before I shoot you in the face."

Katie lifted her head to see a longhaired bearded man in an army field jacket and blue jeans place a very large pistol squarely to the forehead of the invitation grabbing giant. "Now, big fella,"—Rusty guided Mosha to the table next to Katie Zanderfield, pistol to head—"*sit!*"

Freddy unconsciously attempted to pull his fly shut and turned to Peppie. "Jack and the Bean Stalk, ya think?"

"Si, Senor Mango! I know this cop; undercover man, a real bad dude, bro. Might be looking for me!"

Katie, with a big smile, looked at Mosha's angry scowl across his big face. "You boys really know how to put on a New Year's Eve party. Surprise surprise!"

Jimmy Ryan traded places with Candy Sweet, putting himself between her and the potential gunplay. "You're my knight in shining armor, Jimmy." She giggled and blew a large pink bubble. Candy saw guns pulled all the time at the Pussy Cat Club.

June Swift contemplated how wonderful it would be if a real gun battle broke out and she caught a bullet. Save the suicide, and her ex-husband and sons would really feel bad.

Shelby leaned over to the good reverend and said, "Give me my knife back."

J. Andrew III looked at Rusty's big gun now at his side and stretched both hands high over his head. "Don't shoot me! Please don't shoot me."

Rusty shook his head in disgust. "Sit down, you idiot. No one's going to shoot you."

Sean maintained his Irish good humor, although he knew something had really gone very bad. "What'll it be, mate. Scotch?"

Rusty gave him his best undercover barroom smile. "How 'bout a cold Miller Lite, friend! Get the whole bar a round while you're at it. Make it last call!"

Rusty turned his attention to Annie. "Imagine meeting you here!" He pulled her close and could feel her shaking all over. He whispered, "Calm down, sweetheart, calm down. Everything will be okay. I'm here now. Mack's outside watching. Stop shaking, baby, it will be all right. Now listen carefully and do exactly what I say, okay?"

"Okay, Rusty, I'm sorry. I just wanted to find those murdering—"

"I know, baby, I know. But who's the cop here? Now walk out quietly and quickly. Go to your car and wait. Do you understand me?" There was a real *Do It Now* sound to his voice.

"Yes."

"Go and wait, now!"

Annie did as she was told, and Rusty turned back to Sean, taking a sip of his beer. "So then, Sean, where might I find Polly?"

Polly put the finishing touches on the small explosive charge that would ignite the chain reaction throughout the Hikes Point Lounge. Once outside, hit the remote and *whoosh!*

During construction, Polly had rigged ignition cords throughout the ventilation system. Inside the walls attached to the cord were strategically placed containers of gelled petro. Military stuff like they used in Vietnam, phew gas. One tiny spark and a white-hot eruption of liquid fire. Simple as that. Within seconds the place would erupt in flames. In minutes it would fill with toxic smoke. Shortly thereafter they would all die horrible fiery deaths as the Hikes Point Lounge went up in flames, and the screaming souls within would go straight to hell. "*The Beginning,*" Polly whispered.

Rusty saw Polly come up from downstairs. The smile on the adopted son of Borack Abbadon spoke pure evil.

Rusty pointed the pistol directly at Polly, targeting his face. "Polly! Nice to see ya!"

Polly laughed. "Nice to see you too! I'd suggest you put that big gun on the bar."

"Really? Why would I want to do that, Polly, my boy?"

Polly held up the remote control for all to see. "Because, cop, if I take my thumb off this red button, the place goes *boom boom* and all these nice people catch on fire!"

June gasped. She really did not want to die that way.

Freddy let go of his fly and watched Peppie crawl under the pool table.

"So, mister crime fighter, if you want all these good people to live, I'd suggest you put down that big gun of yours."

"Not a chance, maggot. Push the button. Let's all go out together in a blaze of glory!"

"I don't want to die. I want to live. Please, God, help us!" Katie Zanderfield pushed herself up out of the wheelchair, standing weakly on her feet.

"Okay, Polly, okay. You win." Rusty placed the gun on the bar. Polly's evil smirk shook the cop big time. He knew this psycho would indeed kill everyone.

Outside, Turk turned the key, locking the front door deadbolt, and ran back around the building to the alley, where Macklin now kneeled beside the dumpster, gun in hand.

"All right then, John Wayne,"—Polly smirked—"you just stay cool, and Polly will leave through the back door here nice and quiet. All's well that ends well, right?"

"It's your call, Polly."

"You got that right, cop. See ya in hell!"

Polly quickly exited the back door, closed it, and took the heavy brass key from his pocket. Holding the remote detonator high in his left hand, he turned the key to the dead bolt, trapping all the almost millionaires inside.

"What about the drawing?" the TV preacher whispered. "I need a million dollars!"

"Shut up, fool." Shelby knew it had all been a hoax; he just didn't know what for.

Before Polly could turn around, Turk clamped his large paw around Polly's left hand. "Let go, Polly. Take your finger off the button. Be nice boy for Turk."

Polly did as told and turned around to see Turk smiling at him. "But, Turk? Father said it was up to me!" He almost cried like a kid who didn't get his candy. "I want to burn them up! Please!"

"Your father gave me message, Polly. He says good-bye."

Turk placed the nine millimeter to Polly's forehead and pulled the trigger.

"Drop it! Drop the gun to the ground and turn around! Drop it, or I swear I'll drop you!" Macklin stood ten feet away, eyes and gun locked on the gigantic shadow now covered in snow.

Turk slowly turned and faced Macklin. He was smiling. The alley monster raised his pistol, with one less round, which was buried in Polly's brain.

Macklin placed three rounds in a tight circle, chest

high. Turk staggered back against the iron door, firing back twice, hitting Macklin high in the left shoulder and right arm. Mack's gun flew from his hand and slid down the alley in the snow.

Macklin lay on his back, seriously wounded. Turk stood over him, gun pointed at his head. The giant tapped his chest with his huge knuckles. "Bulletproof vest. Good idea, I think. Say bye-bye."

"Stop, Turk. Don't you do it!" A tiny voice filled with a sweet familiarity came through the heavy snowfall. "Please, I beg you, do not hurt him."

Turk did not raise his head, although he wondered if he was hearing angels. Could it be? "I think I kill him anyway."

Muzzle flashes from the angel. White lights in the dark, flying through silent snowflakes *Blam! Blam, blam, blam, click, click.* Gun empty. No more flashing flights.

Turk staggered and dropped to his knees, falling to his side, clutching his neck as each heartbeat pumped a stream of blood upon the snow-covered alley.

Standing over him, he looked into the eyes of an angel covered by a hooded white Russian fox coat. "Grey." The giant smiled, released the red button, and died.

Grey fell on Macklin, pulling his head to her breast, covering him with her warmth. "Macklin! Please, Macklin, hold on. God, please, please keep him."

"Grey?" More question than statement. He squeezed her hand in his. "Left pocket, cell phone, call 9-1-1." His hand went limp.

It wasn't a loud explosion. The sounds were muffled, like small gusts of wind. *Phew, phew, phew,* one after another.

Black toxic fumes began to bellow out of all the ventilation ducts, the one big expansive *whoosh,* and the interior of the Hikes Point Lounge erupted in flames. Terror and panic filled the place from every corner.

Rusty reached for his pistol that he'd placed on the bar. Sean's hand did the same. The narc pulled free and ducked as the Irish bartender swung the liquor bottle at his head. *Bam! Bam!* Rusty placed two shots in Sean's heart. The young Irishman completed his journey. He was now at his crossroad. Next stop: hell.

Rusty turned, only to be in the grasp of the invitation giant. Mosha picked him up like a rag doll and threw him over the bar. The narc came up firing. *Bam, bam, bam!* Three shots to the chest. The giant fell backward, dead, as he landed on the Reverend Tommy Johns, pinning him to the floor and crushing the air from his lungs.

"On the floor!" Rusty screamed, placing a wet bar towel over his mouth and nose. "Everyone on the floor! Cover your face with your clothing! Breath through your clothing!"

Rusty stumbled toward the bar-covered front windows, emptying his remaining bullets into the glass.

Grey took the brass key from her dead brother's hand and opened the heavy metal back door. Great gusts of black smoke poured out, helped by the draft created through the front windows Rusty had blown out moments before.

"Come this way!" Grey screamed through the gagging fumes. "Follow the moving smoke!"

Police cars with flashing lights filled the alley from both directions. Grey didn't know why she'd spoken the words. She'd never heard them before in her sheltered existence. It was as if a tiny voice whispered when she pushed 9–1-1. "Officer down!"

Paramedics frantically worked on Macklin as they loaded him in the ambulance. Grey, hidden in the shadows, not wanting to explain this evil to the men in uniform, dropped to her knees in the snow. "Please, God, please keep him, I pray."

Fire trucks filled the front parking lot as firemen battered the door and cut away the bars covering the windows.

Annie moaned and cried in the front seat of her Mercedes Benz, hoping she had not caused the death of the man she loved so much.

Jimmy and Candy were the first to crawl out of the back door.

Bright high-beam lights and bullhorns gave directions out of the living hell for the special guests, the ones selected for the New Year's Eve million-dollar drawing at the Hikes Point Lounge.

Jimmy crawled forward, his coat over Candy, protecting her from the falling fiery debris. "Our Father, who art in heaven…" It had been a long time since Father Ryan had said that prayer.

Shelby ran over the back of J. Andrew on his way out the back door, leaving the ex-realtor to crawl, sniffling and crying, to safety on his own.

Leon, on his hands and knees, heard Reverend Tommy Johns gasping for air in the blackness. He crawled to him and screamed in the darkness for help. Two courageous firemen made it. Pulling Mosha from the top of the preacher, they placed an oxygen mask on his face and led the preacher and the Jewish hero to safety.

Katie Zanderfield sobbed quiet tears as she staggered out the back door, supporting June Swift in her arms. She could walk, and this was in fact her crossroad.

Then, as the firemen extinguished the remaining blaze, through the smoldering embers of the charred and heavily damaged building, Rusty emerged through the front door of the Hikes Point Lounge. He was dragging Freddy and Peppie in each arm.

Ten unsuspecting sinners enticed by the lust of money and the dreams they hoped would save them, survived and walked away from the evil that brought them there. For each and everyone, this would be life changing. They had been to hell and walked out. They were now at their final crossroad, their new beginning.

Borack Abbadon stood over the old woman lying in a black heap in front of the door. She was dead. She was his mother, and he stood squarely in the middle of his crossroad. *The Beginning* had gone up in smoke!

Mosha, Turk, Polly, and Sean stood somberly before the gates of hell, their final and lasting crossroad.

Grey sat quietly in her motel room on the outskirts of Louisville. She held the phone patiently in her hand. On hold, she awaited the nurse to return and tell her if Macklin, the love of her life, was alive. The answer to that would lead to the final crossroad in her troubled life.

FINAL CROSSROADS

Macklin stood outside the Hikes Point office, admiring the new sign: *"Macklin, Judd, and O'Doul: Private Investigators."*

Rusty and Annie, now Mr. and Mrs., stood at either side of the recovered man.

"Feeling okay, partner?" Rusty put his arm around Macklin's shoulder, and Annie leaned on her tiptoes to kiss his cheek.

"Good as new, my friend. Stronger than ever."

"Ready to get to work?" Annie asked with a cheerful *Hope So* tone in her voice.

Macklin put his arms tightly around them and brought them close to his body. "I love you guys very much. You are my family. But I can't do anything until I find Grey. I must do that."

Rusty and Annie were silent. There really were no words adequate to express their true emotions.

"You see," Macklin continued, "Abbadon will not stop. Evil has no end. Until he is dead, Grey will never be free."

"But where will you look? Where will you go?" Annie's voice was pleading.

Macklin pulled her close, whispering in her auburn curls. "To the ends of the earth."

"Can I—can we—do anything to help?" Rusty too had tears in his eyes.

"Pray for me. Pray for me, friends. Only with the help of God can I save Grey and bring this evil to an end."

Macklin kissed them both, turned, and walked away into the sunlight, on his way to unknown darkness, on his way to the crossroad where good and evil do battle.

"He'll be back," Annie whispered, fighting a flood of tears.

"Sure he will," Rusty stated with outward confidence and little belief that he would.

Jimmy Ryan placed his arm around Candy's waist as they exited the hospital, new baby in her arms. "Who knows, sweetheart?" Jimmy smiled and kissed his wife softly on her lips. "You might be carrying the next pope!"

Pastor Tommy Johns spoke softly and with heartfelt humility. "Thank you, God, for this day and the honor of being in your presence." The seven homeless men at the Crossroads Mission ate their donuts and listened intently to a rousing, inspired sermon.

Leon Schwartz walked among the twelve tables, greeting his customers and welcoming them to Leon's New York Deli, located in Little Rock, Arkansas and closed on Sunday's.

June Swift rocked her granddaughter in her arms as she watched the other three grandchildren play on the jungle gym. Her oldest son kissed her gently on the cheek.

Shelby Gaffney read his Bible in the eight-by-ten-foot cell. The young black man he'd falsely accused watched his children fish in the small river behind the house as his wife prepared their picnic lunch.

J. Andrew wiped the sweat from his brow, admiring the third house he'd helped to build in Honduras as a volunteer for Second Mile Missions.

Peppie Hernandez sold the twenty-year-old Chevy to the young couple with no credit. That's what he did now at Peppie's Buy Now Pay Later. They were hardworking people, and he trusted them.

Freddy Yancey sat quietly in his cell, reading his Bible. Tomorrow he'd hear his sentence for the murder of his wife. Turning himself in had been the right thing to do.

Katie Zanderfield would become a bestselling author with her book, *The Hikes Point Lounge*.

Webster defines "crossroads" as *a road that crosses a main road or runs between main roads.*

But one might argue that point. One might say it's bigger than that. I guess a person could even say it's that moment where good meets evil, a time when love conquers hate, that one opportunity to look inward, not outward, that opportunity when God comes calling.

Ten people, lost and alone, walked into the Hikes Point Lounge looking for magic where none existed. They left in a different direction.

They did in fact find their crossroad. Have you?

e|LIVE

listen|imagine|view|experience

AUDIO BOOK DOWNLOAD INCLUDED WITH THIS BOOK!

In your hands you hold a complete digital entertainment package. In addition to the paper version, you receive a free download of the audio version of this book. Simply use the code listed below when visiting our website. Once downloaded to your computer, you can listen to the book through your computer's speakers, burn it to an audio CD or save the file to your portable music device (such as Apple's popular iPod) and listen on the go!

How to get your free audio book digital download:

1. Visit www.tatepublishing.com and click on the e|LIVE logo on the home page.
2. Enter the following coupon code:
   7605-266d-5bc8-e81a-1a27-7a2e-34f7-157f
3. Download the audio book from your e|LIVE digital locker and begin enjoying your new digital entertainment package today!